THE MAN WHO INHERITED A GOLF COURSE

By the same author

The Medicine Men (1975)
Paper Doctors (1976)
Everything You Want To Know About Ageing (1976)
Stress Control (1978)
The Home Pharmacy (1980)
Aspirin or Ambulance (1980)
Face Values (1981)
Guilt (1982)
The Good Medicine Guide (1982)
Stress And Your Stomach (1983)
Bodypower (1983)
An A to Z Of Women's Problems (1984)
Bodysense (1984)
Taking Care Of Your Skin (1984)
A Guide to Child Health (1984)
Life Without Tranquillisers (1985)
Diabetes (1985)
Arthritis (1985)
Eczema and Dermatitis (1985)
The Story Of Medicine (1985, 1998)
Natural Pain Control (1986)
Mindpower (1986)
Addicts and Addictions (1986)
Dr Vernon Coleman's Guide To Alternative Medicine (1988)
Stress Management Techniques (1988)
Overcoming Stress (1988)
Know Yourself (1988)
The Health Scandal (1988)
The 20 Minute Health Check (1989)
Sex For Everyone (1989)
Mind Over Body (1989)
Eat Green Lose Weight (1990)
Why Animal Experiments Must Stop (1991)
The Drugs Myth (1992)
How To Overcome Toxic Stress (1990)
Why Doctors Do More Harm Than Good (1993)
Stress and Relaxation (1993)
Complete Guide To Sex (1993)
How to Conquer Backache (1993)
How to Conquer Arthritis (1993)
Betrayal of Trust (1994)

Know Your Drugs (1994, 1997)
Food for Thought (1994)
The Traditional Home Doctor (1994)
I Hope Your Penis Shrivels Up (1994)
People Watching (1995)
Relief from IBS (1995)
The Parent's Handbook (1995)
Oral Sex: Bad Taste And Hard To Swallow? (1995)
Why Is Pubic Hair Curly? (1995)
Men in Dresses (1996)
Power over Cancer (1996)
Crossdressing (1996)
How To Get The Best Out Of Prescription Drugs (1996)
How To Get The Best Out of Alternative Medicine (1996)
How To Conquer Arthritis (1996)
High Blood Pressure (1996)
How To Stop Your Doctor Killing You (1996)
Fighting For Animals (1996)
Alice and Other Friends (1996)
Dr Coleman's Fast Action Health Secrets (1997)
Dr Vernon Coleman's Guide to Vitamins and Minerals (1997)
Spiritpower (1997)
Other People's Problems (1998)
How To Publish Your Own Book (1999)
How To Relax and Overcome Stress (1999)
Animal Rights – Human Wrongs (1999)
Superbody (1999)
The 101 Sexiest, Craziest, Most Outrageous Agony Column Questions (and Answers) of All Time (1999)
Strange But True (2000)
Food For Thought [revised edition] (2000)
Daily Inspirations (2000)
Stomach Problems: Relief At Last (2001)
How To Overcome Guilt (2001)
How To Live Longer (2001)

novels
The Village Cricket Tour (1990)
The Bilbury Chronicles (1992)
Bilbury Grange (1993)
Mrs Caldicot's Cabbage War (1993)
Bilbury Revels (1994)
Deadline (1994)

The Man Who Inherited a Golf Course (1995)
Bilbury Country (1996)
Second Innings (1999)
Around the Wicket (2000)
It's Never Too Late (2001)

short stories
Bilbury Pie (1995)

on cricket
Thomas Winsden's Cricketing Almanack (1983)
Diary Of A Cricket Lover (1984)

as Edward Vernon
Practice Makes Perfect (1977)
Practise What You Preach (1978)
Getting Into Practice (1979)
Aphrodisiacs – An Owner's Manual (1983)
Aphrodisiacs – An Owner's Manual (Turbo Edition) (1984)
The Complete Guide To Life (1984)

as Marc Charbonnier
Tunnel (novel 1980)

with Alice
Alice's Diary (1989)
Alice's Adventures (1992)

with Dr Alan C Turin
No More Headaches (1981)

THE MAN WHO INHERITED A GOLF COURSE

Vernon Coleman

Chilton Designs Publishers

Chilton Designs Publishers, Publishing House, Trinity Place, Barnstaple, Devon EX32 9HJ, England

This book is copyright. No part may be reproduced by any process without written permission. Enquiries should be addressed to the publishers.

First published in the United Kingdom by Chilton Designs in 1993.

Reprinted 1995, 1996 (twice), 1998, 2000, 2001, 2002, 2003

Copyright © Vernon Coleman 1993

The right of Vernon Coleman to be identified as the author of this work has been asserted in accordance with the Copyright, Designs and Patents Act 1988.

All rights reserved. No reproduction, copy or transmission of this publication may be made without written permission. No paragraph of this publication may be produced copied or transmitted save with written permission or in accordance with the provisions of the Copyright Act 1956 (as amended). Any individual who does any unauthorised act in relation to this publication may be liable to criminal prosecution and civil claims for damages. This book is sold subject to the condition that is shall not by way of trade or otherwise be lent, resold, hired out or otherwise circulated without the publisher's prior consent in any form of binding or cover other than that in which it is published.

A catalogue record for this book is available from the British Library.

All characters and places in this publication are fictitious and any resemblance to real persons, living or dead, is purely coincidental.

ISBN 0 9503527 9 9

Typeset by Create Publishing Services Ltd, Bath, Avon
Printed in Great Britain by J. W. Arrowsmith Ltd, Bristol

'My doctor forbids me to play unless I win.'
  – Alexander Woollcott
(he was a croquet player but the principle is the same)

THE OUTWARD NINE

CHAPTER ONE

The tube train was crowded and the surprising solid, tweed-clad rear of a plump, stern-looking woman was pressed so firmly against his left thigh that the flow of blood to Trevor Dukinfield's left leg had been halted.

Moving with great caution, lest his entirely innocent motives be misinterpreted, Trevor gingerly lifted his left knee and wiggled his leg up and down a few times. The movement, a vain attempt to encourage a few red blood cells to carry some fresh oxygen down to the muscles of his left foot, provided some slight relief.

The plump woman, who was standing far closer to him than would normally be considered socially acceptable for individuals who had not been formally introduced, forcefully rammed her elbow backwards and then turned her head and glared at Trevor. She had huge bushy eyebrows, a squint, a clearly defined moustache and a bundle of long, black hairs sprouting from each nostril. She was a woman who knew how to glare.

'Pervert!' she hissed.

Trevor, coughing from the blow, blinked, paled, and quickly lowered his left knee. When he had recovered he glanced around at his fellow travellers. Most of them looked just as miserable as he was. There must have been sixty people within whispering distance but there wasn't a smile in view. The carriage was stuffy, the air was smoky and stifling, and a cloud of pungent, cheap aftershave from an unknown traveller failed to mask less pleasant, more intimate smells.

Trevor glanced at a watch on the wrist of a man who was pointlessly holding onto one of the straps attached to the carriage roof. Holding the strap was quite unnecessary because they were all crammed into the carriage so tightly that none of them could have possibly fallen over. Trevor estimated that the train had been stationary for nearly half an hour. Although neither Trevor nor any of his fellow passengers knew it there had been another bomb scare at all main-line London stations and all underground trains were running late. It was the third time in a week that Trevor Dukinfield had been late for an important appointment. Even though it wasn't his fault he wasn't looking forward to having to explain to the editor of Ball Bearing Monthly why he had failed yet again to finish an important assignment successfully.

Feeling a sudden desire to scratch his nose Trevor tried to raise an arm but even this simple action brought a string of disapproving looks from those around him. Surreptitiously, he tried to obtain relief by rubbing his nose against the brim of the bowler hat worn by the man standing in front of him, but the man turned his head just as Trevor leant forward and glowered fiercely at him. At a distance of just six inches a well-aimed glower has considerable force and even the strongest may blink and retreat. And Trevor was not what anyone would call a strong man. He was physically slight and rather underweight and to describe him as shy and self-effacing would be like describing Buckingham Palace as a house. He could not help feeling that in a so-called civilised society it surely wasn't a great deal to ask for enough room to scratch one's itches and to stretch one's cramped muscles.

Trevor wondered whether anyone would notice if he just made the interview up. He felt sure that the businessman he had been due to meet would be far too busy counting his money to bother reading interviews with himself in tiny trade magazines. It occurred to him that if he made sure that he only said nice things about the man there would be little reason for him to complain, even if he did notice the slight fraud. He immediately felt guilty about having harboured this unprofessional thought and felt himself blushing. It is a tribute to Trevor's innocence that he believed that he must have been the first and only journalist ever to have such a thought. It is a further tribute to his innocence that he would not have believed you if you had told him that journalists had occasionally been known to do such things for real.

It was Trevor's first week in London and already he was beginning to wonder if he had made a mistake in trying to make his fortune in the capital city.

* * *

After the completion of his course in Slavonic languages at Mettleham University, Trevor had drifted into journalism more by accident than design. He had never spent much time thinking about a career, but after his graduation had quickly discovered that the demand for Slavonic translators is not a particularly large one.

The careers adviser at the university, a world-weary former lecturer who had been given the post when his own grant had expired and he had been unable to find himself alternative employment, had told Trevor that his lack of any special skills meant that journalism was the only career for which he seemed particularly well-suited. Taking this advice Trevor had applied for, and duly obtained, a job as a junior reporter on a local weekly newspaper in Dorset. He had spent two years attending innumerable council meetings, rewriting reports from the various local Womens' Institutes and occasionally writing obituaries of local dignitaries.

Trevor found these tasks pleasantly undemanding and would have been happy to stay there indefinitely if it hadn't been for Sylvia. She had enough ambition for them both. She had other ideas. Worst of all she had 'plans'.

Sylvia Instow, five years older, fourteen pounds heavier and four inches taller than Trevor, was the daughter of a local plumbing magnate. She worked as a receptionist at the Town Hall, though in view of her social position, and the six months she had spent at an international finishing school in Melton Mowbray, she regarded herself as far too good for the post. She had persuaded everyone, including herself, that she stayed there more through a sense of civic duty than anything else.

The two had first met on one of Trevor's many visits to the Town Hall. Largely under Sylvia's supervision and direction their acquaintanceship had flowered into friendship at a Cheese and Wine Party organised by the Housing Committee.

'You've got to get into Fleet Street,' Sylvia had insisted, nine months after they had first met, five months after the Cheese and Wine Party and three months after she had told her delighted parents that she and Trevor had become unofficially engaged.

'That's where the money is,' she had explained to a slightly puzzled Trevor as they sat together on the overstuffed sofa in the parlour at Mr and Mrs Instow's detached house on the outskirts of the town. Neither of them had realised that the national press had long since left Fleet Street and had migrated to more spacious and luxurious quarters in the East of London.

When, at Sylvia's insistence, Trevor had borrowed a colleague's copy of the UK Press Gazette, so that they could hunt through the classified advertisements for suitable posts, the only acceptable vacancy they had seen was the one for Features Editor on Ball Bearing Monthly, a long-established and reputable, if unexciting publication, which happened to have its offices above a tobacconist's shop in Fleet Street.

Trevor had narrowly won the post against severe competition from a 65 year old unpublished novelist and a feminist mother of three who had done her cause little good by announcing at her interview that she intended to bring her three children with her to the office every day. Trevor had, in due course, handed in his notice to the newspaper, rented a room in Paddington and set off alone to find fame and fortune. Trevor's parents had both died in an aeroplane crash when he was twelve and he was used to being alone. For eight years of his life home had been a boarding school.

Now, despite Sylvia's enthusiasm, he couldn't help wondering whether he might possibly have made a mistake in coming to London. When, after his delayed journey on the Tube, he returned to the offices of Ball Bearing Monthly with his tape recorder empty and his notebook blank, it turned out that his apprehension was not unique.

* * *

Hubert Wrigglesworth, the magazine's editor, regarded himself as a patient man and a sympathetic employer. But he had spent fifty years working as a journalist and, as he never tired of telling anyone who was junior enough or patient enough to listen to him, he firmly believed that no excuse was ever good enough when a story had been lost. He listened with ill-disguised impatience while Trevor explained why he had arrived nearly an hour late for his appointment with the Chairman of one of Western Europe's largest ball bearing manufacturers.

'How many interviews have you lost now?' the editor demanded. 'Four?'

'Er, no, sir,' said Trevor, nervously. 'It's three.'

'Oh, well that's all right, then!' said Mr Wrigglesworth, throwing his arms wide and showering cheap cigar ash over his desk, Trevor's desk and the slight and trembling form of Rose, Editorial Secretary, Production Coordinator, Researcher and Circulation Controller. 'How long have you been here? Three days?'

'Er, no, sir,' said Trevor. 'It's four.'

'So!' said Mr Wrigglesworth. 'Four interviews lost in three days!'

Trevor opened his mouth to correct the editor, thought better of it and stayed silent. Rose pecked at her ancient, sit up and beg typewriter with short, stubby fingers and tried, with rather more success than one might expect possible, to pretend that she wasn't there.

'You're in the big time now, Dukinfield!' said Mr Wrigglesworth with pride. 'This is your chance to make a name for yourself in journalism. But how are you going to make a name for yourself if you never get where you're supposed to be when you're supposed to be there?'

Trevor hung his head and wished he was back in Dorset rewriting W.I. reports. But the thought of what Sylvia would say if he abandoned the career she had helped him choose frightened him rather more than the prospect of facing Mr Wrigglesworth's wrath.

'I don't know what to make of you,' sighed Mr Wrigglesworth. 'Thousands of young journalists would give their right arms to be in your position.'

Trevor, attempting unsuccessfully to suppress the unpleasant image of several thousand one-armed journalists struggling to operate their keyboards, nodded and remained silent.

'I'll give you one more chance!' said the editor. 'And then you're fired! Do you understand what I'm saying?'

Trevor lifted his head and nodded. 'Thank you,' he mouthed.

Mr Wrigglesworth picked up a fistful of press releases from the metal tray on his desk and tossed them towards Trevor. 'In the meantime get some copy for the news pages out of those!' he said. He paused. 'Do you think you can find your way back to your desk?' he asked sarcastically.

Trevor picked up the bundle of press releases and walked a yard and a half across the room to his desk, sat down and started to read through them. As he did so he realised for the first time just how interesting those W.I. reports had been.

* * *

When Trevor got back to his room that evening he slumped down in his solitary armchair feeling very miserable. He didn't like the crowds; he didn't like the dirt and the rubbish in the streets; he didn't like the fact that it was nigh on impossible to get around the city; he didn't like his job; he didn't like Mr Wrigglesworth and he didn't like his grubby little room. In short he didn't really like anything about living in London.

He sat for a few moments staring into space and then suddenly realised that he was hungry. For a few moments he thought about going out to find a cafe but he couldn't bear the idea of facing all that traffic again so he opened the solitary cupboard above his small, stained sink and took out a can of baked beans. He removed the lid with an old-fashioned and slightly rusty can opener and emptied the beans into a small saucepan. He then placed the saucepan on the stove and turned on the heat. While the stove heated the beans he put two slices of white bread into an ancient and rather highly strung toaster and pressed down the operating lever.

As he waited for the beans to bubble and the bread to toast there was a knock on his door.

Trevor walked over and opened it. A woman in her late fifties was standing there holding an envelope. She was wearing a rather scruffy looking grey and blue checked dressing gown which was tied tightly around the waist with a dark blue cord and she had curlers in her hair and fluffy pink slippers on her feet.

'This came for you this morning,' said the woman handing Trevor the envelope.

Trevor looked at it, surprised. 'Thank you.'

'It's been readdressed from your previous address,' she explained unnecessarily, pointing to the writing on the envelope. His last address had been neatly typed on the envelope but had been crossed out and the words PLEASE REDIRECT TO were followed by his name and address in London.

'It's from a firm of solicitors in Mettleshire,' whispered the woman, knowingly.

Trevor was about to ask her how she knew this when the woman pointed to the return address on the back of the envelope. Sure enough, it was a firm of solicitors. And the woman was right: their address was in Mettleshire.

'Maybe it's good news!' said the woman, nodding towards the letter.

'Yes,' agreed Trevor, unconvinced.

'If it isn't you can always say you never got it,' she added, turning and leaving.

'Thank you very much!' said Trevor, speaking to her back.

He shut the door to his room just in time to save the saucepan from permanent damage but not in time to save the beans.

He spread marmalade on his two slices of toast and read his letter.

Dear Mr Dukinfield,
　We represent the estate of the late Mr Archibald Pettigrew of Pettigrew Towers, Butterbury Ford, Nr Mettleham, Mettleshire.
　We have information which might be to your advantage and we would, in consequence, be grateful if you would get in touch with us, at the above address, at your earliest convenience.
Yours sincerely,
Twist, Kibble and Fenshaw

Even though he had spent three years at Mettleham University Trevor had never heard of anyone called Archibald Pettigrew, of a house called Pettigrew Towers or of a place called Butterbury Ford and he had no idea at all what Twist, Kibble and Fenshaw could have to tell him which could possibly be to his advantage. He folded the letter, put it back into the envelope and then put the envelope in his jacket pocket. He wondered why solicitors used phrases like 'at your earliest convenience' instead of 'as soon as possible'. Then he sat down with a copy of 'Ball Bearings Through the Ages' which Mr Wrigglesworth had given him to review.

Trevor studied this well rounded, extraordinarily comprehensive (and monumentally boring) analysis of the ball bearing industry until ten o'clock. He then pulled his bed out of the wall, climbed into it and went to sleep quite unaware of the changes which were about to take place in his life.

CHAPTER TWO

Trevor's short career as Features Editor of Ball Bearing Monthly came to an abrupt halt the following morning.

Things started to go wrong when the bus in which he was travelling to work was in collision with a taxi half way along Oxford Street. While the bus driver and the taxi driver conducted an earnest debate about the way in which blame should be apportioned for the incident Trevor, who had left his home in Paddington with plenty of time to spare, decided to walk the rest of the way to work, innocently believing that this would reduce to manageable proportions the chances of there being any further delay.

What he did not and could not have possibly have allowed for was the accident which took place at the junction of Oxford Street and Charing Cross Road.

Trevor himself was not involved, but when he recognised the Royal Standard flying on the radiator of the Rolls Royce which had collided with the electric milk float he felt a duty to help remove some of the broken milk bottles so that the Royal chauffeur could continue on his way unhindered. Trevor was rewarded for his efforts with a personal Royal wave and a strict ticking off from an officious constable.

'What's your excuse?' demanded Mr Wrigglesworth, the editor, when Trevor arrived with blood stains on his hands and a series of unpleasant stains, produced by a potent mixture of oil and milk, on his trousers.

Trevor explained about the milk float and the Rolls Royce with the Royal Standard.

To Trevor's surprise Mr Wrigglesworth seemed interested,

even strangely impressed, by the excuse. 'Who did you ring with the story?' he asked, leaning forward across his desk.

Trevor stared at him blankly.

'Which of the papers did you ring?'

Trevor continued to stare.

'Come on, fair's fair, we split the take on stories like this,' said Mr Wrigglesworth, with an ingratiating, indeed nauseating, smile.

'I'm sorry,' said Trevor. 'I honestly don't know what you mean. What 'take' are you talking about?'

When Mr Wrigglesworth realised that Trevor had failed to recognise the news potential in the incident which had happened before his very eyes he fired him on the spot.

'Maybe I could ring one of the papers now?' suggested Trevor unhappily.

'Ring them now?' exclaimed the editor, in despair. 'You might as well ring them to tell them that World War II has finished!'

*   *   *

It was an hour later, while standing in front of a Job Centre window and looking for a piece of paper upon which he could write details of employers looking for journalists (there weren't any), that Trevor rediscovered the forgotten letter from the firm of solicitors in Mettleshire.

Forty-five minutes after a short telephone call he was on a train pulling out of Euston Station and heading north to Mettleham.

*   *   *

'I'm here to see Mr Twist,' said Trevor to the receptionist, a girl of about seventeen who had reluctantly interrupted what was clearly a conversation with a friend to attend to him. She had put the telephone receiver down on her desk but she had not severed the connection.

'What Mr Twist?' demanded the girl. She wore a tight white tee shirt that was several sizes too small for her

'Your Mr Twist,' explained Trevor. 'Mr Twist of 'Twist, Kibble and Fenshaw'.'

'Oh, him,' said the girl. 'There ain't no Mr Twist here. I think he's dead.' The gum she was chewing stuck to a tooth and she poked a finger into her mouth to free it.

'Oh. Well, Mr Kibble then.'

'Mr Kibble is definitely dead. He died before I come to work here.'

'What about Mr Fenshaw?'

'He's out at lunch. He won't be back until four.'

'I telephoned from London a few hours ago,' explained Trevor. 'I don't know who I spoke to but they said I should come up here straight away.' He took the letter out of his inside jacket pocket and showed it to the girl.

'Mr Johnson,' she said. 'You want Mr Johnson.'

'How do you know?' asked Trevor, puzzled.

The receptionist handed him back his letter and pointed to a reference at the top of the letter. 'GJ,' she said. 'That's Mr Johnson.' She sat back and picked up her telephone receiver. 'Sorry about that Cynthia,' she said. 'So what did he say?'

'Do you think you could please tell Mr Johnson I'm here?' asked Trevor.

The receptionist, listening to her friend, shook her head. 'He's out,' she mouthed. She looked at her watch, a flamboyant time piece with a fluorescent green dial and a salmon pink plastic strap. 'Come back in twenty minutes.'

Trevor mouthed a silent thank you and went back outside. He stood on the pavement and looked around him. The road looked grey and dirty. The buildings which surrounded him looked grey and dirty. Even the sky looked grey and dirty. The lawyers' offices were in the middle of a rather sombre, rather seedy-looking business area. One or two buildings had been converted into flats but most had been turned into offices for solicitors, accountants, surveyors and other professionals. Trevor suddenly felt hungry and remembered that he hadn't eaten anything since the night before when he had consumed two slices of marmalade laden toast. He looked around and could, at first, see no immediate sign of a cafe or, indeed, any shop likely to sell food but when he walked around the corner Trevor spotted a public house called The Duke of Westminster. It was the sort of place where people go for no other reason than to drink enough alcohol to help them forget why they went there in the first place.

The saloon bar was lit by a single unshaded bulb and it took Trevor a few moments to get accustomed to the darkness. When his eyes finally started to work properly he could see that all the furniture was bolted to the floor. The walls and ceiling seemed to be painted an unusually dark shade of yellow but a rectangular area of light cream which marked the place where a picture of some kind had once hung showed that the dark yellow was simply a result of years of tobacco smoke clinging to the paint. Behind the bar a metal grille that existed to protect the bottles of spirits and the drinking glasses had been pushed up almost out of sight while at the front of the bar another metal grille, presumably there to protect the bar staff, was suspended half way down.

There were just three customers in the pub. Two old men in long, beige raincoats wearing flat hats with greasy peaks were playing cribbage. A third man, dressed in the same sort of raincoat but with his hat rolled and stuffed into his pocket was reading a copy of 'The Sporting Life'.

Trevor ordered half a pint of lager and asked the barman if he could see the menu. The barman, a short, hairless man whose twin hobbies were clearly lifting heavy weights and visiting tattoo parlours, looked at him as if he'd asked for a glass of '49 Bollinger and a look at the Prime Minister's personal diary and sighed wearily as though fed up of eccentric and over demanding customers.

'Mild or bitter?' he demanded.

'Bitter,' replied Trevor.

'Half?'

Trevor nodded and tried to ignore the contemptuous look the man gave him.

'Plain or salt and vinegar?'
'I beg your pardon?'
'Crisps. Plain or salt and vinegar?'
'Plain, please.'

The barman, his sense of camaraderie clearly exhausted by this exchange, pushed a half pint glass of bitter across the counter and then, without looking, reached underneath the bar. He pulled a packet of crisps from an unseen box and tossed the packet onto the bar top. Trevor reached out instinctively to catch the packet but his move was unnecessary for the packet's slide was arrested by a puddle of someone else's stale beer. Trevor's hand and sleeve landed in the same puddle. He wiped his hand on his trousers, shook his sleeve, paid for the beer and the crisps and carried both to an empty table in a far corner of the room.

As he sat there, munching stale crisps and drinking warm beer, he wondered what Sylvia would say when he told her that he had lost his job in London. It was not a conversation he anticipated with any relish for Sylvia was not a particularly sympathetic woman. He sometimes wished that she could be, well, maybe just a little bit *nicer*.

Maybe, he thought, he could just stay in London and pretend that he still had his job. Better still, perhaps he could get another job. Perhaps, he thought, his mind now soaring with optimistic flights of fancy, the firm of Twist, Kibble and Fenshaw would have good news for him.

This thought reminded him why he was in Mettleham. Trevor looked at his watch and saw that it was now a full nineteen minutes since he had left the lawyers' offices. He drank up his beer, finished the broken bits at the bottom of his crisp bag by upending the bag and pouring them into his mouth, looked at the barman, thought about saying goodbye and changed his mind, and headed back round the corner to the offices of Twist, Kibble and Fenshaw. The sky still looked grey and dirty.

* * *

'Do you have any form of identity with you?' asked Mr Johnson, an earnest, bespectacled young man in his mid twenties who sat behind a cheap desk in a small office radiating self importance.

Trevor pulled the now rather battered letter from his pocket and handed it to the young solicitor. Mr Johnson took it, read it and handed it back. 'I'm afraid that won't do,' he said. 'Do you have your birth certificate or passport with you?'

Trevor, who could never remember seeing his birth certificate and did not have a passport, shook his head. He wondered whether there really were people who wandered around the country constantly armed with such documents on the off chance that they might be required as evidence by earnest solicitors.

Mr Johnson sighed. 'I suppose your driving licence will have to do,' he said wearily.

'I'm afraid I don't have one,' said Trevor, apologetically.

'You should always carry your driving licence with you,' said the solicitor sternly.

'But ...' began Trevor.

'If a police officer asks to see your licence then you have to produce it,' said Mr Johnson. 'You should know that.'

'You don't understand,' said Trevor. 'I don't have a licence. I don't drive.'

'You don't drive?' said the solicitor, with a mixture of horror and disbelief.

'I've never got round to it,' said Trevor, weakly. It was his inability to drive which had resulted in his lack of promotion when he had worked on the weekly paper in Dorset. While other young journalists had sped around the countryside collecting stories of burning hayricks, overturned tractors and pony show glories it was an inability to transport himself around the community which largely explained why Trevor had remained glued to the W.I. reports.

'Do you have your national insurance card with you?' asked the solicitor.

Again Trevor was forced to shake his head.

'Well you must have something that proves who you are!'

Trevor rummaged in his jacket pockets and found two credit cards, a press pass and an out of date membership card for the Video Club at the village shop in Little Torrington. He placed these on the desk in front of Mr Johnson who picked them up one at a time, holding them carefully by the edges as though touching them might contaminate him permanently, and examining them as though they were pieces of evidence in a murder case. He then handed them back.

'So,' he said with some distaste, 'you're a journalist?'

Trevor felt as thoroughly and irretrievably condemned as if he had the wrong skin colour or the wrong blood type. 'Yes,' he admitted. 'Well, I was,' he said, correcting himself. 'I lost my job this morning.'

'So!' said Mr Johnson, his distaste increasing by the second. 'You're an unemployed journalist!'

'Yes,' said Trevor. 'I suppose so.'

Mr Johnson sighed and shook his head as though he could not understand why a man of his calibre should be forced to deal with such people. He opened an orange-coloured cardboard file that lay on his desk and took out a sheaf of papers.

'As you know,' he sighed, 'we represent the estate of your late uncle Mr Archibald Pettigrew who died twenty one days ago.'

'He was my uncle?' asked Trevor, surprised. 'I didn't know that.'

'Indeed he was,' said Mr Johnson who was clearly not startled to find that Trevor was the sort of person who mislaid his relatives.

'What did he die of?' asked Trevor.

'I'm afraid I don't know,' said Mr Johnson, clearly uninterested in such distasteful details.

'How old was he?'

Mr Johnson flicked through the papers in front of him. 'According to the information I have here he appears to have been 87 years old when he died,' he said, cautiously.

'Good age anyway,' said Trevor.

'Indeed. Shall I continue?'

'Yes. Sorry.'

'As your uncle's sole surviving relative you are the only heir to the estate,' said Mr Johnson. 'Though I must warn you that your uncle's affairs were not well managed.'

'I just wish I'd known about him when he was alive,' said Trevor, who was genuinely sad to know that his only living relative had died without his having had a chance to meet him.

'Quite,' said Mr Johnson, who clearly found this sort of emotional nonsense unnecessary. 'The main house, Pettigrew Towers, was heavily mortgaged to the banks and there will not, of course, be anything due to you from that quarter. Mr Pettigrew himself sold off all the valuable furniture and paintings to help stave off his creditors and so there is little or nothing in the house of any value.'

'Maybe I could pop in and see if there's anything of sentimental value?' asked Trevor. 'There might be some old photographs, letters, that sort of thing. There could even be something about my parents.'

'About your parents?'

'They died a long time ago,' explained Trevor. 'I don't really know very much about them.'

'I see,' said Mr Johnson rather coldly. 'I'll have a word with the bank,' he added, rather impatiently. He looked down at the papers in front of him again. 'The one part of the estate which you will inherit is the golf course.'

'The golf course?' said Trevor, incredulously.

'Your uncle was an extremely enthusiastic golfer,' explained Mr Johnson. 'Forty-five years ago he laid out a private, eighteen hole golf course in the grounds of Pettigrew Towers. Eighteen years ago, when his finances first began to cause concern at the bank, he built a clubhouse, appointed a professional and opened the course to the public in an attempt to provide some income. It was his first and last, and therefore both his least and his most successful, commercial venture.'

Mr Johnson paused, apparently waiting for Trevor to say something. He was met with total silence as Trevor was far too preoccupied with digesting all this new information to even consider making any comment. Faced with the non-responsive beneficiary, Mr Johnson continued. 'Unfortunately, the success of the venture was only relative,' he went on. 'Your uncle steadfastly refused to mortgage the course until fairly recently but had no money to improve it or to maintain it, so you won't be surprised to hear that during recent years the enterprise has steadily deteriorated.'

'Oh, that's rather a shame,' said Trevor, finally gathering his thoughts enough to make some sort of comment. 'Especially if the old chap was particularly fond of it.'

'Yes,' said Mr Johnson, rather coldly.

'You said that the golf club is mortgaged,' said Trevor. 'How much is the bank owed?'

'Fortunately for you just slightly less than the market value of the club,' said Mr Johnson. 'We had the club surveyed last week and despite the condition of the clubhouse our surveyor came to the conclusion that if you put the property on the market immediately you would be able to raise £10,000 more than the outstanding loan.'

'Ten thousand pounds!' said Trevor, to whom such a sum seemed astronomical.

'Precisely,' nodded the lawyer. 'We anticipated that you might want to sell the club and so on your behalf we asked Ogilvy, Patterson and Yolland...'

'Ogilvy, Patterson and Yolland? Who are they?'

'Estate agents,' explained Mr Johnson, as though talking to a child. 'They specialise in commercial property and have a very good reputation both locally and nationally. They say they have found a prospective buyer who is prepared to pay off the bank loan, pay all the necessary fees and give you a cheque for £10,000.'

Trevor again failed to notice his cue to offer some sort of reply to the solicitor.

'I trust you find the news satisfactory?' prompted Mr Johnson.

'Oh, absolutely!' said Trevor with sudden enthusiasm. 'Very satisfactory!'

'Of course,' said the solicitor, 'you could keep the golf club yourself and try to make a go of it but were you seriously to consider that possibility there is a codicil to the will which might influence your thinking.'

'A codicil?'

'A supplement.'

'Oh,' said Trevor. 'What does it say?'

'Do you play golf, Mr Dukinfield?' asked the solicitor.

'Er ... no, not exactly,' confessed Trevor. 'Though I was once a bit of a demon on the crazy golf course in Weston-super-Mare.' The memory of this distant success brought a contented smile to his face. 'They had one hole that was a real terror,' he told Mr Johnson. 'No 14 it was. You had to send your ball up a slope, over a drawbridge, down through a castle with a red roof and along a narrow walkway to land on a tiny island in the middle of a little lily pond.'

'Really,' murmured Mr Johnson, skilfully resisting whatever temptation may have passed his way to show interest in this anecdote.

'I was the only person to get a hole in one on No 14 for the first two weeks in August,' said Trevor.

'Do you have any business experience?' asked Mr Johnson, apparently unimpressed by the memory of this golfing success.

Trevor hesitated. 'Not really.'

The solicitor lifted up the piece of paper which lay on his desk in front of him and started to read from it. 'Insofar as the undernamed ...'

'Excuse me,' said Trevor, apologetically, 'But do you think you could just tell me what it says? In plain language?'

The solicitor smiled condescendingly. 'The gist of the codicil is that if you choose to take control of the golf club then it will only remain yours if at the end of three months you can satisfy two very specific requirements.'

'Which are?'

'Firstly, your uncle states quite clearly that you should be able to play a full round of golf on your own course in less than 100, observing all the rules of golf.'

Trevor blanched.

'Secondly,' continued Mr Johnson, 'your uncle also states, with equal clarity, that you and a selected nonprofessional playing partner should play a handicap match play competition against two representatives of the bank. Once again the normal rules of golf will operate. If you win the match *and* complete a round of golf in a score of under 100 then the course will be yours.'

'Will the bank be prepared to put forward a team?' asked Trevor, puzzled.

'I'm sure they will,' said Mr Johnson. He paused, though whether this was for effect, for pleasure or merely in order to breathe Trevor had no idea. 'Under the rules of your uncle's will the bank will inherit the golf club if you and your partner lose.'

Mr Johnson fiddled with his pen for a moment. And then he smiled. 'The codicil may help you make up your mind about what to do,' he said.

CHAPTER THREE

The bank had given Trevor permission to visit Pettigrew Towers so that he could look through what was left of his uncle's belongings, and Trevor had decided to stay the night in Mettleham.

And so it was from a small unmemorable hotel foyer that he telephoned Sylvia to tell her his news.

'I'm in Mettleham,' he said.

'What on earth are you doing there?'

'I had a letter from a solicitor here. My uncle died.'

'I didn't know you had an uncle in Mettleham.'

'Neither did I.'

'I didn't know you had any uncles at all!'

'Neither did I.'

'How on earth can you not know that you've got an uncle?'

'I don't know how I didn't know. I just didn't know.'

'Have you got to go to the funeral?'

'No. That was last week. They didn't bother to tell me about the funeral.'

'So what are you there for?'

'My uncle owned a big house and was quite rich. Well, he wasn't *really* rich because he owed a lot of money to the bank. But he also owned a golf club which I seem to have inherited.'

'Just one? I thought people usually had them in sets?'

'No. Not that sort of golf club. The sort with buildings and people and so on.'

'A golf course?'

'Yes.'

'But what on earth do you want with a golf course? You don't even play golf!'

'The solicitor says they'll sell it for me and that I'll get £10,000.'

'£10,000 doesn't sound an awful lot for a golf club.'

'It's rather heavily mortgaged, I'm afraid.'

'Oh. That's a pity!'

'I'd rather my uncle was still alive. I'd like to have known him.'

'Yes, of course. But since he isn't it's rather nice that he's left you some money isn't it? Even if it isn't very much.'

'Yes. I suppose so.'

'Does your editor mind you taking time off from work'

Trevor hesitated. If he hadn't had some good news to tell Sylvia he might not have told her that he had lost his job. But he no longer thought that the loss of his job was quite the disaster it had originally seemed. 'I rather seem to have been fired,' he told her rather bluntly.

'Fired?'

'Yes.'

'What on earth for? How did you manage to get fired? You've only been working there for a week!' Sylvia paused and thought about it. 'Less than a week!'

'It's rather complicated.'

'I don't care how complicated it is. I want to know. I'm entitled to know Trevor!' Sylvia sounded very cross.

'I saw the Queen in a collision with a milk float but I didn't ring anyone with the story and so the editor fired me.'

The telephone was silent for a moment. 'I don't understand,' said Sylvia at last.

'No,' agreed Trevor. 'I'm not entirely sure that I do.'

'Well, have you submitted a formal complaint?' Sylvia demanded.

'What do you mean?'

'They can't just sack you without a good reason,' said Sylvia. 'Not even in Fleet Street!'

'I was also late a few times,' said Trevor. 'It wasn't my fault,' he added quickly.

'Oh dear Trevor,' sighed Sylvia wearily. 'What on earth are

we going to do with you. All that effort we went to to get you that job'

'It wasn't a very good job,' said Trevor. 'I didn't like it.'

'How on earth can you know whether or not you liked it?' asked Sylvia. 'You didn't have the job for long enough to know whether or not you liked it,' she pointed out. 'Anyway it was in Fleet Street!' she added. 'Sometimes I despair of you, Trevor. Really I do' And with that Sylvia put down her telephone receiver with a crash.

'Sylvia? Sylvia?' called Trevor.

But she had gone.

When Trevor put the telephone down he felt quite miserable.

* * *

The next morning Trevor travelled by taxi to Pettigrew Towers where he was due to meet Ms Nancy Boyes from the bank. Since the bank owned the entire contents of the house – as well as the house itself – Ms Boyes had the authority to decide what, if anything, Trevor could take away and whether or not there would be a charge for it.

The driveway leading to the house had probably looked very impressive before Mr Pettigrew had lost his money. The entrance was marked by huge wrought iron gates, each of which had a painted crest in the middle. Impressive rows of oak trees stood guard along the sides of the twisting, turning driveway.

But the wind, the rain and the years had taken their toll, and the entrance to Pettigrew Towers no longer looked quite as grand as it obviously once had. The gates, which stood open, were rusting and didn't look as if they had been closed for years. The colours on the two crests were hardly discernible. Two of the oaks had been blown down and although somcone had cut away the branches which had blocked the driveway the huge trunks, half covered in moss, lay where they had fallen. Even from the gateway Trevor could see that the driveway itself was scarred with thick tufts of grass, while the lawns alongside it, which badly needed cutting, were marked with a dozen or more mole hills.

Trevor looked at his watch as the taxi slowed and started to turn into the driveway. 'You can drop me here, if you like,' he said, realising that it would be twenty minutes before the bank's representative arrived.

'It looks like a long walk, guv,' said the driver. The car bumped up and down as it slowed to a halt on the cattle grid which guarded the driveway.

'That's all right. I'd like to walk.'

The driver shrugged and pulled on his handbrake. 'Suit yourself.' He turned, looked at the meter and told Trevor what he owed. Trevor paid him, climbed out of the car and watched as the taxi driver drove rapidly back towards Mettleham.

Pettigrew Towers had been built in the middle of the 18th century by John Pettigrew, who had made his fortune as a pirate. The architect commissioned to design the house had been instructed to build something impressive, and the turreted towers and dark, stone facade showed that he had followed his brief to the letter.

The skies, which had merely been grey when he had arrived, started to blacken as Trevor began the walk up the driveway towards the house, and the rain started just as the Pettigrew Towers came into view. By the time he arrived at the end of the driveway and stood on the edge of the huge, gravelled parking area at the front of the house it was raining heavily. Trevor stood with hands in pockets and shivered as he stared upwards at the empty flagpole standing on the tall stone tower above the huge wood and iron front door. Just then a small BMW sped into the parking area and slid to a gravel-splattering halt a couple of yards away from the front door. A tall, thin woman of about Trevor's age climbed out of the car, slammed the door and darted into the huge stone entrance porch.

'Trevor Dukinfield?' she called, shaking the few drops of water from her silk suit and taking a huge iron key out of a thin leather briefcase.

Trevor nodded. 'Ms Boyes?'

'Come on in. You'll get soaked. Where's your car?'

'I walked. Well, from the gates anyway.'

Ms Nancy Boyes, showing no signs of her surprise at this admission, opened the front door to Pettigrew Towers and stood aside to let Trevor walk in ahead of her.

Trevor had no idea what the inside of Pettigrew Towers would look like but even so he was astonished by what he saw. The floor in the hallway consisted of bare stone flags and there was no furniture to be seen at all. The ceiling of the hall was some sixty feet above. Rain dripped through holes in the roof in half a dozen different places, splashing noisily onto the flagstone floor.

'I'm afraid we've already moved all the furniture to our auction rooms,' apologised Ms Boyes. 'Normally we would have left it here and had the auction in the house but our insurance people insisted that we move it.' She looked upwards. 'As you can see the fabric of the building isn't in terribly good condition.'

'Do you expect the sale of the furniture and the house to cover the loan my uncle had taken out?'

Ms Boyes shook his head. 'Very unlikely,' she said. 'But that's our problem not your's. As you know your uncle refused to include the remains of his golf club as security against his loan with us, though to be honest it wouldn't have made a lot of difference if he had. Do you want to see the rest of the place?'

'Yes, please. Very much so.'

Even with no furniture in the rooms the guided tour of Pettigrew Towers took nearly three-quarters of an hour of steady walking. Trevor had never been into a private house that had its own ballroom, library, armoury, gun room, flower room and chapel.

In one of the many bedrooms Trevor spotted an enormous pile of clothes thrown in a corner. Next to them were three untidy and unsteady-looking piles of documents. 'Whose were those?'

'This was your uncle's bedroom,' explained Ms Nancy Boyes. 'He couldn't afford to heat the place and so for the last few years he virtually lived in this one room. The clothes were his and the papers were found in his desk.'

'That's all that's left of all his personal belongings?'

'I'm afraid so!'

'Can I take the papers with me?'

'Certainly! Do you want the clothes?'

Trevor hesitated. 'They could perhaps go to a local charity shop?'

'That's what we thought. Let's see if we can find anything to put those papers in.'

They found a cardboard box and two large plastic carrier bags in the kitchen and crammed them full with old Archibald Pettigrew's accumulated paperwork.

'What do you think will happen to the house?' asked Trevor, as he walked down the stone staircase with a cardboard box full of papers in his arms.

'Heaven knows!' admitted the banker, who was carrying the two plastic bags. 'It's probably too big to be bought as a private house but it would need an awful lot of money spending on it to convert it into a hotel or anything like that.'

'It seems such a pity,' said Trevor, sadly.

'Are you heading back into Mettleham?' asked Ms Boyes. She put down the two bags she was carrying and opened the front door.

'To the railway station,' nodded Trevor, walking through into the porch. The rain was still pouring down. 'There's not a lot of point in my staying around here. Mr Gittings said he'd get in touch with me as soon as he had any more news about the golf club.'

'You're going to let the solicitors sell it for you?'

'I think so. It seems the only sensible thing to do.'

'Absolutely. Very wise of you. Use your money as a deposit on a nice little semidetached house somewhere.'

'Yes, I suppose so,' agreed Trevor, who suddenly realised how mundane and unimaginative this alternative appeared.

'You're going back to London then?' asked the banker.

Trevor nodded, though it did occur to him that with no job

to return to there wasn't a lot of point in going back to the capital.

'I'll give you a lift to the station,' said Ms Boyes. She took the key out of her briefcase and relocked the front door. Fifty-five minutes later Trevor found himself sitting on a crowded Inter-City express heading back to Euston Station.

*   *   *

When he had first seen the pile of papers that Archibald Pettigrew had left behind Trevor had, not unnaturally, assumed that his uncle must have been something of a hoarder. He had expected to find that most of the papers were simply old bills, dull bank statements and irrelevant letters. He had only taken the papers with him in the rather vain and forlorn hope that he might find one or two old family photographs or letters among the dross. He had expected to find that by the time he arrived back at Euston Station he would have sorted the papers into one very small pile worth keeping and one very large pile to throw away.

But that first impression had been unfair and grossly misleading, and it wasn't long before Trevor decided that all the papers which he had rescued from Pettigrew Towers were well worth keeping; at least, until he could sort through them more carefully than was possible on the crowded train.

At Euston Station he had to find a trolley and then hire a taxi to take him and his uncle's papers, still packed in the cardboard box and the two plastic bags, back to his room in Paddington. He got the taxi driver to stop at a burger bar on the way home so that he could buy a double cheeseburger and a large portion of chips

Once safely back in his room Trevor ate the cheeseburger and chips and then put a spoonful of instant coffee into his solitary mug which he filled with hot water straight from the tap. He then cleared the remains of his meal from the kitchen table, wiped the surface clean of crumbs with his arm and emptied the first plastic bag of papers onto the table so that he could start the task of sorting through them properly.

An hour and a half later he found a letter in an envelope addressed to him.

When he saw his name written in a hand which he now recognised as his uncle's Trevor froze for a moment and went quite cold. For a while he didn't open the envelope but just rested it up against his coffee mug and stared at it. Up until that moment he had had no idea that his uncle had even known of his existence.

Eventually, Trevor reached out, picked up the envelope and slit open the top with his thumb. Then, as though handling a precious piece of manuscript, he carefully unfolded the letter.

My dear Trevor,

It feels strange knowing that by the time you get this I will be dead. But one advantage of writing from beyond the grave is that you don't have to worry too much about saving face or avoiding embarrassment.

The first thing I want to do is to apologise to you. I know that I should have contacted you long ago and I feel very guilty about that. I've known of your existence ever since you were born, though I strongly suspect that you've never known of mine. When your parents died I kept meaning to get in touch but every time I almost wrote or picked up the telephone to call you I managed to find yet another very good excuse for not doing so. And in the end I was so ashamed at having left it so long that I just couldn't get in touch with you at all.

Your father and I had a fierce falling out before you were born. It was, as you can imagine, over a woman; your mother, of course. Your mother and I went out together for two years and we were going to get married. Then, gradually, your mother fell in love with my brother and, to cut a long story short, she decided to marry him instead of me.

I was devastated and I blamed your father. I know it wasn't fair of me, for your father didn't deliberately set out to take her away from me. But I was hurt and I couldn't bear to see the two of them together.

I was two years older than your father and so I had inherited the family house and the land that went with it when our parents died – I was about your age when I inherited Pettigrew Towers. I had originally intended to give your father some of the land but when he and your mother got married, well, as you can imagine that good intention was quickly forgotten and I'm afraid I made it pretty clear that your father wasn't going to get anything.

Your father wasn't a man to complain. He was a proud man. He went away from the area and when he got married he took your mother's name. That's why you are a Dukinfield instead of a Pettigrew. He didn't know, but I kept an eye on him and your mother. I don't know why I did it. Partly curiosity I suppose, and partly a strange sense of responsibility. I think I rather hoped that he'd be a failure at whatever he chose to do so that I could go riding in and save him – and take your mother away with me.

I knew about your birth but I didn't say or do anything. I didn't even send you anything for your christening. I wanted to but I was ashamed because I knew that if I did your parents would know that I'd been secretly watching them. I've never admitted this to another soul but I even paid a firm of private detectives to send me monthly reports about you and your family. Through their eyes I watched your father build up his business and I watched you growing up. But I never wrote or called and then, by the time of your parents' accident, it was somehow too late to get in touch.

I've made quite a mess of my life and although I've had some fun I have a lot of regrets.

After I lost your mother I went a bit wild for a few years. I spent a fortune just wandering around with the wrong sort of people. I went to Gstaad for the skiing Monte Carlo for the gambling, Paris for the women and so on.

When I got tired of all that I came back here and discovered golf. That's when I built the golf course; my one achievement. I'm rather proud of it, though I know it's rather gone to seed in recent years. I readily confess that I didn't start out to build the course out of any sense of altruism. I had a row with the club I was a member of – they were a terribly stuffy lot – and decided to build my own club where I could play without any interference.

I'm afraid you won't inherit the Towers. The banks will take that. But I've made sure that the golf course remains separate, and although *there's a thumping great mortgage on it you should be able to make a go of it if you want to. It's all I've got left to leave you.*

Of course, I wouldn't blame you if you decided just to sell it. After all you certainly don't owe me a thing and I know you don't play golf. But if you decide to keep it and make a go of it you might find that you enjoy it. I was older than you are now when I first discovered golf and it's been a great source of joy to me.

Well, Trevor, that's about it. My eyes are terrible and my hand is a bit shaky and it has taken me most of a day to write this letter. I did think of posting it but in the end I've decided to leave it in the top drawer of my desk. If you're the sort of man I hope you are you'll want to look around Pettigrew Towers and you'll find it.

I'm sorry we never met, Trevor. It was entirely my fault and I feel very guilty about it. I hope you're a better man than I ever was and that you can forgive me.

Take care and God Bless,
Your loving Uncle,
Archibald Pettigrew

P.S. I hope you don't mind the business about getting you to play a round in under 100 and beating those damned bankers. But you can't really own a golf club without playing the game. And you'll enjoy it once you start to play.

When Trevor put down the letter he felt a lump in his throat and tears pricking his eyes.

He could hear Sylvia's spirit shouting at him to accept the money. He thought about all the things that he could do with £10,000. He could put down a deposit on a semidetached house with two and half bedrooms and a small garden; buy a middle of the range Japanese motor car with velour upholstery and an integral radio-cassette player; invest in government stocks and have an extremely small, private income for the rest of his life; go on a round the world cruise with a group of seventy year olds he had never met before; start a business of his own and lose the money; or rent a remote cottage in an uncivilised part of Scotland for a year and shiver as he struggled to write a novel.

It was, he realised, going to be difficult to satisfy his uncle's stipulations. He knew that it wasn't going to be easy to play a round in under 100 in such a short time.

But, however difficult it was, and however long the odds against him, he knew that he would now try to keep the golf club.

He had never before felt that he had any roots, and he suddenly realised how much he had missed them. Finding at least part of his past had put purpose into his hitherto rather aimless life. In finding his past he rather thought that he might well find his future.

* * *

'Have you *seen* the golf club you're planning to try to run?'

'No, not yet,' admitted Trevor. 'But I intend to pop out there this afternoon,' he added enthusiastically.

'Don't you have any career plans of your own?'

'Well, oddly enough I don't really have too much on at the moment,' confessed Trevor. 'I'm rather in between engagements.'

'I see,' said Mr Johnson. 'And do you have any capital?'

'No, not much.'

'You do realise that if you decide to take over the running of the golf club you won't get any cash from your uncle's estate?'

'Oh yes.'

'And you'll owe the banks a fairly huge amount of money?'

'Yes, I suppose I will.'

'And when the golf club goes under – as it surely will – you'll lose your chance of making £10,000 out of it?'

'Yes, I realise that,' said Trevor. 'I know it might seem strange but I'd really rather like to give it a go.' He hesitated a moment. 'He was family, you know.'

'Family? You never knew the man!' protested the lawyer.

'But he was my uncle!'

Mr Johnson lowered his voice in an effort to sound comforting. He sounded about as friendly as a shark eyeing up a swimmer's plump calf. 'Can I be frank with you, Mr Dukinfield?'

'Of course,' said Trevor, rather warily.

'That golf club is never going to be profitable,' said Mr Johnson. 'The only chance of making any money out of the course is to sell it for building houses or factories. £10,000 is a very fair offer.'

'I think I'd rather keep the club,' said Trevor.

'Well, be it on your own head,' sighed Mr Johnson.

'The way I look at it is this,' said Trevor. 'When I first received your letter I was broke and unemployed. If I fail to make a go of the golf club I won't be any worse off but I will at least have tried.'

'Very well, Mr Dukinfield,' said Mr Johnson, as though humouring a man intent on squandering his last few coppers on a gamble certain to fail. 'If that's what you're determined to do with the consequences of your good fortune ...!' Mr Johnson paused for a moment as though expecting Trevor to change his mind at any moment. 'But I do suggest that before you make any final decision you go and take a look at what you're letting yourself in for. Would you like me to give them a ring and tell them that you're coming?'

'Er, no, thanks,' said Trevor. 'That's very kind of you but there's no need for that.

CHAPTER FOUR

It was a gloriously sunny day. The sky was blue and cloudless. A perfect day to view the golf club you've just inherited.

'Excuse me,' shouted Trevor to a boy on a tractor. 'Can you tell me how far it is to the clubhouse?'

The boy on the tractor, who wore a voluminous, shapeless, grubby, green oilcloth coat with several tears in it and had rather large quantities of longish, light brown hair escaping from underneath a long peaked baseball cap, bent forward and fiddled with something on the right of the steering wheel. The tractor slowed and the noise the engine was making dropped appreciably. The tractor was so old and covered in rust and dried grass cuttings that it was impossible to see what colour it was painted when it had left the factory.

'Pardon?' shouted the young tractor driver, who had been cutting the fairway grass on the part of the course on the right-hand side of the roadway.

Trevor repeated his question.

The boy looked around. 'Where's your car?'

'I came by taxi. I got the driver to drop me off at the entrance to the drive,' shouted Trevor, who had made the same mistake as he had when he had visited Pettigrew Towers. 'I didn't realise it was such a long way!'

'Pardon?'

Trevor repeated what he'd said.

'Where are your clubs?'

'Clubs?'

'Golf clubs!'

'I haven't got any!'

'Sorry?'

'What?'

'Say it again, please. I didn't hear. When I've been on the tractor for an hour or so I can't hear very well for ages.'

'You should wear ear protectors!'

'What did you say?'

'I haven't got any.'

'Oh,' said the boy, looking puzzled.

'I've only come to have a look round.'

'There isn't much to see. Are you thinking of joining?'

'Is there a waiting list?'

The boy laughed. He pointed forward. 'Keep straight on. It's about half a mile,' he said. Then he fiddled about with the something to the right of the steering wheel again and shot off back onto the fairway. The grass cutters behind the tractor sprang into action, whirling grass cuttings high into the air and hiding the tractor cab behind a wall of green mist. In the distance Trevor could just make out a solitary golfer who seemed to be attacking the turf with one of his clubs, repeatedly raining blows upon the grass.

Trevor trudged on along the unmade road and gazed out at what he could see of the golf course. The land was naturally hilly and well stocked with a dozen different varieties of mature, broad-leafed trees including oak, chestnut, beech, sycamore and elm. If he turned his head and looked to the left he could see that there were several fairways on that side of the rough roadway too.

Suddenly, the noise of the tractor dropped a few dozen decibels again. Trevor looked across to where the ancient vehicle had stopped and watched the boy jump down from the cab, land lightly on the grass, and run forwards and slightly to his left, into the light rough that bordered the fairway. The boy bent down, picked up something small and white and slipped it into his pocket before running back to the tractor, climbing back aboard and driving off again. The boy was, of course, doing what all greenkeepers do; supplementing his paltry income by collecting stray golf balls to clean, sort and sell back to the members who had lost them in the first place. But Trevor knew so little about golf that he thought the boy had jumped down off his cab merely to pick a mushroom he had spotted.

* * *

Ten minutes later Trevor walked over the brow of a small hill and suddenly found himself walking not on the rough and uneven stony roadway to which his feet had rather reluctantly grown accustomed but on a worn and frost damaged stretch of tarmac which was so thin that it looked as if it had been spread by a mean-spirited British Rail chef wielding a butter knife.

The tarmac had been laid as a car park and whoever had ordered the laying of the artificial surface seemed to have been unreasonably optimistic for although there was room for over a hundred cars there were no more than half a dozen vehicles parked there. The parking spaces nearest the entrance to the clubhouse were marked with small wooden signs. Each of these small boards was painted white and had one or two words neatly painted on it in black capital letters. The signs said: PRESIDENT, VICE-PRESIDENT, CAPTAIN, LADY CAPTAIN, SECRETARY, PROFESSIONAL. There were cars parked only in the last two of these marked spaces.

The oldest part of the clubhouse was built of wood in the style of a Victorian village cricket pavilion, complete with a modest clock tower, but at various times small additions had been made. On the left of the original building there stood an extension built from concrete blocks and on the right there was a small prefabricated extension. Both supplements to the main building were painted white; or, rather, they had been painted white when they had last been decorated some years earlier. Wind, rain and sunshine had managed to remove most of the paint. The original part of the clubhouse had a roof made of grey slate; the concrete block extension had a roof made of large red tiles, some of which were missing, and the prefabricated part of the building had an invisible flat roof.

About fifty yards or so to the right of this architectural lucky bag there was a large, green and cream static caravan which, judging from the notices leaning against the side of it, served as the professional's shop. And fifty yards even further to the right there were two smaller caravans. Both of these had probably been white when they had been delivered by their manufacturers but many years of sunshine and rain had turned them a rather unpleasant shade of cream. Although both caravans had clearly been originally intended to travel neither of them looked as if they had moved for some considerable time.

Trevor's first impression was that Butterbury Ford Golf Club was not in the first tier of clubs. It was, he realised, unlikely to be playing host to the British Open in the immediately foreseeable future.

'I say! You there!'

Trevor turned towards the direction from which this unfriendly cry had come. He shaded his eyes against the sun with his hand.

'Yes, you!'

A small, stoutish man, dressed in a smart blue blazer and a pair of neatly creased, cream flannels, had appeared at the entrance to the clubhouse and was standing at the top of the short flight of steps which led down into the car park. His hair was neatly parted just above his left ear, with the longer strands being used to hide some of what was an almost entirely bald head. He wore a small toothbrush sized brown moustache on his upper lip and the breast pocket of his blazer was decorated with a gold braided badge. He stood as though to attention. Two of the shiny gold buttons on the blazer were fastened.

'Hello!' said Trevor, cheerily, turning and starting to walk towards him.

'I'm afraid this is a private club!' said the man in the blazer, walking slowly down the steps. 'Are you a member?' He stopped on the bottom step.

'No,' admitted Trevor. 'But I thought I'd take a look around. I'd rather like to learn to play golf.'

'I don't know about that. It's not a school!' said the man. 'This is a very exclusive club, you know.'

'Are you the secretary?' asked Trevor.

'Good heavens, no!' replied the man. 'Name is Jarrold. Captain Jarrold. Ex-Army. Royal Engineers.' He checked the buttons on his jacket and pulled himself up to his full five feet seven inches. 'Member of the Committee and Deputy Chairman Elect of the Finance and General Purposes Committee.'

'Pleased to meet you,' said Trevor. He introduced himself, though, through a mixture of natural modesty and a rather cunning desire to find out as much about the club as he could, did not mention that he was legally the owner of the club and the course. 'Who should I see about getting some lessons?'

'Never played before?'

'No,' confessed Trevor. 'Well, only on the crazy golf course in Weston-super-Mare.'

'Hrrmph!' said Captain Jarrold, scowling. 'You'd better have a word with the professional.'

'Do you know where he is?'

'Try his shop,' was Captain Jarrold's suggestion, with a nod in the direction of the static caravan. 'If he isn't there Mrs Weatherby will know where he is.' And with this advice the man in the blazer turned, made his way back up the pavilion steps and disappeared once more inside the building.

* * *

The inside of the static caravan was well stocked with golfing paraphernalia. In addition to the rows of clubs and the selection of bags which Trevor had expected to find on sale there were special, multicoloured golfing umbrellas; three plastic mannequins modelling tasteless plaid trousers in three sickly combinations of green and red together with pastel coloured jumpers decorated with neatly embroidered slogans and small yellow giraffes; golf shoe boxes piled from floor to ceiling; three plastic buckets filled with used golf balls ('Take Your Pick: 50p, 75p, £1.00'); wet weather gear specially designed and marketed for golfers; golf gloves; golf socks; patented pitch repairing devices; videos demonstrating how well-known professional golfers win championships and, for some unexplained reason, two dozen, shiny, chromium-plated coffee making machines all still in their presentation boxes.

At the far end of the caravan, behind a small collapsible table upon which were piled score cards, a cardboard box containing patented 'all weather' golf tees and a small plastic rack holding round tins of special 'golf sweets', sat a pleasant looking but rather shapeless woman of about fifty who wore a grey cardigan over a blue and grey patterned dress. It wasn't cold in the caravan but she wore green, fingerless gloves

'I'm looking for the professional,' said Trevor. 'Are you Mrs Weatherby?'

'Iris Weatherby,' said the woman, with a kindly smile. 'Gunther is on the practice green with Mrs Dussenberg.'

'Is Gunther the professional?'

Iris nodded. 'Gunther Schmidt.'

'How long has Mr Schmidt been the professional here?'

Iris pursed her lips and thought for a moment. 'It must be three or four years,' she replied at last. 'I've been here nearly that long.'

'What's he like?' asked Trevor.

Iris laughed and leant forward confidentially. 'He's a bit of a ladies' man,' she told Trevor with a wink. She had a small growth on her right upper eyelid which wobbled when she winked.

'Is he a good golfer?'

Iris looked puzzled by this question. 'I don't know,' she said. 'He's the professional so I suppose he must be.'

'Don't you play?'

Iris laughed; a glorious, full-throated laugh. 'Me? Don't be silly. Not with my legs. Not at my age.'

'Can you tell me where the practice ground is?' asked Trevor.

Iris levered herself up out of her chair and bent down towards the window nearest to Trevor. He couldn't help noticing that she had elastic bandages wrapped around both legs. 'Just go round behind the back of the clubhouse and then walk about three hundred yards to the left. There's a small copse and you'll find the practice area behind it. You should see Gunther and Mrs Dussenberg there'.

Trevor thanked Iris for her help and went outside in search of Gunther Schmidt.

* * *

Iris Weatherby's instructions were entirely accurate and Trevor spotted the golf professional and his pupil immediately. It wasn't difficult. Mr Schmidt was wearing a pair of the sort of plaid trousers which were on display in his shop together with a bright red sweater and a plaid Tam O'Shanter cap which matched his trousers. The bottoms of his trousers were tucked into long patterned socks, but instead of making them look like plus fours (which was, presumably, the intention), the result was that the professional's trousers simply looked as though they had been tucked into his socks. He was standing directly behind a tall, statuesque, dark-haired woman whom Trevor assumed must be Mrs Dussenberg. She was wearing a short, tight lilac-coloured skirt, a tight-fitting pink sweater with a tiny giraffe embroidered over her left breast and a rather fetching Tam O'Shanter, worn at a very jaunty angle. A huge red leather golf bag lay nearby alongside a red plastic bucket full of balls and a curious looking three foot long yellow cylindrical plastic tube for which Trevor could imagine no useful purpose.

Mrs Dussenberg and Mr Schmidt had managed to get into probably the only position which enabled them both to hold the same golf club at the same time while facing in the same direction. Mrs Dussenberg was bending forward slightly and gripping the club firmly with both hands. The professional, the front of his body pressed very tightly against Mrs Dussenberg's rear, had his arms wrapped around her chest and waist, and his hands wrapped around her hands. He seemed to be holding her very firmly. He was whispering something to her and Mrs Dussenberg was giggling.

Trevor, who had approached unnoticed, and had originally intended to wait until a suitable moment before making his presence known, suddenly realised that the suitable moment was not getting any closer for neither Mrs Dussenberg nor Mr Schmidt seemed in the slightest bit interested in using the golf club as anything other than a prop. He was tempted to retreat and had started to do so when his natural sense of discretion was overwhelmed by courage. Rather to his own surprise, he found himself making a polite and entirely artificial coughing sound. Mrs Dussenberg and Mr Schmidt responded immediately to this delicate interruption and sprang apart as though they had both suddenly acquired matching magnetic polarities.

'I'm terribly sorry to bother you,' said Trevor, slightly embarrassed and genuinely apologetic.

'What are you wanting?' demanded the professional, his face visibly reddening with startling speed despite his suntan. He had dark, bushy eyebrows, wrinkled and heavily weathered skin and copious amounts of black hair emerging from his nostrils and his ears. The escaping hair looked rather thick and wiry, and this aspect of Mr Schmidt's appearance reminded Trevor of a burst sofa. Mrs Dussenberg, who had retained hold of the golf club and who was now standing at least six feet away from Mr Schmidt, used one free hand first to adjust her jumper, then her Tam O'Shanter and finally to re-tousle her already carefully tousled hair.

Trevor swallowed and began to stutter. 'I, er, I j-j-j-just, er, w-w-w-wondered if I could b-b-b-book a few lessons?' He had not stuttered since he had been at school where a German maths teacher had terrified the life out of him. If he had spent a year with a psychoanalyst he would have discovered that the stutter had been revived by the professional's heavy German accent.

'What are your names?'

Trevor looked around. Not counting Iris Weatherby, invisible in the static caravan, there was, to the best of his knowledge, no one else within half a mile. 'I b-b-b-beg your p-p-p-pardon?'

'Your names!' shouted Mr Schmidt. 'What are your names?'

'Me?'

'Yes, you!' roared the German. 'Who else are there? Do you not English speak? What are your names?'

'T-T-T-Trevor,' replied Trevor. 'T-T-T-Trevor D-D-D-Dukinfield.'

'One half of an hours!' said Schmidt. 'You are to my shop in one half an hours coming. Yes?'

'Y-y-y-yes,' agreed Trevor. 'F-f-f-fine. Thank you.' He waved a hand in salute, turned and hurried back towards the clubhouse. Behind him he heard a woman giggling and a man snorting. He assumed that the giggling came from Mrs Dussenberg and the snorting from Mr Schmidt though he did not dare to turn round to confirm this suspicion.

* * *

Iris wasn't in the shop when Trevor got back and the car park was still more or less deserted. Only the steady drone of the grass cutting tractor confirmed that there was any other human activity in the neighbourhood. Trevor walked slowly across the car park towards the clubhouse entrance, climbed the steps and went in through the front door.

The entrance led into a small hallway, and in contrast to the brightness of the sunlight it was dark inside the clubhouse. As Trevor's eyes grew accustomed to the lack of light he could see that there were a dozen or more notices pinned to the wall in front of him and to the doors on his left and his right.

Two or three of these notices gave advance notice of club competitions and invited members to sign their names if they wanted to take part. None of the notices had attracted more than half a dozen signatures, and if Trevor had bothered to examine them carefully he would have probably harboured doubts about their validity for it is surely unlikely that one club could boast members with such illustrious names as 'Mickey Mouse' and 'Adolf Hitler'.

Most of the notices, however, contained instructions, admonitions and warnings. These were largely written in red felt-tip pen and although all seemed elderly and rather dog-eared, and judging by the pin holes in their corners had been up long enough to need to be repositioned on numerous occasions (one or two had faded and become almost completely unreadable), they were presumably all still intended to convey important information to the members.

He discovered that he was not to enter the clubhouse if he wore shoes with spikes in them, shorts or denim trousers. He was warned that he was under an obligation to replace all his divots, repair all pitch marks, give way to faster players and regard the ditch between the 7th and 8th fairways as 'ground under repair'. He learned that his membership fee would include a modest (though unspecified) contribution to the Christmas Staff Fund, that any member who parked in the Secretary's Car Parking Space would automatically be suspended from the club for six months, that until a new septic tank had been installed members were asked to use the toilets as sparingly as possible and that members who wanted a 10% discount off golfing holidays in Palm Beach should see the professional as soon as possible.

After studying these notices for a few moments Trevor opened the door on his left, which was marked LOUNGE, and walked into a room which had all the charm of a waiting room at a provincial railway station. There were half a dozen people in the room. Captain Jarrold, Deputy Chairman Elect of the Finance and General Purposes Committee, sat playing bridge with three other men in blazers. A large, unhealthy looking man wearing green checked trousers and a pale blue sweater with a giraffe embroidered on the right breast sat on a bar stool smoking an enormous cigar and wheezing noisily. A painfully thin man who was wearing a short white coat and a black, clip on bow tie which had become loose and was hanging rather precariously from one collar point stood behind the bar wearily wiping a pint glass with a rather unhygienic looking tea towel.

Trevor was uncomfortably aware that several pairs of eyes were staring at him. 'Good afternoon, gentlemen,' he said.

For a moment no one said anything in response to what they

seemed to regard as a controversial and presumably impertinent affront.

Captain Jarrold eventually broke the silence.

'I did explain to this visitor that this is a private club,' he said, speaking to a man in the blazer who sat on his left.

'Yes, you did,' agreed Trevor, delighted to hear that his stammer had disappeared. 'But I've arranged an appointment with the professional for a lesson and I thought that I could perhaps get a drink while I wait. A cup of coffee perhaps?' He paused. 'And maybe I could talk to someone about joining the club.'

'I'm afraid not,' said the man in the blazer who was sitting on Captain Jarrold's right. He seemed genuinely apologetic. 'The lounge is for members only.' The man had to twist round in order to speak to Trevor. 'I bid two hearts,' he said.

'How do I join the club?' asked Trevor, terribly tempted by the rudeness of this response to declare his hand; to tell them that he now owned the club; that it was his chairs they were sitting in and probably even his cards which they were using to play bridge. But he said nothing. The time, he felt, was not yet right.

'I'm afraid you need to get an application form from the secretary's office and get it signed by two members,' said the man in the blazer.

'Three spades,' said the man in the blazer on the right of the man in the blazer who had told Trevor that he needed to get an application form from the secretary's office.

'Oh, right,' said Trevor. 'Where do I find the secretary?'

'I'm the secretary,' said the man in the blazer. 'Trout's the name. Bartholomew Trout. Wing Commander Bartholomew Trout.' Every time he spoke he twisted round so that he could look at Trevor and every time Trevor replied he twisted round so that Trevor was speaking to his back.

The man in a blazer on the right of the secretary, whose turn it was to bid, shook his head.

'Oh, jolly good,' smiled Trevor. 'Do you think I could trouble you for an application form then, please?'

'I'm afraid not!' said the man in the blazer. 'Sorry. But you're not allowed in here. The lounge is for members only.' He seemed genuinely saddened by the fact that the rules were so restrictive.

Trevor scratched his head. 'Well, if I go outside would you bring me a form?' he asked.

'I'm afraid I can't do that,' said Wing Commander Trout, as though he had been asked to do something illegal.

Trevor thought for a moment. 'So, how do I get hold of an application form?' he asked.

'You can write in for one but you must enclose a stamped, self-addressed envelope,' replied Wing Commander Trout.

'Five spades,' said Captain Jarrold.

'Oh,' said Trevor. 'Well, if that's the only way ... !' He was beginning to understand why the club had such a small membership.

'I'm afraid it is. Six hearts.'

After a moment's thought Wing Commander Trout shook his head. The player on his right then quickly shook his head too. The enthusiastic player on the left of the secretary started to lay out his cards.

Trevor left the clubhouse, trotted down the steps and walked back across the car park towards Mr Schmidt's shop and his first golfing lesson.

*   *   *

'So are you wanting golf to learn to play?'

'Y-y-yes, p-p-please,' said Trevor. They were standing together in the static caravan and Trevor's stutter had come back. The golf professional rather frightened him. Iris Weatherby was back behind her small table. She had smiled when she'd seen Trevor and had, he thought, winked at him in an unusually friendly, rather motherly sort of way.

'Good, good!' said Mr Schmidt, rubbing his hands together with undisguised glee. He had taken off his Tam O'Shanter cap to reveal a large bald patch surrounded by a thick growth of black hair. From the ears up it made him look a little like a monk. 'That is very good. But first we must be making you with the equipment.'

'C-c-c-couldn't I j-j-j-just have the lesson and see how I g-g-get on?' asked Trevor. 'I might not like it or be any g-g-g-good at it.'

'Nonsense!' cried the German, brushing aside these fears with a wave of his hand. He reached up and pulled down a long club with a large, round reddish brown head stuck to one end and a corrugated rubber grip wrapped around the other. 'The driver!' he said. 'With this you will hit the big time. Yes?'

The professional handed the club to Trevor. 'There, you see, it a perfect fit is!' he said. 'It might have been for you made. When the balloon goes up you will be barking up the right tree with this.'

Trevor looked down. He could see no way in which a piece of metal with a rubberised grip on the handle could possibly satisfy this professional forecast.

'Now you must this have, and one of these, and of these one, and of those, and these, and this and that and all of these.' As he spoke Mr Schmidt pulled down club after club and handed them all to Trevor. 'These are good, you know. The very best. With these you will have the irons in the fire that you need. And now you need a bag in which they to store.'

Trevor looked down at the armful of clubs he was holding. 'I need s-s-s-something to hold them,' he agreed. 'But c-c-c-couldn't I maybe just buy a second hand set? Do I really need all these c-c-c-clubs?'

'It important is that you with the best equipment start,' said the German. 'A bad working man will ...,' he stopped, obviously lost. 'How do you say?'

'B-b-b-blame his t-t-t-tools?' suggested Trevor.

'You have it!' cried Mr Schmidt. 'A bad working man will blame his tool! Otherwise he will be in the hole.' He raised a finger high to mark this pronouncement. 'You must yourself give no chance your tools to blame.'

'N-n-n-no, I suppose not,' said Trevor reluctantly, privately thinking that he might soon be grateful of a chance to blame his tools. 'H-h-how much will all this c-c-cost?'

'Pfui!' said the German, with a flamboyant wave of his hand and arm. 'What is this with the costings? You must not cut off your skin to spite your nose.'

'We usually say either that you m-m-must not c-c-cut off your nose to spite your face or that it is no skin off your nose,' said Trevor boldly.

'You do?' frowned Mr Schmidt. 'I have been taken for a ride.' He scowled. 'I have a book on your English sayings but there are so many sheep in the clothings of the wolves.'

'I m-m-might not have the m-m-money,' explained Trevor.

The German turned to him suddenly. 'You are poor?' he asked, anxiously. 'You do not have two stones to rub together?'

'Well, sort of,' said Trevor.

'Ah, sort of poor!' said the German gleefully. 'When you English are rich you always say you are sort of poor.'

'I'm not rich,' insisted Trevor. 'And I haven't even m-m-managed to j-j-join the c-c-club yet.'

'Pfui. This is nothing of a problem,' said Schmidt. 'No problem.' He winked.

'Oh,' said Trevor. 'Right. Thank you.'

'My pleasure,' beamed the German. 'You are to scratching my bottom and I am doing likewise with yours.' He looked around the shop. 'Now what else are you needing? Shoes, yes? What size in shoes do you have?'

Trevor, wondering if the fact that he owned the golf club meant that the shop and its contents were his, told the professional his shoe size.

'Splendid!' cried the German, pulling down a shoe box and handing it to Trevor. 'And you are the glove and balls needing? Yes?'

'I suppose so,' agreed Trevor reluctantly, removing his own shoes and putting on the spiked shoes the professional had handed him.

Twenty minutes later, laden down with more equipment than he could comfortably carry, walking uncertainly in his first pair of spiked shoes and dressed for the part in golfing clothes which the professional assured him were the very latest in golfing fashion, Trevor followed Mr Schmidt out of the caravan into the sunshine and headed off towards the practice ground for his first golf lesson.

* * *

They stopped by the side of a small flat area of grass which was decorated with two small tee markers which Trevor rightly assumed had been made by pouring concrete into plastic flower pots.

'Right!' said Mr Schmidt, grinning broadly and handing Trevor a plastic, cellophane and cardboard packet. 'Put on your glove and we then start the game.' The concrete tee markers had at one time been painted white and someone had painted what looked vaguely like a P on each of them. Clods of earth which had been dug out of the grass tee were strewn on the fairway a few yards away.

Trevor laid his bag of clubs down on the ground and with some difficulty tore open the packet he had been handed. He examined the contents carefully. 'Er, I'm afraid there's only one g-g-glove here,' he pointed out.

'Yes?' said the golf professional, examining the contents of the opened packet and nodding his agreement. 'This is correct.'

'But surely there should be two...!'

'Two?'

'One for each hand?' suggested Trevor. He held out his arms to amplify the point he was making.

Mr Schmidt looked puzzled. 'In golf we only wear gloves on one hand,' he explained.

'Oh,' said Trevor. 'Why?'

'Because the gloves are sold in singlets,' explained Mr Schmidt.

Trevor decided that he could think of no suitable response to this. He shrugged and pulled the solitary glove onto his left hand. Looking around and finding nowhere to throw the now unwanted packaging he pushed it into his pocket.

'Now like a golfer you are looking!' beamed Mr Schmidt.

Trevor looked down at his black and white spiked shoes with their tasselled laces, his green and red plaid trousers dutifully tucked, as he had been instructed, into white and blue checked calf-length socks and his fluorescent pink mohair sweater with a small embroidered giraffe marking the position of his left breast and wondered idly whether looking like a complete and utter pillock was an essential part of the game of golf. He felt relieved that no one he knew was there to see him. The golf professional bent down and carefully selected a club from Trevor's bag.

'Will I really n-n-n-need this many c-c-c-clubs?' asked Trevor. 'They don't b-b-break do they?'

'Break?' said Mr Schmidt, puzzled. 'These clubs will not break!' He lifted the club he had chosen high into the air and smashed it down onto the ground a few inches away from Trevor's left foot. Trevor, who thought that the professional had taken offence and had been aiming at him leapt backwards. Or, rather, he tried to leap backwards. He discovered, however, that the spikes on his shoes had secured his feet firmly to the ground. The result was that although his body leapt backwards his feet remained exactly where they were.

'See?' said Mr Schmidt, smiling. 'It has not broken! I will not flog you a dead horse!'

'No,' said Trevor, lying flat on his back on the ground and trying to look impressed. 'That's g-g-g-good! Very good.' He pushed himself up into a sitting position and rubbed his left elbow which hurt.

*   *   *

Twenty-five minutes later Trevor gazed in astonishment and delight as the small white ball which had, a moment earlier, lain unmoving on the grass before him, soared high into the air and sailed away towards the practice green.

It was his first proper golf shot; his first moment of unalloyed pleasure; his first taste of the joy that comes from an almost perfect hit. It was, in truth, his only decent golf shot of the morning.

He had missed the ball more than he had hit it. His club had hit the ground so often that his elbow ached. He didn't know it at the time but that one good shot was a complete fluke. And that shot hooked Trevor Dukinfield as surely as a perfectly tied fly will catch a salmon.

Mr Schmidt the golf professional was wise enough to know that he had arrived at the right moment to stop for the morning.

'You have hit the big time!' he cried with unconcealed delight. 'Any professional would have with that shot been as pleased as a punch. Here's mud in your eye! Same time next week?'

'Maybe we could make it sooner than that?' suggested Trevor, his stammer conquered by the new found confidence born of success; blissfully unaware of the heartache yet to come; quite unaware of the fact that for every perfect shot there will be a thousand shots exhibiting varying degrees of imperfection.

Like a million other golfers Trevor had been suckered into a love for the game of golf by a single, apparently effortless and successful shot. And like the other million golfers he would eventually learn that the difficulty in golf is not to play a single good shot (anyone can play one good shot) but to play a sequence of good shots.

'Certainly!' said Mr Schmidt, with a broad smile. 'I'll be on top of the moon and as happy as a cat with nine tails to see you tomorrow!'

CHAPTER FIVE

Although Trevor's moment of glory on the practice ground may have sealed his affection for the game of golf it had not softened his brain entirely.

'It isn't going to be easy,' he warned Sylvia, when he telephoned her that evening from London. 'But it's a tremendous challenge and I think I owe it to my Uncle Archibald to try to make a go of it.'

Sylvia, who had not yet said anything apart from 'But...' and 'Er...' in response to Trevor's announcement that he intended to turn down a £10,000 inheritance and take on the responsibility of running a golf club, finally managed to speak.

'Don't I get a say in this?' she demanded. The venom in her voice was unmistakable. Not even Trevor could avoid noticing it.

'Of course you do, dear,' said Trevor, suddenly conscious for the first time of the fact that Sylvia was not quite as excited as he was by the prospect of owning and running a golf club.

'I think you're being absolutely stupid,' said Sylvia firmly. She wasn't a woman who was shy about speaking her mind. 'You don't know anything about running a golf club. It's bound to be an absolute disaster. You are a fool sometimes, Trevor Dukinfield.'

Trevor hesitated. 'I know you're not quite as enthusiastic as I am at the moment,' he said. 'But that's probably just because I rather sprang it all on you.'

Sylvia sighed. 'You don't even play golf!' she pointed out. 'You don't know a thing about the game.'

'Ah, well you're wrong there,' said Trevor, feeling that he was now on slightly firmer ground. 'I had my first lesson this morning and even if I do say so myself I think it was pretty successful.' He paused, closed his eyes and visualised his final shot of the morning. 'There was this one shot I played which was absolutely tremendous. I was using a seven iron – that's a fairly lofted club – and although I suppose there may have been a little bit of luck in it I must have caught the ball just right. The professional said afterwards that he couldn't have played the shot better himself.' Trevor did not bother Sylvia with details of the other 99 muffed shots he had played for he felt that these would be unlikely to attract her interest in the same way. Besides, he thought, the good shot had been his last shot of the morning session and it did not seem unreasonable to argue that all the other shots had merely been in preparation for that moment of golfing glory.

'It's really not a terribly difficult game,' he told Sylvia, with all the calm confidence of a man who knows virtually nothing of the game but has learnt the one fundamental truth of any sport: that the greatest joy is not playing but talking about it afterwards. 'You should try it. I hope you will!'

Sylvia was not impressed by Trevor's account of his morning's success. 'I have absolutely no interest in taking up golf,' she insisted coldly. 'And I'm surprised that you want to waste valuable hours hitting a silly little ball around a field.' She paused. Trevor started to point out that golf wasn't played in a field but Sylvia wasn't interested in the minutiae of the argument. 'Anyway,' she went on, 'whether or not you start playing golf is hardly the point. What I really find difficult to believe is that you are being so stupid.'

'But ...,' began Trevor, rather tentatively.

Now that Sylvia had started, stopping her was not going to be easy.

'For one thing,' she said, 'how on earth do you expect to be able to run a golf club in the Midlands when you're living in London?'

'I'm giving up my room in London,' said Trevor immediately.

'It just won't be possible,' continued Sylvia. 'You'll spend all your time travelling and you'll always be in the wrong place. Besides, all the travelling will cost you a fortune. It's not even as though you can drive up and down.' She paused as Trevor's last sentence sank in. 'What did you say?'

'What do you mean? I didn't say anything.' said Trevor.

'Yes, you did. A moment ago. You said something about giving up your room in London.'

'Oh, yes.'

'But, but, but how on earth are you going to get another job in Fleet Street if you don't live in London?' demanded Sylvia. She blew out air like a whale surfacing. 'Oh good heavens,' she said. 'I don't know what I'm going to do with you. I'm beginning to think that mother was right.'

'What do you mean?' asked Trevor. 'What did your mother say about me?'

'Never mind. It doesn't matter,' said Sylvia, hurriedly. 'You can't really be serious about this,' she said. 'Please tell me you aren't really throwing away your career to run a bankrupt golf club in the Midlands!'

'It isn't bankrupt!' said Trevor. 'And I don't have a career to throw away.'

'It can't be far off bankrupt if it's only worth £10,000!' insisted Sylvia. 'And what do you mean you don't have a career? You've worked in Fleet Street!'

'It was a terrible job, Sylvia!' protested Trevor, plaintively. 'I hated every moment of it. And I'm not really cut out for that sort of work anyway.'

'And I suppose you are cut out for running a golf club?'

'I don't know,' said Trevor honestly. 'But I'd like to try.'

'Well, if you want ever to see me again,' said Sylvia in her 'This is an ultimatum and just you take notice!' voice which Trevor knew so well and dreaded so much, 'you can jolly well tell that wretched little solicitor of yours that you've changed your mind; that you want the £10,000 they promised you and that they can sell the ...,' at this point Sylvia paused, as though summoning up words from some distance away, 'damned golf club to anyone silly enough to want to buy it,' she finished in a rush. The mild profanity brought an undisguised blush to her voice.

'I can't tell him that!' said Trevor. 'It's too late now.'

Strictly speaking this was not true. However, since Trevor had his fingers crossed when he told Sylvia that it was too late, the lie didn't really count.

'Well you know how I feel about it,' said Sylvia firmly. She sighed. 'What you do is up to you now.'

And she put the telephone down so firmly that Trevor jumped away from his handset as though it had exploded.

*   *   *

Trevor was back in his flat scraping the burnt bits off a round of toast when his doorbell went. At first he didn't know what the noise was. His doorbell hadn't ever rung before. When he eventually realised what the ringing denoted he put down the toast and the knife, opened his front door, walked out onto the landing and peered downstairs. Through the frosted glass in the front door he could just see the shadow of a visitor.

'Yes?' he shouted, hoping that the visitor might hear him and push open the never locked front door. The visitor was, he thought, almost certainly for someone else in the house. The response to his shout was, however, simply another ring of the doorbell.

With a weary sigh Trevor walked down the stairs and opened the front door. A thin, rather neatly dressed fellow stood there. He was wearing a dark brown leather jacket, a pair of dark green corduroy trousers and a flat cap worn at an unmistakably rakish angle.

'Willie!' said Trevor, unable to hide the surprise from his voice.

'Hello, Trevor!' grinned the visitor. 'How are you? It took me ages to find you. Aren't you going to invite me in?' He bent down and picked up a well-filled brown canvas and leather holdall that was parked on the step beside him. He had the build of a jockey and moved with the same easy grace and confidence.

Trevor opened the door wider and stood back. 'What on earth are you doing here?' he demanded.

Willie walked into the hall and Trevor shut the door behind him. 'Can you put me up for the night?'

'Well, there isn't much room, but, yes, I suppose so!'

Trevor turned and the two of them started to climb the stairs. 'Why? Whatever's happened? Where's Julia?'

Willie frowned. 'Julia?'

'Your wife,' explained Trevor.

'Oh Julia and I got divorced months ago,' said Willie. 'The current model is called Brenda.'

'Oh,' said Trevor. 'You didn't mention it when we spoke last.'

'Didn't seem important,' said Willie.

'No,' Trevor sighed. 'Maybe not. So, what's happened to Brenda?'

'Bit of a story, old chap,' said Willie. 'But the short version is that we've split up temporarily.'

Trevor stopped and Willie collided with him. Trevor turned round. 'I'm sorry!' said Trevor, apologising both for the collision and the collapse of Willie's most recent marriage.

Willie shrugged and grinned. He had a rather lopsided grin which, Trevor remembered, had for some inexplicable reason always made him attractive to women and a charm that had been known to sway traffic wardens in the pursuit of their duty. The two of them had been at university together and had shared a flat. 'These things happen,' he said.

'How on earth did you find me?' asked Trevor.

'I rang Sylvia.' Willie sniffed noisily. 'Is that cooking I can smell?'

'That's funny. She didn't say anything,' said Trevor. 'I was on the phone to her a few minutes ago.' He led the way into his tiny flat. 'Toast,' he said. 'Not really cooking.'

'I didn't actually tell her that I was coming to see you,' admitted Willie, looking around. 'I just asked for your address.' He frowned and paused. 'I don't think Sylvia has ever really approved of me.' He put down his bag. 'Is this where you live?'

Having spotted what he had been looking for he strode quickly across the kitchen and picked up Trevor's piece of burnt toast.

'No,' agreed Trevor. 'I don't think she has. Mind you, I don't think she entirely approves of me at the moment.' He looked around the flat as though seeing it for the first time. 'The flat is only temporary. I'm leaving tomorrow.'

'Leaving! Where are on earth are you going?' demanded Willie, opening a drawer and finding a knife. 'I was hoping I could doss down with you for a few days.' He opened and shut all of Trevor's cupboards in rapid succession. 'Haven't you got anything except marmalade? Any jam? Butter? Margarine?'

'I've inherited a golf club,' answered Trevor, as though he'd inherited a cracked Wedgewood plate and £10 worth of savings certificates. 'And no I'm afraid I haven't got anything except marmalade. And that was my last piece of bread.'

'My uncle left me a whole set,' said Willie.

'No, not that sort of club,' said Trevor. 'I mean the whole thing. Clubhouse, greens, fairways – the lot. It's up near Mettleham.'

'You've *inherited* a *golf club*?' said Willie, smearing marmalade onto the dry toast. 'You wouldn't want this anyway,' he said. 'It's burnt. A whole golf club?'

'I know it's burnt,' said Trevor. 'I was just scraping the burnt bits off when you arrived.'

'Well you didn't do a very good job of it,' said Willie, holding up the toast so that Trevor could inspect the inadequacy of his handiwork. 'Is that where you're going?' he asked. 'To your golf club?' He stuffed the toast into his mouth and tore off a third of it with white and expensively capped teeth.

'Yes.'

'You lucky beggar!' said Willie, or at least that was what it sounded like. He sprayed bread crumbs around the kitchen as he spoke. 'Sounds like we'll have more fun there than in this place anyway,' he added, looking around and assuming without hesitation that he would be travelling to Mettleham with Trevor.

'It's not as great as it sounds,' confessed Trevor. 'The banks own most of the club and I lose the bit I've got now if I can't satisfy the conditions of my uncle's will.'

'Which are?' asked Willie, stuffing the toast into his mouth again, despite the fact that the first chunk had still not disappeared.

Trevor explained.

'Easy!' cried Willie, finishing off the toast. 'No problem!'

'Oh, I don't know about that!' said Trevor, far less confidently.

'You'll pick it up in no time!' promised Willie.

'I didn't know you played golf.'

'Of course I do! I've played since I was a kid. Our house backed onto a golf course and I used to nip over the fence after school and bash my way round with a couple of old clubs.'

'I don't suppose you ever bothered joining the club or paying green fees?'

'What would I want to do that for? There was only a broken down old fence between us and the course.' He sighed. 'In fact it was golf that led to my splitting up with Brenda.'

'Golf!' repeated Trevor, genuinely surprised. Willie had always had something of a deserved reputation as a ladies' man and Trevor had assumed that the breakdown in his marriage had been a consequence of an unauthorised dalliance.

'The sales manager had organised a golf day to entertain some Japanese customers,' explained Willie. 'We were all under strict instructions to make sure that we let the managing director of the Japanese company win the trophy.'

'So, what happened?'

'After fifteen holes I was five over par,' said Willie excitedly. 'I knew I had a chance of a cracking round. Our sales manager, who had finished his round, came back to tell me that the Japanese chap, who was two holes ahead, was three strokes behind me and to tell me to hit a wild drive off the 16th and play three off the tee.'

'But you didn't?'

'Trevor, my old love, I really intended to but when it came to it I just couldn't do it. The 16th was a short hole and I knew I could get a par three there fairly easily. I thought it would add a bit to the excitement if I kept the tension going for another hole or so.'

'So you got a three?'

'I got a two. My tee shot ended up nine feet from the pin.'

'Which left you four strokes ahead?'

'Six. The Japanese chap put his drive into a stream on the 18th.'

'So what happened then?'

'I told the sales manager that it would look too obvious if I threw the match at that point,' said Willie. 'I said the Japanese would think we were patronising them.'

'What did he say?'

'He said the Japanese chap didn't give a stuff about being patronised, he just wanted to win the trophy.'

'But you didn't want to lose it?'

'I didn't give a monkey's for the trophy but by this time I knew that if I did the last two holes in par I would beat my previous best ever round!'

'What happened?'

'I did the last two holes in par, beat my previous best score and won the trophy, the Japanese broke off negotiations for an 11 million dollar contract and I was made redundant.'

'They sacked you because you won a golf tournament?'

'Not really. They sacked me because without the contract the company didn't have any work to do.

'And Brenda threw you out because you lost your job?'

'It's a bit more complicated than that,' admitted Willie. 'Her old man is a big shot in the bank which was financing the company I was working for and when the Japanese pulled out of the contract his bank took a bit of a bath.'

'Oh.'

'Brenda was a bit miffed about it all,' said Willie. He shrugged. 'She never liked golf anyway. I think I'll just keep out of the way for a while. Absence makes the heart grow fonder and all that.'

'Why on earth doesn't she like golf?' asked Trevor, who was

still innocent enough to think of golf as a genteel game, played by gentlemen.

'Oh, she said she thought that golf encouraged gambling and bad language and cost too much money.'

'Couldn't you get her to believe the truth?'

Willie looked at Trevor for a moment. 'That *is* the truth,' he said. 'Show me an honest golfer and I'll show you someone who has only been playing for a week. I've seen a priest kick his ball into a better lie when he thought no one was looking.' He paused, 'Still,' he added, with a grin. 'It was worth it.'

'Worth it? How do you make that out? You lost your job, the company you were working for went bust and you've had to leave home!'

'It was a cracking round!' said Willie defiantly.

Trevor, the novice golfer, thought for a moment. 'I see what you mean!' he said at last.

* * *

Trevor's personal belongings fitted comfortably into a blue cardboard suitcase and two plastic carrier bags. His golf bag, clubs, shoes, glove, balls, tees, trousers, sweater and other essential golfing paraphernalia had stayed in the professional's caravan at the Butterbury Ford Golf Club.

Standing on the pavement in the rain Trevor looked up at the ancient and grubby building where he'd stayed for such a short time and realised that he didn't have a single regret about leaving London. The sky was grey and he thought he could feel the acid in the rain burning into his skin. He hated the crowds and the queues and the fumes and the noise and the dirt and the weather, he hadn't enjoyed his job in the slightest and his room had had all the attractive qualities of a Turkish prison cell. He hailed a passing taxi, tossed his suitcase and his plastic bags into the back and climbed in beside them. Willie, clutching his bag, bounded into the cab as though he were an afterthought.

'Euston station, please!' said Trevor, cheerfully.

'Quick as you like, cabby!' added Willie.

'Not so much of the cabby,' snarled the driver over his shoulder. 'And I ain't doing no Stirling Moss impression in this traffic.'

'Sorry, old chap,' said Willie. 'I didn't mean...!'

'It's people like you, always in a hurry, that have given me my ulcer,' moaned the driver. 'I had a bloke in the cab two weeks ago, desperate to get to Paddington to catch his train and get off home to his missus. Some anniversary dinner or other. I felt sorry for him, did him a favour, went as fast as I could and some half blind bugger in a red Escort put a dent in my door in Sussex Gardens. What thanks do you think I got? Bloody fifty pence tip that's what I got. Fifty pence!'

'Sorry,' apologised Willie again. 'Take your time. No hurry.'

'There you go, you see,' said the cab driver, taking both hands off the wheel and throwing up his arms in despair. 'I try to be reasonable. I try to explain things to you and what do I get? Sarcasm that's what I get. 'Take your time' that's what I get.' He put his hands back onto the wheel just in time to steer his cab around the back of a bus which had stopped in front of him.

Trevor stayed silent and decided to enjoy his departure from London. He wasn't going to miss England's capital city one little bit.

CHAPTER SIX

On his arrival back in Mettleham Trevor, temporarily abandoned by Willie who had made a detour to pick up more of his belongings (in particular his golf clubs), had gone straight to the offices of Twist, Kibble and Fenshaw to see Mr Johnson.

'I've made my mind up,' Trevor said, firmly, when he was shown into Mr Johnson's office. 'I'm going to try and make a go of the golf club.'

Mr Johnson stared solemnly and gloomily at Trevor's suitcase and plastic bags. 'It seems a rather reckless decision, if I may say so,' he drawled, looking rather put out. 'Have you found somewhere to stay?' the lawyer asked.

'Well, I noticed that there were a couple of caravans parked at the golf club. I thought I might move into one of them.'

'And if they're already occupied?'

'Oh, I hadn't thought of that,' Trevor replied. 'They didn't look occupied.'

'Well, just let me know when you change your mind and decide that you want the money,' said Mr Johnson. 'I can't promise that you'll get the £10,000 you've been offered but if you change your mind in the next week or so I should be able to get you something near to that.'

'That's very kind of you,' said Trevor. 'But I won't change my mind.'

*   *   *

In contrast to his first visit, which had been on foot, Trevor rather felt that it would be appropriate to return to Butterbury Ford Golf Club in a more stylish manner.

And this he duly did; travelling in as much style as is possible when your mode of transport is a rather elderly Volvo saloon with a broken exhaust pipe and copious amounts of hideous pink primer dotted all over the paint work, and your chauffeur is an unshaven pensioner with a greasy, peaked cap pulled down low over his eyes, a large plastic hearing aid, connected to a rather conspicuous ear piece, hung around his neck on a piece of knotted string and a cigarette butt stuck firmly to his upper lip.

''Ere, you are, guv!' said the taxi driver, using the handbrake to help him bring the Volvo to a halt and sending a shower of loose tarmac flying against the walls of the clubhouse. 'Butterbury Ford Golf Club.'

Trevor did not get out of the car straight away but paused for a few moments to try to give his heart a chance to start beating again with some degree of regularity. The taxi driver had not shown any of the caution exhibited by his London colleague and had thrown the ancient Volvo around like a man driving a hire car.

When Trevor felt that his cardiovascular system had recovered enough to be trusted with the task of sending regular supplies of oxygenated blood gurgling merrily into his muscles and organs he opened the car door and stepped out. Despite the horrors of his journey he was glad to be back, and not even the mismatched architecture of the clubhouse could dampen his enthusiasm for Butterbury Ford Golf Club.

The sun was shining, the trees were in leaf and the birds were singing. The taxi driver had by this time already lifted Trevor's suitcase and plastic bags out of the boot and placed them on the floor by the clubhouse wall.

Trevor paid the sum the driver asked for and added a large tip, and although this was intended more as a gesture of thanksgiving than as a reward the driver misinterpreted the gesture. 'Thanks, guv,' he said, gratefully, momentarily grasping the peak of his cap between a grubby thumb and an equally grubby forefinger. 'Next time you ask for a cab I'll make sure you get me.'

'Thank you,' said Trevor, weakly. 'That's very kind of you.'

He stood and watched for a moment as the driver put the Volvo into gear and sped away back down the driveway, turning away only when the cloud of dust thrown up by the Volvo engulfed him.

Leaving his suitcase and plastic bags where the driver had abandoned them Trevor climbed the steps to the clubhouse and entered the lounge. It was like walking into yesterday, and for a brief moment Trevor wondered if he might be hallucinating. Exactly the same people were sitting and standing in exactly the same positions and doing exactly the same things.

'Good afternoon,' he said, looking around at the gloomy and familiar faces. This time the dark and gloomy lounge bar reminded him more of a funeral parlour than anything else. He walked across to where Wing Commander Trout was sitting and took a letter out of his inside jacket pocket.

'This is from Mr Gittings of Twist, Kibble and Fenshaw,' he said. 'My solicitors,' he explained. 'You'll find that it confirms that I am the new owner of the club.'

Some people would have made this announcement with arrogance or bravado. Trevor managed to sound apologetic about it. However, it was the message which was important, and the message, not the method of its delivery, which made its impact.

Six lower jaws fell and six pairs of tonsils got an unaccustomed airing as the four members, secretary and barman listened to this simple statement.

The secretary did not say anything immediately but took the letter from Trevor and then put a hand inside his jacket and pulled out a pair of spectacles. He put the spectacles on and read the letter and as he did so he paled even more.

'This says that a Mr Trevor Dukinfield is the new owner,' he croaked.

Trevor nodded. 'That's right.'

'And you're Mr Dukinfield?'

'Yes,' said Trevor.

'A relative of Mr Pettigrew's?'

'He was my uncle.'

Wing Commander Trout handed the letter back to Trevor and stood up. He swallowed hard, pulled out a bright red handkerchief and dabbed at his brow. 'I'm sorry about that little misunderstanding yesterday, sir,' he said. 'But I'm sure you wouldn't want us to let strangers into your clubhouse.' He paused for a moment and bent forwards slightly. 'Why didn't you say anything about this yesterday, sir?' he asked.

'I wasn't entirely sure whether or not I was going to take on the club then,' said Trevor, honestly. 'I thought I'd like a look around first.' He rather thought he preferred the offhand, arrogant secretary to the unctuous, obsequious one.

'And may we assume that your impression of the club was a favourable one, sir?' asked Wing Commander Trout. There were, Trevor noticed, fresh beads of sweat on his brow.

'Mixed,' said Trevor thoughtfully. 'I think the word 'mixed' would be a more accurate description of my first impression.'

'May I congratulate you, sir,' said Captain Jarrold, standing up and holding out a liver spotted hand.

'Thank you,' said Trevor.

'I'd very much like to associate myself with the secretary's apology,' said Captain Jarrold. 'If there were any misunderstandings yesterday then I'm sure that they were occasioned by our earnest desire to do our best for the club.'

'Do you know if those two small caravans are occupied?' Trevor asked Wing Commander Trout.

'The one nearest the clubhouse is, sir' answered Wing Commander Trout. 'I believe that the woman who helps the professional lives there.'

'Iris Weatherby?'

'That's the name,' agreed the club secretary. 'She also does some cleaning in the clubhouse. She lives there with her daughter and her son. If you'd like me to get rid of them I could do that straight away, sir.'

'Good heavens, no!' said Trevor, genuinely shocked. 'But there's no one living in the other caravan?'

'No, sir,' answered the secretary.

'I thought I'd move in if it was empty,' replied Trevor. 'Do you have a key?'

The Wing Commander shook his head. 'I don't think there is one, sir,' he said. 'I think it's open.'

'Jolly good,' smiled Trevor. 'I'll go and have a look.' He started to move away and then paused. 'I think we ought to have a meeting of the committee and the members,' he said. 'Would you arrange it?'

'Certainly, sir,' said Wing Commander Trout. 'We're due to have our next committee meeting on the fourth Thursday of next month. We could arrange a general meeting then.'

'I'm afraid I think we need to arrange something a little more urgently than that,' said Trevor. 'Perhaps you'd fix something up for this evening?'

'This evening?'

'That's right,' agreed Trevor. 'This evening.'

'But what shall I tell people, sir,' asked Wing Commander Trout, 'Do you have any, er, plans for the club?'

But Trevor had gone.

'Let me know if I can help in any way, sir' called the secretary after him, rather plaintively. 'Any way at all ...!'

* * *

The empty caravan was no bigger than the room Trevor had rented in London. At the far end of the caravan there were two bench seats and a collapsible plastic-topped table. The two bench seats could be pulled together to create a bed. Along one side of the caravan there was a tiny sink, a stove and a couple of cupboards. And at the other end of the caravan, the end nearest the door, there was a tiny bedroom with two bunk beds.

It may have offered cramped accommodation but the caravan did have one big advantage to offer: a splendid view of the 18th fairway and the 18th green. Had Trevor ever chosen to look out of his window in London he would have found himself staring at a blank and grimy brick wall; far too high to attract the interest of spray can artists, graffiti writers or even the ubiquitous, uncaring and much-wanted Bill Stickers. But here, deep in rural England, the view from his window was far more congenial, and with a promise of a constantly changing cast of characters it certainly looked as if it was going to be far more entertaining.

Having unpacked the belongings from his cardboard suitcase and plastic bags and crammed them into the tiny wardrobe and chest of drawers, and having opened all the windows and the skylight in order to get rid of the rather musty smell which hung in the air, Trevor squeezed into the cramped dining section of the caravan and drank in the view.

A tall, thin, miserable-looking man wearing bright yellow trousers and a green, short-sleeved, open-necked shirt with something embroidered on the left breast was walking towards the green, dragging behind him a heavy-looking metal trolley which was laden with clubs and other essential impedimenta. It was strange, thought Trevor idly, that such a simple game should require more luggage and equipment than your average explorer would consider necessary for a trip around the world.

The man, who seemed to be deeply depressed, was looking around him as though he knew he had lost something but didn't know quite where he had lost it.

Approaching from an entirely different direction, a tall, dark-haired woman wearing a bright red skirt and a sky blue blouse with something embroidered on the left breast, and with a white visor shading her eyes, came purposefully hurrying up the 18th fairway. Trevor rather thought he recognised her but couldn't remember why. She too looked as if she was more at home feeling miserable than feeling happy but she had a strangely, almost cruelly, satisfied look on what Trevor could see of her face. She looked as though, despite a life full of sadness and despair, she was gaining some satisfaction and inspiration from the fact that at least one other person on the planet was having an even worse time than she was.

It wasn't terribly difficult to guess who the other person was, and Trevor suspected that such hatred must mean that the two combatants were partners in more than a game of golf. A cynical friend had once told Trevor that more marriages are held together by the glue of mutual hatred than by the cement of mutual love, and although Trevor tried hard not to share such deeply cynical despair he sometimes found the evidence in support of the contention difficult to deny.

She also had a trolley loaded with clubs, but instead of pulling her trolley she was pushing it in front of her. The trolley also carried a black box the size of a car battery.

Just short of the green the woman stopped her trolley and stood still for a moment with her hands on her hips while she watched her partner's progress. At last, in response to a wave and a shout that Trevor couldn't quite decipher, the woman pulled a club from her bag and walked forwards purposefully for a yard or two. Peering through the dirty caravan window Trevor could just make out a ball lying cleanly on the fairway. He watched as the woman carefully settled herself into her stance, took a tentative practice swing, then took a more determined practice swing and, finally, after shuffling forwards a couple of inches, played her shot.

When the ball bounced first, right on the front of the green, it was clear that it wasn't going to be able to stop anywhere near the flag. By the time it had bounced three times it was clear that it wasn't going to stay on the green. The grass was as hard and as smooth as polished marble and the ball didn't look as if it was ever going to slow down.

The woman, her club still in her hands, leant forward and Trevor could almost *feel* her willing the ball to grip the green or, at least, to find a small, miraculously moist patch that would arrest its progress. Neither of these things happened and the ball bounced right across the green before rolling through a collar of slightly longer grass, launching itself gracefully into the air and then, finally, landing with a muffled plop into a bunker full of soft sand just a dozen yards away from Trevor's caravan. Trevor suddenly remembered where he'd seen the woman before. It was Mrs Dussenberg, Mr Schmidt's pupil.

Mrs Dussenberg could not possibly have seen exactly where her ball had landed but she certainly knew that it wasn't on the green. Trevor watched as, almost in slow motion, her facial expression changed from gloat to fury. She then slammed her club back into her bag and started to push her trolley around the green without waiting to see what her partner was doing.

Meanwhile, the woman's husband (for Trevor was now firmly convinced that they were indeed a permanent twosome) had found his ball and was busy pacing out the distance between it and the flag. When he had done this he selected a club and with surprisingly little preparation gave the ball a wholesome thwack. The ball cleared the green easily, slammed into the side of the woman's trolley and bounced back onto the putting area where it came to rest less than two yards away from the pin.

Trevor watched all this with growing curiosity and a steadily deepening sense of foreboding. Red faced with anger the woman abandoned her trolley and marched onto the green to meet her partner. He had exchanged the club he had used to such good if surprising effect for a putter and this he held tucked under his arm as he removed the glove from his left hand and slipped it into his back pocket.

'You get a two stroke penalty for that!' Trevor heard the woman shout.

'Of course I don't!' retorted the man. 'It hit your trolley not mine.'

'It doesn't matter!' said Mrs Dussenberg.

'If anyone gets penalised it's you!' said the man. He took a rule book out of his back pocket, flicked through the pages and read out loud. 'Look, here it is! It says that there's a two stroke penalty for an opponent who deflects a player's ball.'

'Don't be so stupid,' snapped the woman. 'Why on earth should *I* be penalised? Look at it!' she nodded towards her opponent's ball. 'If the damned thing hadn't hit my trolley it would have gone into the trees.'

'Don't tell me not to be stupid,' said the man. 'I put so much back spin on it that the ball would have probably spun back onto the green anyway.'

'I've never heard such absolute rubbish in all my life!' exclaimed the woman. 'Back onto the green, indeed! Are you going to take a two stroke penalty?'

'No!'

'Well, we'll see about it later,' said the woman. 'I'm going to take it up with the committee.'

'You do that.'

'I will, don't you worry!' With this retort the woman strode back across the green and wheeled her trolley and clubs towards Trevor's caravan and the bunker wherein lay her ball. Abandoning her trolley and selecting a suitable club she clambered down the grassy bank alongside the bunker and then stood and gazed in obvious despair at her ball. Trevor could see that it was very nearly buried in the sand.

The fact that the woman was furious probably didn't help her to play a decent shot. She swung at her ball more with anger than skill and although she succeeded in digging a large quantity of sand out of the bunker and spreading it all over the green she didn't manage to move the ball; that stayed exactly where it was.

'It doesn't seem to have come out,' called the man. 'Perhaps you'd better have another go'

Mrs Dussenberg said nothing but stood and glared down at her ball. Then, Trevor watched with absolute amazement as, hidden from her partner's view by the wall of the bunker, she deftly and surreptitiously kicked her ball into a more playable position. She then played a relatively easy shot up onto the green and sank her ball with two putts. Her partner sank his short putt successfully and, from his demeanour, clearly won both the match and the hole.

But Trevor felt distinctly uncomfortable about what he had seen and he felt that he had to say something. He scrambled out from the caravan and met the two golfers as they came off the last green and headed towards the clubhouse.

'I feel a bit embarrassed about this,' he said, addressing his remarks to the man. 'But I saw your partner kick her ball out of what looked like a rather difficult lie in the bunker.'

The two players stared at him as though he made an indecent

proposal or offered to sell them a time share apartment in Marbella.

'What on earth are you saying?' demanded the man. 'Do you *know* what you're saying?'

To show that he did, indeed, know what he was saying Trevor repeated what he had said.

'What an absurd suggestion!' said Mrs Dussenberg, who had gone a quite unbecoming shade of red.

'I will not stand here and allow you to accuse my wife of cheating' said the man quite firmly. 'Besides,' he added, 'I won the match anyway so the incident would be of purely academic interest.'

'Are you suggesting that I might have cheated but that it doesn't matter because you won?' demanded the woman, horrified.

'If you like,' answered the man.

'Well!' said the woman. 'That's it! I've never been so insulted in all my life.' And with that she stalked off towards the clubhouse, pushing what Trevor could now see was an electrically operated trolley in front of her.

'Now look what you've done!' said the man to Trevor crossly. 'We've just had a lovely round of golf and now you've gone and spoilt it all.' He followed his wife and headed for the clubhouse.

Trevor, feeling rather glum, headed back towards his caravan; as he did so he saw the young tractor driver hurrying towards the neighbouring small caravan.

'Hello!' called Trevor cheerily.

The boy, apparently ignoring him, opened the door to his caravan and disappeared inside.

Trevor, not realising that his young neighbour was still deafened by his lengthy stint on the tractor and hadn't heard his cheery greeting felt depressed and rather lonely as a result of this minor slight.

* * *

Trevor's gloom and loneliness were despatched with great

efficiency by the arrival twenty minutes later of Willie who turned up at the wheel of a rather impressive looking and exceedingly noisy sports car.

'What's that?' asked Trevor, who had seen his friend skid to a halt outside the clubhouse in a choking cloud of dust.

'What's what?' asked Willie, pulling a bag of golf clubs from the front passenger seat.

'The car!'

'It's a Porsche!'

'I can see that it's a Porsche. But is it yours?'

'More or less.' Willie walked round to the back of the car and opened the rear door. 'For now.' He then proceeded to extract a seemingly never ending collection of matching luggage.

'What do you mean by 'more or less'?'

'Well, strictly speaking I suppose it's Brenda's. Her father bought it.'

'So it isn't yours!'

'It is for now,' said Willie. 'Possession is nine-tenths of the law and all that.' He looked around. 'Where are we living?'

'In there!' said Trevor, nodding towards the caravan he'd just left. 'But you can't just... !'

'There?' interrupted Willie, clearly unimpressed.

'Are you going to take it back?'

'What?'

'The car.'

'No, of course not. But if Brenda turns up to collect it I'll give her the keys.'

'Oh,' said Trevor, quietened for a moment. 'Does she know where you are?'

'Of course not!' snorted Willie, picking up two of his suitcases and carrying them towards the caravan. 'Give us a hand with these, will you, old chap?'

'So how is she supposed to know where her car is?'

'If she wants it she'll find it!' said Willie.

CHAPTER SEVEN

Despite the fact that the meeting had been called at such short notice the golf clubhouse was packed with members who were desperately keen to find out what was going on. Throughout the day, ever since Wing Commander Trout had made his first telephone call, rumours had spread rapidly among the members. The latest rumour, repeated with increasing conviction by members whose sense of certainty was matched only by their total ignorance, was that Trevor Dukinfield was a financial whizz kid from the city who had bought the golf club and Pettigrew Towers and intended to turn the whole lot back into a private estate.

Trevor had never been a keen public speaker and consequently this was not an area of life in which he had gained a great deal of experience. His only previous attempt had been at school where he had once stuttered his way through a two minute discourse on his summer holidays. The memory of that rather painful incident surfaced from somewhere deep within his subconscious as he stared with some horror at the assembled multitude.

The members of the golf club were a disparate looking bunch and to Trevor it seemed that the only two things they had in common was that they were all members of the club and that they all wore clothes which had been bought from Mr Schmidt's shop.

If Trevor had known them better he would have also realised that they did have one other thing in common: for one reason or another none of them had been able to join any of the larger, more fashionable golf clubs in the area. Some of them had been blackballed because they didn't have the right ancestry or because they earned their living in some socially unacceptable way; some simply found the fees at the other clubs impossibly high.

It was this that made them particularly concerned at the prospect of losing their club; it wasn't much but it was all they'd got.

'Excuse me, sir.'

Trevor looked down to his left. Captain Jarrold was standing there rubbing his hands together like an embarrassed bank manager calling in a loan from a social superior. Trevor produced a rather weak imitation of a smile; he was so nervous that it was all he could manage.

'Your tie, sir!' whispered Jarrold.

Trevor looked down. 'I'm not wearing a tie.'

'Exactly, sir,' said Captain Jarrold, apologetically. 'I'm afraid it's a club rule ...,' he looked around. 'In the clubhouse ... !'

'Oh dear,' said Trevor, rather miserably.

'It is rather a silly rule,' said Captain Jarrold helpfully. 'Would you like us to repeal it?'

Trevor brightened visibly. 'I think that would be a rather good idea.'

'Yes, sir,' said Captain Jarrold. 'When would you like it repealed?'

'I think we should repeal it straight away!' said Trevor.

'Very good, sir!' agreed Captain Jarrold. He hurried off. As he disappeared the club secretary approached. 'I think we can start whenever you're ready,' he said, looking around. 'It's a very good turn out.'

'How many people are here, do you think?'

'Around 124,' replied the secretary, promptly. He leant in closer. 'It'll do the bar takings a power of good!' he confided.

'Perhaps we should have emergency meetings every evening!' suggested Trevor.

'Oh I'm not sure we could do that ...,' protested Wing Commander Trout.

'Don't worry,' said Trevor. 'It was just a joke ...,' he explained rather lamely.

The secretary laughed and nodded. The nod was real. The laugh was as forced as February rhubarb.

'How many members are there?' asked Trevor.

'Altogether?'

'A hundred and seventy six,' answered Wing Commander Trout, promptly.

'That isn't many, is it?'

The secretary leant in and whispered again. 'We haven't conducted a recruiting campaign for quite a while,' he said. 'Old Mr Pettigrew didn't want too many members.' He looked around. 'Besides,' he paused. 'The facilities ...,' he waved an arm around to indicate the smoke-stained walls, the water-stained ceiling and the beer-stained, threadbare carpet. The atmosphere in the room was thick with stale cigarette, cigar and pipe smoke. It was, truly, a room with a phew.

'I see what you mean,' said Trevor. He noticed the couple he'd seen earlier in the day playing the 18th hole. Mrs Dussenberg was wearing a sky blue skirt and a yellow blouse with a small embroidered giraffe above her left breast. Her husband was wearing black and yellow checked trousers and a green shirt. There was, Trevor was not surprised to see, a small giraffe embroidered on his left breast. They were clearly not talking to one another.

Trevor felt someone tugging at his sleeve. He looked down at Captain Jarrold, who looked very pleased with himself.

'I thought you'd like to know that the Social Committee has just met,' he reported. He pointed over his left shoulder. Trevor looked in the direction he was pointing and saw a group of men in blazers all staring in his direction. They nodded as one when they saw him looking. 'We've repealed club rule 97b,' said Captain Jarrold.

Trevor stared at him, puzzled.

'The tie rule, sir,' whispered Captain Jarrold. 'You don't have to wear a tie in the clubhouse.' The Captain looked like a dog who's just performed a trick.

'That's splendid,' said Trevor. He turned and picked a bowl of peanuts up off the bar counter. 'Have a peanut!'

'Thank you, sir!' said Captain Jarrold, taking Trevor at his word and helping himself to a single peanut. 'Thank you very much.' He looked at the peanut for a moment, as though contemplating keeping it as a souvenir. Eventually, he decided against this and popped the peanut into his mouth.

'Why don't you take your tie off?' asked Trevor. 'Now that rule 97b has gone...!'

'Me, sir?'

Trevor nodded.

Captain Jarrold went rather red for a moment. Then, very slowly he untied his tie and pulled it away from his collar. When he had rolled his tie up into a neat ball and placed it carefully in his jacket pocket he unfastened the top button of his shirt. He then looked around nervously, as though rather expecting people to point at him and laugh.

'There you are,' said Trevor. 'Doesn't that feel better?'

Captain Jarrold swallowed hard. His face had gone quite red, though whether with shame or embarrassment there was no way of knowing. 'Oh yes, sir,' he said. 'Much better!'

'How would you like me to introduce you?' asked the secretary, who was still standing on Trevor's other side.

Trevor turned in his direction. 'Whatever you think appropriate,' he said. He swallowed hard. 'I suppose we might as well get on with it...!'

Wing Commander Trout coughed loudly and then rapped his knuckles loudly against the bar counter. Slowly, the buzz of conversation began to reduce in volume. The secretary rapped his knuckles once more and then cleared his throat loudly.

'Ladies and gentlemen,' he said, when the conversation buzz had subsided sufficiently for him to make himself heard without shouting. 'The new owner of the club, Mr Trevor Dukinfield, would like to say a few words.' He waved a hand in Trevor's direction and then led what was clearly intended to be a polite and welcoming round of applause. Sadly, however, this good intention was not fulfilled. Apart from Captain Jarrold, who joined in the applause with spirited enthusiasm, the response from the other members was, to put it politely, muted.

When he realised that apart from the secretary he was the only person clapping Captain Jarrold arrested his hands in mid air and tried, rather in vain, to pretend that he hadn't been clapping at all.

'Thank you,' said Trevor. He turned to Wing Commander Trout. 'Thank you,' he said again.

The secretary smiled thinly at him and then turned and waved his almost empty glass in the barman's direction to order himself a refill.

'Though I n-n-n-never met him Archibald P-P-P-Pettigrew was my uncle,' began Trevor, horrified to realise that his stutter had returned. 'Until a c-c-c-couple of days ago I didn't know that he or this g-g-g-golf club existed.'

'Pity it didn't stay that way,' called an anonymous voice from the back of the room.

Trevor felt a flush of anger rising within him. He had never been heckled before. That sort of thing wasn't allowed in Miss Cavendish's class. 'The s-s-s-solicitor who told me that I'd inherited the g-g-g-golf club wanted me to sell it,' he told the members. 'A bank has offered me a large sum of m-m-m-money – £10,000 – to sell the c-c-c-club and have nothing more to do with it.'

'So, why didn't you take the money?' demanded a second heckler. The question was greeted with a sharp murmur of approval.

'For a while I was t-t-t-tempted,' agreed Trevor. 'But then I d-d-discovered one or two things that changed my mind.' He swallowed hard. 'My uncle was very p-p-p-proud of this g-g-g-golf c-c-c-club – I gather that he is said to have d-d-d-designed the c-c-c-course himself – and I felt I owed it to his m-m-memory to try to k-k-keep it alive.'

'Don't kid yourself you're doing us any favours. We were managing quite well without you,' called the first heckler.

'I n-n-n-need your help if I'm g-g-g-going to make a success of running the c-c-c-club,' admitted Trevor. 'And you n-n-n-need my help too.' The palms of his hands felt moist and he wiped them on the sides of his trousers. 'That's why I asked for this m-m-m-meeting this evening.' He paused and swallowed. 'We don't have -m-m-much time,' he said.

'What do you know about running a g-g-g-golf c-c-c-club?' shouted someone else, deliberately mimicking Trevor's stutter and gaining rather a lot of cruel laughter as a reward.

'I don't know anything about running a g-g-g-golf c-c-c-club,' admitted Trevor. 'B-b-b-but I'm keen to learn.'

'Why on earth would a bank bother taking over a golf club?' demanded yet another voice.

'They d-d-d-don't want the club,' replied Trevor. 'They want the land it's on.' He was beginning to feel rather angry now. 'If I had agreed to sell the c-c-c-club you wouldn't have a g-g-g-g-, a g-g-g-g-g-,' he took out a handkerchief and wiped his brow. 'You wouldn't have a course at all.' He swallowed hard and then realised that his audience was, for the first time, waiting to hear what he said next. 'The solicitor who made me the offer told me that the prospective buyers have got outline p-p-p-planning p-p-p-permission,' he continued. 'They want to b-b-b-build an industrial estate here.'

Someone started to shout something else but the silence which met Trevor's revelation was so dense that the shout died before it took any recognisable shape.

'Good heavens!' said Wing Commander Trout after a moment or two. He emptied his gin. 'Good heavens!' He had gone very pale.

'You may not like me or approve of me being here,' said Trevor, speaking very quietly. 'But even though we may have different reasons we both have the same aims. You want the golf course to stay open so that you can play golf on it. And I want the golf course to stay open because my Uncle Archibald built it and if he'd wanted to build an industrial estate that would have been what he would have built.'

This simple and honest statement drew a spontaneous and perfectly genuine burst of applause from Trevor's audience. Trevor realised that his stutter had disappeared.

'Bravo!' shouted Captain Jarrold, standing up and clapping his hands. Wing Commander Trout looked at him as though he had pulled out his tie and was whirling it round and round his head. 'Bravo!'

'One last question,' asked a gentleman in a tweed jacket. 'May I ask if you intend to learn to play golf now that you're the owner of the club?'

'I certainly do!' said Trevor, enthusiastically. 'I've got my second lesson tomorrow morning.'

He didn't think that this was an appropriate moment to burden them with the knowledge that unless he learnt to play golf pretty quickly the banks would very quickly turn the course into a small industrial estate packed with factories making plastic accessories for Japanese cars.

The owner of the tweed jacket nodded sagely, clearly satisfied with this reply. There were loud murmurings of approval from the other members.

Judging his moment to perfection Wing Commander Trout stood up. 'I'd just like to remind members that the profits from the bar help keep the club's deficit smaller than it would otherwise be. The more drinks you buy tonight the more you'll be helping the club to survive!' He looked around him. 'I think we'd better have an emergency meeting of the Club Committee tomorrow evening,' he announced, looking around and acknowledging the nods of those committee members whose glances he managed to catch.

Trevor, Captain Jarrold and Wing Commander Trout were then swept aside as a rush of members stormed the bar in a desperate attempt to help improve the club's finances.

CHAPTER EIGHT

At five minutes to ten the following morning, feeling slightly conspicuous in his plaid trousers, bright red sweater (with the little giraffe embroidered over the left breast) and Tam O'Shanter cap, Trevor Dukinfield, golfer, stood silently and slightly nervously outside the professional's caravan and waited for his mentor Gunter Schmidt to return from the practice ground where, so Iris Weatherby had told him with a nudge-nudge look that said far more than words, he was busy showing Mrs Dussenberg a thing or two.

By Trevor's side stood his aluminium 'Ever-So-Lite' golf trolley which held his red imitation-leather golf bag (individual compartments for fourteen clubs, four spacious zipped pockets, quick release umbrella clips, towel holder and tee caddy). In the bag rested his fourteen clubs (including a carbon and molybdenum shafted and metal headed No 1 'wood' guaranteed to add forty yards to any player's drive), his breathable wind and showerproof clothing system, a supply of individually wrapped golf balls (special aerodynamically designed oval dimples guaranteed to add thirty yards to the average player's drive) and a brand new packet of coloured and unbreakable golf tees (unique head design shown by trials to add twenty yards to the average player's distance 'off the tee'). Trevor may have lacked talent, skill and experience but he certainly did not lack equipment.

His feet were clad in 'waterproof, breathable, multi-spiked non-slip shoes', his eyes were shaded from the sun by a white, 'non sweat' sun ray visor and his left hand was safely encased in a soft, leatherette golf glove with 'unique palm and finger texturing for added contact and special grooves to ensure a close grip in the wet'.

No mighty golfing warrior of the past, neither Bobby Jones nor the immortal Tom Morris, ever faced a golf course so well equipped for success. The equipment he was carrying was guaranteed to improve his first drive by well over one hundred yards.

'Aha, so!' cried a slightly breathless but familiar, Teutonic voice. 'Here already you are! No?'

'No. I mean, yes!' replied Trevor, turning round and coming face to face with the club professional, still red faced and breathing heavily from his exertions on the practice ground. Of his pupil, Mrs Dussenberg, there was no sign.

'So!' cried Mr Schmidt, looking Trevor up and down and rubbing his hands together. 'You are ready for the course, today, yes?'

Trevor looked at the professional and blanched. 'The course?' he said. 'You mean, the golf course?'

'Of, course! You have a course on the course!' said Mr Schmidt, who looked pleased with this far from subtle play on words. He reached out and slapped Trevor on the shoulder. 'You and me are ready to tango, no?'

'Er, yes, I mean, I'm not sure, probably not,' stumbled Trevor. 'Don't you think I ought to spend a little more time on the practice ground, first?'

The professional waved a hand in a dismissive fashion. 'Pfui!' he said, again pronouncing every letter of the word. He had found it, like most of the other phrases he favoured, in a guide to colloquial English but had never heard it pronounced. He thought himself rather a master of the English language. 'When you are a player you can practice! But how can you practice before you can play?'

Trevor had no answer for this superficially logical statement. 'Well, all right, then,' he mumbled, without much enthusiasm. 'I suppose I c-c-c-could give it a t-t-t-try.' His stutter reappeared as his confidence waned.

'That's the spirit! Here's mud in your ear!' cried Mr Schmidt, clapping his hands together and leading the way from the caravan. 'Let us go and put our noses under the grindstone.' He took hold of his trolley and headed off towards the first tee.

Two minutes later Trevor stood on a proper golf tee for the first time in his life and stared in stark horror at the apparently endless miles of neatly mown fairway which lay before him. He looked away again, averting his eyes from the terror.

'Right!' said Mr Schmidt. 'I'll play off the yellow tees with you today.'

'Yellow tees?' said Trevor. He bent down, unzipped one of the pockets of his golf bag, took out his plastic pack of golf tees and obediently began to pick out the yellow ones.

'Vot is it that you are doing?' demanded Mr Schmidt, puzzled.

'Picking out the yellow tees,' explained Trevor, patiently. He bent down to pick up a red one which had slipped through his fingers.

'No, no, no!' cried Mr Schmidt. 'White is for professional, yellow is for men and red is for ladies!' As he spoke he pointed far behind him to the two white inverted concrete flower pots which marked the edges of the professionals' tee, at the two yellow inverted concrete flower pots which marked the edges of the tee upon which they were standing and then at the two red, inverted concrete flower pots which marked the edges of the ladies' tee some thirty to forty yards ahead of them.

'Ah' said Trevor, understanding. 'And it doesn't matter what colour tee I use?'

'You can use any colour you like!' cried Mr Schmidt magnanimously. 'As the actor said to the bishop,' he added with a wink. 'I will go first.'

He pulled his No 1 wood from his bag and removed the leather cover from it with a flourish. He casually tossed the cover onto the grass, plucked a tee from a trouser pocket and stuck it into the ground, pulled a ball from the same pocket and balanced it on the tee, swung his club with a nonchalant ease and hit the ball with a speed, certainty and skill which removed what tiny element of confidence Trevor still retained.

'There you are!' said the professional, bending down to pick up his tee and slipping it back into his pocket. 'I am crying all the way to the bank. Now you do the same.' Trevor peered into the distance looking for the professional's ball but could see no sign of it anywhere.

'Where did it go?' he asked.

'Down the middle, of course!' said the professional, as though there was not and never could have been any possible doubt about this. He pointed down the middle of the fairway. 'Like a lamb to the slaughter.'

'Good heavens!' said Trevor when, a moment or two later, he spotted a small white speck sitting in the middle of the fairway. 'Is *that* it?'

'I wasn't very lucky with the bounce,' complained Mr Schmidt. 'I was batting on a sticky wicket and must have hit a soft patch.'

Trevor swallowed hard. 'It's gone a long way,' he said.

The professional shrugged nonchalantly for though he was secretly pleased with the shot he would never have admitted it to Trevor. To admit that it was a good shot would have been to admit that he was capable of playing a bad shot. Since being in England Mr Schmidt had learned the gentle art of self-effacement and, like most Englishmen who are good at sport, used it to imply to his opponents that, however well he played, he was capable of playing much better.

'Where's the green?' asked Trevor, squinting into the distance. 'I can't even see the green?'

'Oh, don't worry about that,' said Mr Schmidt, dismissing the green with an airy wave of a hand. 'It's just over the hill and far away. You just play straight up the fairway.' He paused. 'But mind the bunkers or you will be up in a creek without a paddle,' he added, pointing to two large bunkers, one on each side of the fairway about two hundred yards away.

Trevor took out his No 1 wood and tossed the leatherette cover casually onto the grass. He took a brand new ball out of his bag, unwrapped it, threw the wrapper into a small, wire mesh waste basket, and then balanced the ball on top of a yellow, plastic tee. He wrapped his hands around the grip of his club, backed away from the ball and started to swing.

'No, no, no!' cried Mr Schmidt. 'Your grip is all wrong.'

He moved forward and adjusted Trevor's fingers until they felt strangely uncomfortable. 'Hands at the top of the club. Not right at the top. Half an inch away or so. And firm. But not too firm. Firmly with the last three fingers of your left-hand. Right hand like so. That's better!' he cried. 'Now! Off you go! And you must relax!'

Trevor started to swing his club back.

'No, no!' cried Mr Schmidt. 'You are not standing right!' He stood behind Trevor, took hold of him by the shoulders and moved him twelve inches backwards and six inches to his left.

'There you are!' he said. 'That is better!' He frowned. 'Cock your wrists a little more. Transfer your weight when you feel your shoulder beginning to drop. Show me more of your knuckle. This is all you have to remember and you will have an ace in the hole.'

'Yes,' said Trevor.

'Relax!' shouted Mr Schmidt. 'You are not relaxing!'

'I'm sorry,' apologised Trevor, genuinely contrite. Once again he began to swing his club. He could feel beads of sweat forming on his brow.

'No, no! More smoothly!' said Mr Schmidt. 'You must move your hands first, control the club with your left arm, no your right arm. No, not so stiff. Move your hips from the one side to the other and rotate your shoulders as you go. As you move your hips put more weight on this foot, no that foot, but do not move your head. Do it slowly. Turn your body until your shoulders are at right angles to the direction of the ball and then bend your knee slightly in and keep your arms close in your body and cock your wrists. And all the time you must stay relaxed. It's all so simple!'

He spoke with increasing speed and excitement and by the time he had finished Trevor had no idea whether he was about to hit a golf ball or boil an egg.

He swung his club back, brought it down in a huge arc and missed the ball by a good yard.

'Very good!' lied Mr Schmidt enthusiastically. 'But you must relax more. If you relax more you will hit more of the ball. Remember, whenever you are on the horns of a dilemma that there is more than one way to swing a cat.'

'Right,' said Trevor, who was now wondering why he had decided to learn to play golf at all. He felt as relaxed and as calm as a tightrope walker who suddenly realises that he's developing cramp.

One of the most comforting and most immutable laws of nature is the one which decrees that if you wave two square inches of golf club around in the vicinity of a golf ball, the club head and the ball will eventually collide.

In Trevor's case this law of nature was fulfilled on his fifth swing.

'Bravo!' cried Mr Schmidt, who was genuinely delighted by Trevor's success. 'I can see you are man with a card well up your sleeve!'

'Where did it go?' demanded Trevor, anxiously peering into the distance. 'Can you see it?'

'I can see it!' Mr Schmidt reassured him. 'It's just over here.' Trevor looked around and saw with a mixture of shame, embarrassment and horror that his ball had not left the tee at all but was lying about three yards to the left and two yards behind its starting point; it was, he realised, now further from the hole than it had been before he had hit it.

'What on earth happened?' asked Trevor.

'Oh, don't worry! It happens to everyone!' said Mr Schmidt, reassuringly, although he had never seen anything quite like it before. 'When I first started to play this game I too was not hitting the ball good. But don't worry. You can soon pick yourself up by your bootstraps.'

* * *

Like most of the really great golf courses Archibald Pettigrew's course had been designed to take full advantage of the natural contours and hazards of the countryside in which it was situated. No bulldozers had been used to create artificial hills; no diggers had been employed to make artificial lakes; no streams or rivers had been diverted and no trees had been planted to create artificial woods or copses. The lake, the river, the woodlands and the hills around and upon which Archibald Pettigrew had built his golf course had all been there long before anyone had thought of using them as a natural backdrop for a sporting arena.

The most extraordinary thing about the course was that on none of the first six holes was the green visible from the tee. Trevor, never having played on a golf course before, was surprised by this but, in his ignorance, assumed that it must be normal and merely took guidance from his mentor, Mr Schmidt. Since Trevor's skill with his clubs was, to put it kindly, rudimentary, his inability to see the target he was supposed to be aiming at was not the disadvantage it might have been to a more skilful player.

Trevor's clear objective as he struggled to leave the first tee was simply to get around the course without losing too many balls, breaking too many clubs or having to employ men with torches to light his way back to the clubhouse.

In the end his inaugural round came to a premature but glorious conclusion on the sixth hole. In completing the first five holes in a little under two hours Trevor had taken 64 strokes and lost five balls.

He stood on the sixth tee with an aching back, blistered hands and a deep feeling of despair in his soul. He was quite convinced that he would never make a golfer. Indeed, he couldn't help wondering why he had ever thought he could make a golfer. It was, he had decided, a stupid game; a game for oafs; a game dominated by fortune and chance.

'Don't forget the hands, the feet and the shoulders,' said Mr Schmidt. 'Keep your head still and relax. Do not look so much down in the dumps. You are playing like a fine kettle of fish.'

Trevor no longer cared. He just wanted to get back to his caravan and lie down.

He put his ball onto a small red, plastic tee (he had long since lost all the yellow ones), took the club which Mr Schmidt handed to him without even looking at it and swung the latter at the former without a care or a thought for the consequences. Little did he know then that the shot he was about to play would transform his life, that a few moments later his despair would be gone, replaced with a glorious, joyful feeling of achievement.

Trevor didn't even know whether or not he had made contact with the ball, so sweetly did he hit it. He had grown accustomed to the jarring feeling you get when it is the heel or the toe of your club which hits the ball, and he had never before experienced the exquisite feeling that you get when the ball is hit with the sweet spot on the club.

The ball flew from Trevor's club like an arrow fired from a longbow. It soared high into the air, travelled straight down the middle of the fairway, and seemed to hang in the sky for minutes before plummeting to earth, bouncing once as it rolled over the edge of the bank leading down to the green.

'Bravo!' cried Mr Schmidt. 'A marvellous shot! I am over the moon!'

'Where is it?' asked Trevor, who had, as usual, absolutely no idea where the ball had gone.

'Straight down the fairway!' replied the professional, beaming. 'I couldn't have played a better shot myself!' he admitted. 'On this hole I am playing second fiddle while you blow your trumpet.' He had pulled his own shot from the tee and his ball had gone clattering into the trees on the left of the fairway.

'Really?' said Trevor.

'Really!' exclaimed Mr Schmidt. He took hold of Trevor by the shoulders and shook him so severely that Trevor's teeth rattled. 'Your ball may even be on the green!'

'On the green!' Trevor repeated. He had taken nine shots to reach the green on the last hole, and that had not included penalties for the two balls he had lost in the rough.

'You see!' said Mr Schmidt. 'You relaxed and now you are in a bed of roses!'

But Trevor didn't hear him. He wouldn't have heard anything. He had dropped his club and was racing down the fairway towards the green. He wanted to see where his ball had landed. He ran so quickly that his lungs had difficulty in drawing enough air into his body. Nothing, short of concentrated machine gun fire or a massive coronary could possibly have stopped him.

As Gunter Schmidt struggled off the tee pulling two trolleys Trevor arrived at the top of the small slope leading to the green. He could hardly believe what he saw. He could not have been more thrilled if he had seen a stack of gold bars piled on the green. He stared for a moment, then turned and waved to the professional.

'It's right by the hole!' he shouted, the words interspersed with gasps as his body tried to repair its oxygen debt. He held his hands out in front of him, about three feet apart. 'This far away!' he exclaimed, exaggerating only slightly and wheezing noisily.

'Congratulations!' shouted Mr Schmidt. 'I can see I am teaching my grandfather to suck an egg.' He was genuinely delighted that his pupil had played a good shot. He knew that unless the Gods are feeling particularly cruel even the weakest player will play one good shot in a round of golf, but up until that moment he had been beginning to wonder if maybe the Gods were too busy elsewhere to remember to glance down that morning. One of the trolleys he was pulling hit a divot and nearly turned over. Seeing this Trevor started to run back to help him.

'It's about a foot from the hole!' said Trevor, grinning broadly and exaggerating a little more. Thanks to the bizarre effect that time can have on spacial relationships Trevor's ball would, by that evening, have landed even closer to the flag. By dinner time the ball would have landed no more than six inches from the hole. Fishermen and golfers share a quite remarkable ability to remember and enhance the good and to forget and diminish the bad. 'It was very nearly a hole in one!'

'It was a glorious shot!' agreed Mr Schmidt. 'Jack Nicholson himself would have been proud it to have played.'

'Do you really think so?' asked Trevor, who had by now completely forgotten the 64 strokes which Jack Nicklaus would not have been so proud to have played. 'Jack Nicklaus, surely?' he said, suddenly realising the professional's mistake.

'Himself!' said Mr Schmidt, gloriously unaware of his error.

Trevor blushed with pride.

'But now you must follow your nose and help me to find my ball,' said Mr Schmidt, parking his trolley and walking off the fairway into the trees on the left of the hole. 'We must leave no stone unturned,' he muttered to himself.

When they found the professional's ball it was nestling in a rabbit hole behind a huge oak tree and was quite unplayable.

'I will take the drop,' said Mr Schmidt, picking up his ball and dropping it in a small clearing. He fetched a sand iron from his bag and played a recovery shot which would have been quite good if it hadn't hit a low branch and fallen down behind a large beech tree. In the end he had taken six shots to get his ball onto the green. A long, curling and rather improbable putt from thirty-five feet enabled him to complete the hole in seven strokes.

'You've got five putts to win the hole, six to halve it!' Mr Schmidt reminded Trevor. 'But just two putts will give you your first par, and if you can get the ball in the hole in one you'll have to watch the birdie. Your position is not to be sneezed at; not by a long chalk!'

'A birdie?' asked Trevor, puzzled by the expression. 'What's a birdie?'

'A birdie is when you are playing the hole in one less than par,' explained Mr Schmidt.

'Why?' asked Trevor, whose ignorance about golf was comprehensive.

'I beg your pardon?'

'Why is it called a birdie?'

Mr Schmidt stared at him and frowned. 'I'm not sure,' he admitted. 'But it will be a birdie.'

'Right!' said Trevor. 'Then I shall try and get a birdie!' He bent down as he had seen the professionals do on the television and stared at the grass. He wasn't at all certain about what he was looking for but the grass seemed very neat and flat so that was quite comforting.

'Just be careful not to get egg on your face!' warned Mr Schmidt. 'Remember not to hit the ball too hard. You must make sure that your ball does not end up further from the hole than it is starting.'

Trevor bent over his ball and concentrated hard. He concentrated so hard that every fibre of every muscle in his body became as taut as a bow string. He took his putter back, brought it forward to strike the ball and sent it flying nearly twelve feet past the hole.

'Oh no!' he cried, instinctively reaching out as though desperate to grab his ball and slow it down. 'Oh no! What have I done?'

'You have hit the ball too hard,' replied Mr Schmidt, with Teutonic precision. 'It has gone too far. You have put too much egg in the pudding and now you are all at sixes and sevens.'

Trevor did not reply.

'Do not despair!' said Mr Schmidt. 'All is not yet lost. You can still get a par.'

Trevor walked hurriedly over to his ball and stared down at it.

'Be careful!' warned Mr Schmidt. 'Not too hard!'

Trevor looked up, nodded, then bent over his ball again. He took his putter back slowly and then swung it forwards rapidly. The ball shot off the putter blade as though fired from a cannon. If the shot had been wayward the ball would have doubtless disappeared off the far side of the green, down the hill and into the undergrowth.

Fortunately Trevor's aim was accurate and the ball headed straight for the hole.

It was going so fast that neither Mr Schmidt nor Trevor thought for a moment that the putt would sink. They watched without breathing as the ball shot across the hole, hit the rim on the far side, bounced into the air and then dropped down into the hole where it bounced up to the rim again, rattled around in the metal cup for a few agonising micro seconds and then settled down as it admitted defeat.

Trevor stared at the hole and felt his heart stutter into action once more.

'Congratulations!' cried Mr Schmidt with a genuine and cheery smile. 'You have scored a hole in three, which is par, and you have defeated me by a landslide!'

'Thank you,' said Trevor, modestly.

'I am definitely playing second fiddle,' said Mr Schmidt.

Trevor took the professional's outstretched hand and smiled shyly. 'I think I was just lucky,' he said, not meaning a word of it.

'Not at all!' said the professional, also not meaning it. 'You played with great skill and courage. You deserved your success. I am over the moon and away with the fairies.' He looked at his watch. 'But now I think we walk back to the clubhouse. That will be enough excitement for one day.'

'Oh, dear,' said Trevor, clearly disappointed. 'Do we have to stop now?'

'I'm afraid so,' said the professional, feigning sadness. 'I have another lesson to give half an hour previously.' He was relieved that Trevor's first encounter with the course had ended on such a high note.

'What a pity!' sighed Trevor. 'Just as I was getting the hang of things.'

'Golf is a wonderful game,' he thought to himself as he and Mr Schmidt pulled their trolleys back to the clubhouse. 'How did I manage to live for so many years without it?'

It was, he thought, a game of tremendous skill, a game which rewarded hard work, patience and talent.

'Now that I've got it licked,' he thought to himself, 'I can turn professional if I want; maybe even win the Open!' Such a feat sounded perfectly reasonable to a man who had just played a shot that Jack Nicklaus would have been proud of; a man who had scored a par and had beaten the club professional on his own course by a clear four strokes on a single hole!

As he walked back to his new home he saw an exceedingly pretty young girl coming out of Iris Weatherby's neighbouring caravan. She was carrying a small bag of golf clubs that was almost as big as she was.

'Hello!' he said, slowing down.

The girl blushed and lowered her eyes. 'Hello!' she answered quietly. But she didn't slow down. Trevor turned his head and watched her walk over to the first tee.

CHAPTER NINE

Trevor, freshly showered after his success on the course, was sitting in the men's changing room describing his par three to Captain Jarrold and two slightly deaf pensioners when Wing Commander Trout came bustling through the door from the bar.

'There's a lady here asking for you,' hissed the secretary.

Trevor frowned. 'A lady?'

'She says she's engaged to you,' added Wing Commander Trout, putting the emphasis on the second word and making it clear that he wasn't prepared to take her word for it.

'Oh God!' said Trevor. 'It must be Sylvia. Did she give you her name?'

Wing Commander Trout shook his head.

'What does she look like?'

There had undoubtedly once been a time when the secretary would have noticed exactly what a young woman looked like but that time had long since gone. He waved a hand around airily. 'Very attractive,' he said at last. 'Young,' he added. He thought for a moment. 'Very self-confident,' he concluded. He thought about this. 'Yes,' he said with certainty, 'very self-confident.'

'That's Sylvia!' said Trevor. 'How on earth did she find me?' He shivered involuntarily. He had never realised before just how much Sylvia actually frightened him.

'I don't know, sir,' said the secretary. 'Would you like me to tell her that she's come to the wrong place?'

'No, that won't do any good,' said Trevor miserably. 'If she's tracked me down she won't be fobbed off.'

'I could tell her that you're out on the course,' suggested Wing Commander Trout.

'No, it's no good,' sighed Trevor. 'I'd better come out and face the music.' He stood up, removed the towel from around his waist and took his shirt down from the coat hook above his head.

*   *   *

The secretary had settled Sylvia down at the cleanest table he could find.

'Can I get you anything to drink?' he had asked, wringing his hands obsequiously. Fawning was the one thing he knew he was good at.

'I'll have a coffee,' Sylvia had said. 'Decaffeinated.'

'Certainly, madam,' Wing Commander Trout had muttered before hurrying off to pass on the instructions to the barman.

Five minutes later the coffee still hadn't arrived but Trevor had.

'Hello!' said the world's greatest golfer, smiling nervously and standing diffidently beside his beloved's chair.

Sylvia looked up. 'Do you know how difficult it was to track you down?' she demanded.

'No,' replied Trevor, who didn't.

'I had to telephone every solicitor in the Mettleham area to find the right one!' said Sylvia.

Trevor hesitated. 'I thought solicitors all swore an oath of confidentiality,' he said, smiling nervously.

'That certainly made it more difficult,' agreed Sylvia, who had a rule that she never allowed other people's ethical codes to stand in her way when she wanted something.

'Would you like some coffee?' asked Trevor, anxious to delay more serious conversation.

'That funny little man who tried to stop me coming in here was supposed to have ordered me one absolutely ages ago,' said Sylvia.

'Funny little man?' asked Trevor.

'A chap in a rather nasty, cheap, blue suit who had a few strands of hair combed over a very large bald patch.'

Trevor looked around anxiously. 'That's the club secretary,' he whispered, though this description could have applied to a good third of the club's members.

'Well I must say he gave himself lots of airs and graces for a secretary,' said Sylvia.

'I'll go and see what happened to it,' said Trevor. 'I shan't be a moment...' Grateful for the excuse to drift away before Sylvia explained the real reason for her visit Trevor wandered over to the bar.

'Were you getting a coffee for the lady in the window?' asked Trevor quietly. 'I think Wing Commander Trout may have ordered one for her.'

'Oh, yes,' said Jake the barman who was reading a tabloid newspaper. Jake hated his job, the golf club and just about everyone in the world. 'He did.'

Trevor waited for a few moments. The barman merely continued to read his newspaper.

'How long do you think it will take?' he asked at last.

The barman looked up. 'What?'

'The coffee.'

'She wanted decaffeinated,' said the barman, as though Sylvia had asked for a whisky in a mosque.

'That's right. She always drinks decaffeinated.'

'We don't keep decaffeinated,' said the barman. 'There's no call for it.' He continued reading his newspaper.

'Oh.' said Trevor. He paused. 'I don't suppose you could get some, could you?'

The barman sighed and looked up. 'No,' he said simply.

'Oh,' said Trevor. 'Well thank you very much anyway.'

The barman just ignored him and Trevor returned slowly to Sylvia's table. He pulled out a chair and sat down beside her.

'I'm sorry,' he apologised. 'The club doesn't seem to have any decaffeinated coffee.'

'I thought you owned the club?' said Sylvia.

'Well, yes, I sort of do,' agreed Trevor.

'Well can't you send someone out to get some?'

Trevor hesitated, torn between his fear of Sylvia and his fear of the barman. 'I don't really like to,' he confessed. 'It's an awfully long way to the shops. I could get you a glass of water if you like.'

Sylvia breathed in deeply through her nose and let the air out through her mouth. This simple but eloquent and surprisingly threatening act always terrified Trevor.

'I could call a taxi and we could pop into town if you like,' he offered.

'Don't be silly,' said Sylvia, with a snap in her voice. 'We've got to talk about our future. Where are you staying?'

'Er, here,' admitted Trevor, going cold at the prospect of discussing his future with Sylvia.

'Here?'

'In a caravan.'

Sylvia raised an eyebrow and her voice. 'A caravan?'

'It's just temporary,' explained Trevor, quickly.

Sylvia stood up. 'I want to see it.'

Trevor stood.

Two minutes later they were sitting in Trevor's cramped new home.

'It's cosy, isn't it?' said Trevor, looking around.

'It's cramped,' agreed Sylvia.

'It's handy for the golf course.'

'You don't play golf.'

'I'm learning,' said Trevor. 'I beat the professional this morning!'

'He can't be very good.'

'It was only on one hole,' admitted Trevor. 'I got a par three. He beat me on all the other holes.'

'Why on earth do you want to learn to play golf?'

Trevor hesitated.

'Don't try hiding things from me,' said Sylvia. 'You know it always ends in tears.'

Trevor did not have to think about this to realise that she was right. He wondered how much the solicitors had told her about the rules of his uncle's will and decided, quite accurately, that they had probably told her everything. He decided that honesty was the best of the unpleasant alternatives and explained to her that he had to learn to play golf in order to keep his inheritance.

'So if you find you can't play golf you lose everything?'

Trevor nodded.

Sylvia did the business with the air again. Trevor felt his heart do an impression of an overwound cheap watch.

'Why don't you accept the money?' demanded Sylvia. 'You would if you cared about us.' She pouted.

Trevor opened his mouth but couldn't think of anything suitable to say. He had never got used to the fact that Sylvia would change her moods without warning; changing from aggressive, firm, woman of stern masculine authority to meek, powerless, defenceless woman of delicate femininity in an instant.

'We could use the money to buy a house,' Sylvia said. She took out her handkerchief. 'Sometimes I think you don't love me,' she said.

Trevor, who had realised some time ago that he didn't love Sylvia but who was too nervous to tell her, wondered if this might be the appropriate moment to break the news.

'Oh, Sylvia,' he heard himself saying and realised that he didn't have that much courage. He reached out, grasping for her hand but she moved at the last moment and he caught her knee instead.

'Oh, Trevor,' said Sylvia. 'I know how you feel. I've missed you too.'

Trevor looked down at his hand and intended to move it but he was too slow. Sylvia put her hand on top of his. 'It's been a month,' she said huskily. 'I really missed you when you were in London. I spoke to your editor yesterday. You can have your old job back.' She lifted his hand and placed it a little higher on her thigh.

'Oh,' said Trevor, who didn't want his old job back but realised that employment was not the immediate problem.

Sylvia licked her lips in what she thought was a sexually

provocative gesture and leant forward with her mouth slightly open. She put her free hand behind Trevor's neck and drew him towards her. 'If you promise to take the £10,000 and you draw the curtains you can have your way with me,' she whispered, her voice silky with promise.

Suddenly, the caravan door burst open and a golf bag was thrown in through the opened door. 'Hello, Trevor!' said Willie loudly, following his bag into the caravan. He caught sight of Trevor and Sylvia at the other end of the caravan and wagged a finger reprovingly. 'That sort of stuff will ruin your short game!' he warned.

'Willie!' cried Trevor, who had never been so pleased to see his friend.

'Oh, no!' cried Sylvia, leaping away from Trevor as quickly as she could. 'What is he doing here?' she screamed, pointing at Willie as though he was a vampire.

'You two do know each other, don't you?' said Trevor weakly.

'Trevor Dukinfield!' said Sylvia. 'I've told you I don't approve of him!' She stood up and cracked her head on an overhead cupboard.

Trevor blanched. Since he had been a child he had always known that trouble was coming when anyone addressed him by his full name.

Sylvia pursed her lips and sought for a suitable curse. 'Damn you!' she said in the end.

'Are you all right?' asked Trevor.

'I'm leaving!' said Sylvia. 'For ever!' she added dramatically. 'You won't see me again!' Holding her head high she made her way to the door and disappeared.

'Oh dear,' said Willie. 'Have I arrived at a bad moment?'

THE INWARD NINE

CHAPTER TEN

Not counting Wing Commander Trout, there were ten members of the Butterbury Ford Golf Club committee and it was unusual for them all to turn up at the same meeting. They were all there that evening when Trevor told them about the conditions in his uncle's will.

Under the secretary's supervision, Jake the bar steward had pushed four small tables together, covered them with a rather threadbare brown chenille tablecloth and spread a dozen chairs around them in a crude attempt to create a committee table.

The chairman, Mulliner Park-Ward, councillor, freemason, purveyor of fine meats and joint proprietor of Park-Ward's Family Butchers ('Our Meat Is A Cut Above The Rest'), sat at the head of the table with Wing Commander Trout on his left and Trevor on his right. Alfred Petherick, a retired tailor's assistant with thinning hair and a thickening waist, sat on the secretary's left and Bert Grubb of Grubb and Son, ('Electrical Repairs Done In Your Home – Rewiring Our Speciality'), sat on Trevor's right.

The Prendergast brothers, Winston and Spencer, proprietors of Prendergast Carpets, ('Your Floors Are Our Passion'), sat together, as they always did, with Bert Grubb on Winston's left and Elvis Ramsbottom, the chiropodist, on Spencer's right.

Karl and Arlene Dussenberg, the couple whose antics on the 18th green had so entertained Trevor and who were the joint proprietor's of Dussenberg's Genuine English Antiques (far too grand an establishment to have a slogan), sat between Elvis Ramsbottom and Peregrine Falmouth, the owner and proprietor of Falmouth's Pharmacy, ('Treat Yourself to Our Expertise') while Captain Jarrold sat between Peregrine Falmouth and Alfred Petherick. The Dussenbergs both smiled at Trevor to show that they were happy to forget the words they had exchanged.

Although it wasn't in the slightest bit necessary, since everyone there already knew exactly who he was, Wing Commander Trout began the meeting by introducing Trevor and explaining that he was the nephew of the late Mr Pettigrew and the new owner of the golf club. Having been invited to say a few words to introduce himself Trevor wasted no time in informing the committee members of the conditions which his late uncle had applied to his bequest. The committee received this news in a lengthy and embarrassing silence that was eventually broken by the chairman, Mulliner Park-Ward.

'Would you tell us exactly what happens if you fail to satisfy these conditions?' he asked.

Trevor explained.

Once again the committee stayed silent.

'Er, I hope you don't mind my asking,' began Elvis Ramsbottom apologetically, 'but could you tell us how much golf you have played?'

'I went out onto the course for the first time today,' said Trevor. 'I got a par three at the sixth,' he added, still finding it hard to hide his pride at his achievement. He beamed at each of the committee members in turn but was disappointed to find that they did not seem to share his cheerfulness.

There was, indeed, a general air of gloom in the room. Everyone there knew that a beginner who plays one hole well is heading for a fall.

'Spencer Prendergast,' said Spencer Prendergast, standing up and introducing himself. 'What is the time limit on these conditions?' he asked. He sat down. Spencer Prendergast was a bluff and rather blunt man who believed that honesty was the best policy in every area of life with the obvious exception of business. 'How long have we – you – got?'

'Three months' replied Trevor. 'Well, a bit less than that now. My uncle knew that I hadn't played golf before but he seemed to think that ought to be long enough.'

Again there was a long and pregnant silence as the members of the committee contemplated this gloomy news. The silence was so profound that Jake, the bar steward, looked up from the racing page of the Daily Globe to make sure that there hadn't been a deadly gas leak.

'We must obviously do everything we can to help,' said Peregrine Falmouth finally. He spoke firmly, as though this was his last word on the subject and as though defying anyone to disagree. Peregrine had a reputation as something of an optimist, and anyone who had ever watched him use a wooden club from the first tee would have confirmed that this reputation was sound.

'Well said, sir!' said Winston Prendergast, who harboured secret parliamentary ambitions and had been a keen listener of broadcasts from parliament since their inception.

'Absolutely!' agreed Captain Jarrold, raising his glass and then emptying it in a solitary toast. He levered himself to his feet and staggered off towards the bar to replenish his glass in case there were any more toasts to be drunk. 'Anyone else want a drink?' he muttered to himself when he was safely out of earshot.

'I would certainly appreciate your help and support,' said Trevor. 'After all, we all want the same thing, don't we?'

'You just tell us how we can help and we'll do what we can,' said Peregrine Falmouth. He looked around expectantly. His offer was greeted with much nodding and mumbling of support.

There was a slight commotion as Captain Jarrold returned from the bar, put his drink down on the table and fell over his chair. 'My apologies,' mumbled Captain Jarrold, pulling his chair upright and sitting on it. 'Would anyone else like a drink?'

Heads were shaken and unconvincing denials uttered.

'Mr Chairman,' said Wing Commander Trout, suddenly rather formally, 'Would you be kind enough to consider asking the meeting to pass a motion supporting a vote of confidence in our new owner?'

Mr Park-Ward, the chairman, listened carefully to this request, nodded and then cleared his throat. 'Er, gentlemen,' he paused, 'and Mrs Dussenberg,' he added, nodding in Mrs Dussenberg's direction, 'I have received a request that we pass a vote of confidence in the club's new owner. In view of the fact that such a report has not previously been included in the agenda for this meeting I would like to have your approval. Could we, therefore, please have a vote on this.' He took a gold plated propelling pencil from his inside jacket pocket and fiddled with it in an attempt to produce a lead point with which to write. Unfortunately, the pencil did not seem to contain any leads.

'Here, use mine,' said Trevor, offering the chairman a cheap ballpoint pen which he had bought from a railway station bookstall.

'Thank you,' said the chairman, accepting the pen as though it was made of solid gold. 'Now then,' he said to the committee, 'Can we please have votes for this amendment to our original agenda?'

'I haven't seen an agenda,' said Bert Grubb, speaking to no one in particular. 'Has anyone else seen an agenda?'

There was a general murmuring of agreement confirming that no one had seen an agenda for the meeting.

'Mr Chairman, I'm afraid we didn't have time to produce an agenda,' apologised Wing Commander Trout. 'This is an emergency meeting.'

'Yes,' agreed the chairman. 'Quite so, quite so. Well, then in that case let us simply have a vote confirming that we would like the committee to vote to show our confidence ...' he looked around and the sentence rather tailed off.

'I'll propose the motion,' said Bert Grubb.

'I'll second it,' said Captain Jarrold, who was always happy to second any motion.

'Good,' said the chairman. 'All those voting for the motion?'

Everyone put their hands up except Trevor and Wing Commander Trout who didn't have a vote.

'So shall we call it unanimous?' asked the secretary.

'Oh yes,' said the chairman. 'I think so.' Then he caught sight of Trevor again. 'What about you? Did you vote?'

'No,' said Trevor. 'I don't think I'm allowed to vote am I? I'm not on the committee.'

'Good heavens,' said the chairman. 'Aren't you on the committee?'

'No,' confirmed Wing Commander Trout. 'He isn't.'

'Well, is he entitled to be here if he isn't on the committee?' asked the chairman.

'Spencer Prendergast, Mr Chairman,' said Spencer Prendergast, standing up and introducing himself. 'We ought to have a vote inviting him to stay,' he suggested. He sat down. Spencer Prendergast had read a book on how to manage a committee and secretly felt that he could do much better than Mr Park-Ward.

'Perhaps it would be easier if we just invited Mr Dukinfield to join the committee,' suggested Wing Commander Trout, quietly.

'Splendid idea,' said the chairman. 'Would you like to be on our committee, young fellow?'

'Well, yes, that's very kind of you,' said Trevor.

'I don't want to be pernickety,' said Mr Grubb, who did, 'but is he a member? And can he be on the committee if he isn't a member?'

'Are you a member?' the chairman asked Trevor.

'I don't think so,' admitted Trevor, ruefully.

'Oh dear,' said the chairman. 'Well in that case I don't think you're really entitled to be here. Officially.'

'Officially he isn't supposed to be in the clubhouse,' Winston Prendergast pointed out.

'That's right,' said Karl Dussenberg. 'If he's not a member then he's not really entitled to be in the clubhouse.'

'But he owns the club!' Wing Commander Trout pointed out quietly.

'Do you know anyone who could propose you?' asked the chairman.

Trevor looked around him hopefully.

'I'll be proud to propose you,' said the chairman.

'I'll second that,' said Captain Jarrold, who would have seconded his own expulsion from the club.

'Right,' said the chairman to Trevor, 'you just pop outside for a moment and we'll vote on your membership application and then when you come back in we'll co-opt you onto the committee.'

Trevor popped outside and a few seconds later was called back into the room by Wing Commander Trout.

'Congratulations!' said the chairman, standing up and offering Trevor his hand. 'Welcome to the club!'

'Thank you,' said Trevor, who was quite overwhelmed by all this. He had not previously had any experience of golf club management.

'Now,' said the chairman, 'I propose that we co-opt Mr Dukinfield onto the committee. All those in favour?'

Wing Commander Trout again confirmed that the vote had been a unanimous one.

'The committee doesn't normally agree on things so well,' whispered the secretary to Trevor. 'Two years ago Karl Dussenberg fell out with Spencer Prendergast over whether there should be a shaver socket in the ladies' changing rooms.'

'Right!' said the chairman, pleased with the progress so far. He looked around. 'Is there any more business?'

'We were going to have a vote of support for our new owner,' said Mrs Dussenberg.

'Spencer Prendergast, Mr Chairman,' said Spencer Prendergast, standing up. 'In view of the fact that he is the owner, should our new member be entitled to vote on whether or not we offer our support to the club's new owner?' He looked around and then sat down.

'He is on the committee,' Wing Commander Trout pointed out.

'Point of order, Mr Chairman,' said Winston Prendergast. 'Wing Commander Trout isn't really entitled to contribute to the committee's deliberations on these issues since he is here purely on a de facto basis as a club official.'

'What does de facto mean?' Bert Grubb asked Alfred Petherick in a whisper.

'I haven't the foggiest idea,' Mr Petherick whispered back.

'Maybe we should have another vote,' said the chairman.

'What are we voting on?' asked a confused Captain Jarrold.

'Heaven knows!' sighed Mr Dussenberg.

'Again?' asked Captain Jarrold. 'Isn't once enough?'

'We haven't done it yet,' said the chairman. 'Let's have a vote. All those in favour please raise their hands.'

Everyone present raised their hands and the chairman duly reported that the motion had been carried. The secretary made a note of this vote in the minute book.

The meeting then broke up.

Trevor was on his way out when Jake the barman called him over.

'There's someone on the phone for you,' said the barman, rather brusquely. 'I was in the middle of my break when it rang,' he added in protest.

'I'm sorry,' said Trevor. 'Do you know who it is?'

'A woman,' said Jake.

Trevor picked up the telephone receiver. 'Yes?' he said rather tentatively.

'Is that Mr Dukinfield?' asked a woman whose voice Trevor didn't recognise.

Trevor hesitated.

'Trevor Dukinfield?'

'Who's that?'

'I was hoping it was you.'

'Yes. It is.'

'My name is Morris. I'm a reporter with the Daily Globe. I gather you've recently inherited a golf club!'

'Did you say the Daily Globe?' said Trevor, shuddering involuntarily at the thought that he might have in some way attracted the attentions of the Daily Globe, a newspaper which usually seemed to fill its pages with stories of naughty vicars and errant scout masters.

'That's right!' said the woman, brightly.

'Why do you want to speak to me?' asked Trevor.

'Oh, it's a wonderful story!' said the woman. 'Our readers will be fascinated to read about The Man Who Inherited A Golf Course.' She spoke in capital letters. Trevor didn't think it was much of a story at all. It occurred to him that he definitely hadn't been suited to a career in journalism.

'I just want to come and talk to you, maybe take one or two photos,' said the woman.

'No, thank you,' said Trevor.

'But why on earth not?' asked the woman.

'I just don't want to,' said Trevor. 'Thank you for calling. Goodbye.' He put the telephone down and realised that he was sweating and shaking slightly.

* * *

When Trevor got back to the caravan the door was shut. The lights were on and he could hear noises so he knew that there was someone inside. However, when he tried to get in he found that the door was bolted. After five minutes of knocking and banging, first on the door and then on the windows, Trevor heard the flimsy bolt on the inside of the caravan door being drawn back. The door opened slowly and Willie's head appeared.

'Yes?' said Willie's head, peering out into the darkness of the night. 'Who is it? What the hell do you want?'

'It's me! I want to come in!' said Trevor, wearily. 'It's getting chilly. And I want to go to bed!'

'Oh, it's you!' said Willie, opening the door wider. He grinned broadly. He didn't seem to be wearing anything except one of Trevor's towels which was wrapped around his waist. 'I thought you'd found somewhere else to spend the night!' he winked.

Trevor was climbing up into the caravan when he heard a strange voice, a woman's voice.

'What is it darling?' the voice asked. 'Is everything all right?'

'It's OK!' replied Willie. 'I'll be back in a moment.'

Trevor peered down the length of the dimly lit caravan and could just make out the unmistakable form of a tall, well-built woman with red hair. She was completely naked apart from what looked to Trevor remarkably like a pair of golf shoes and a driving glove.

'Who's that?' he asked Willie, in a whisper.

'Thelma,' Willie whispered back.

'Who?' demanded Trevor, still whispering.

'Thelma,' said Willie again, but slightly louder this time.

'Where on earth did Thelma come from?' whispered Trevor.

'I met her on the putting green,' said Willie. He leant forwards. 'Why are we whispering?' he whispered.

'I don't know,' admitted Trevor, not whispering.

'I think you'd better get dressed, love,' Willie called to Thelma. 'The landlord is back,' he explained, nodding towards Trevor.

'Oh,' said Thelma, clearly disappointed. She sounded as if she was pouting. 'Must I?'

''Fraid so!' said Willie. 'I'll call you,' he promised.

While the redhead dressed Willie and Trevor stood crammed together in the tiny kitchenette. Willie filled the kettle with water and lit the calor gas stove.

'You look glum,' said Willie, when Thelma had gone and the kettle had boiled.

'I feel glum,' admitted Trevor. Willie picked up a small coffee jar from the tiny work surface to the right of the sink. A quick glance was enough to tell him that the jar was empty.

'It's not what you'd call a thriving business opportunity, is it?' said Willie. He opened the cupboard above the stove. 'Where do you keep the coffee?'

'Isn't there any more?'

'No.'

'Oh. Well I must have run out. Is there any tea?'

'No.' said Willie, peering into the cupboard. 'You've got one and a half digestive biscuits, a tin of mustard powder and an almost empty bottle of brown sauce. Pop along to the bar and see if the barman can lend us a few grains of coffee, will you?'

Trevor blanched at the thought of asking Jake the barman to lend him anything. 'I think the bar will be shut by now,' he said.

'Well, try the neighbours then!' suggested Willie. 'I can hardly go dressed like this,' he said, adjusting the towel around his waist. 'I'll freeze to death.'

'No, I suppose not,' agreed Trevor. He paused. 'Which neighbours?' he asked, puzzled.

'In the caravan next door!' said Willie. 'Who lives there anyway?' He bent down slightly, pulled back a curtain and peered outside.

'Mrs Weatherby and her son and daughter,' replied Trevor. 'Mrs Weatherby works in the professional's shop and her son is the assistant greenkeeper.'

'Well their light is still on so they haven't gone to bed yet,' said Willie. He handed Trevor the empty coffee jar. 'Just ask them to put a couple of inches of coffee in here – that should last us until you can get to the shops.'

With reluctance born of shyness Trevor took the proffered empty coffee jar, opened the caravan door and stepped back out into the darkness of the night. 'You won't fill the caravan with strange women while I'm gone, will you?' he said to Willie as he stepped outside.

'You're as bad as my wife!' said Willie. 'I invite one female friend to share a lonely evening with me and you immediately jump to conclusions.'

'I suppose you were helping her with her golf swing?' said Trevor. He stopped on the caravan step. 'Why was she wearing golf shoes and a golf glove?' he asked, puzzled.

'Go and get the coffee,' said Willie firmly, pushing the caravan door until it clicked shut, leaving Trevor on the outside.

Trevor, clutching his empty coffee jar, walked nervously over towards Mrs Weatherby's caravan. His shyness seemed to come in suffocating waves. Fortunately, the door to Mrs Weatherby's caravan was no more than five or six yards from his own; if it had been further Trevor might never have got there. Trevor raised a knuckle and timidly knocked on the door.

He had waited two or three seconds and was about to go

back and tell Willie that there had been no reply when Mrs Weatherby opened the door to her caravan. She was dressed in a rather threadbare candlewick dressing gown which covered her from neck to ankle. Her hair was decorated with a couple of dozen bright pink, plastic curlers. When she saw Trevor she needlessly pulled the two sides of her dressing gown tightly together. Her worries were quite unjustified; the only areas of skin which were visible were her hands and her face.

'Excuse me,' said Trevor. 'I'm terribly sorry to bother you but do you think you could lend me a few teaspoons of coffee?' He held out his small but empty coffee jar, feeling like Oliver asking for more gruel.

'Of course I can, dear,' said Mrs Weatherby, smiling. She took the jar, turned and moved back inside her caravan. Trevor stood on the caravan step and waited for her to return. 'Here you are, dear,' said Mrs Weatherby, returning with Trevor's coffee jar now full to the brim.

'Oh,' said Trevor. 'You didn't have to fill it. That's very nice of you. I'll bring it back to you tomorrow as soon as I've been to the shops.'

Mrs Weatherby raised a hand. 'Don't be silly, dear,' she said. 'Are you all right for sugar? Milk? Do you want some biscuits?'

'A few biscuits would be very welcome,' said Trevor.

'Digestive, bourbon or Garibaldi?'

'I beg your pardon?'

'What sort of biscuits would you like? Digestive, bourbon or Garibaldi?'

'Digestive please,' said Trevor.

'With or without?'

Puzzled, Trevor frowned. 'With or without what?'

'Chocolate.'

'Oh, with please!' said Trevor enthusiastically. 'If it's not going to put you to too much trouble. I'll make sure I replace them for you tomorrow.'

'Don't be silly,' said Mrs Weatherby. She disappeared and returned a moment later clutching a new packet of chocolate digestive biscuits which she handed to Trevor.

'Could I ask you something?' asked Trevor, shyly.

'Of course you can, dear,' replied Mrs Weatherby.

'Was that your daughter I saw coming out of your caravan the other day?'

Mrs Weatherby hesitated for a moment. 'Er, yes,' she replied, sounding rather flustered. Trevor said goodnight and Mrs Weatherby closed the door of her caravan.

Trevor didn't feel like going straight to bed. He went for a walk across the golf course. When he finally got back to the caravan Willie was fast asleep. Trevor, who still wasn't in the slightest bit sleepy, made himself a cup of black coffee and ate half a packet of chocolate digestive biscuits.

CHAPTER ELEVEN

'So what happened to you last night?' demanded Willie, sipping black coffee and munching a chocolate biscuit. 'Do you think we could get a bit of bacon in?' he asked plaintively. 'I do rather like a decent breakfast.'

'I went for a walk,' said Trevor, sleepily. 'I'm sorry.' He stood in the kitchen rubbing the small of his back with one hand and his eyes with the other.

'Walking? For God's sake Trevor, I waited an hour for you to come back. I nearly came over to see if you were OK.' Willie pushed the remains of the biscuit he was eating into his mouth and took another from the packet. 'Shall I make you out a shopping list? We need beer, bacon, eggs, coffee and biscuits. I think that's all the essentials. What else do you reckon?' He paused, thinking. 'Oh, and some tomato sauce!' he added.

'I wasn't really planning on going shopping,' said Trevor, yawning. 'I need to practise my golf.'

'So do we all, old chap!' said Willie. 'My short irons have really been letting me down lately. I thought I'd get out there this morning and do some serious work with my eight iron.' He licked a smear of chocolate from his thumb, finished his coffee, stood up and looked at his watch. Then he squeezed past Trevor and went in search of his trousers.

Trevor tentatively felt the side of the kettle with the back of his hand. It was still warm so he put a spoonful of coffee into a cup and filled it with water from the kettle. Having taken a sip he reached across the table towards the packet of biscuits. The packet was empty. 'You've eaten all the biscuits!' he protested.

'What?' called Willie from the bedroom.

'You've finished off all the biscuits!'

Willie's head appeared around the bedroom door. 'Sorry. What did you say?'

'Never mind,' sighed Trevor. 'It doesn't matter.' He thought for a moment. 'Willie?

'Yes? Have you seen my clothes?'

'They're under the table.'

'Oh, right. Thanks.' Willie pounced upon his trousers. 'Great. Now, do you want me to write out this shopping list for you?'

'Couldn't you go, Willie? You've got a car.'

'Of course I can't! I've got to get some practice in. Besides, what if someone recognises me? Or the car? What if someone recognises me *and* the car?'

'Who on earth is going to recognise you in our village shop?' asked Trevor. 'And what does it matter if they do?'

'If my wife finds out where I am there will be lawyers swarming all over the place! I'm in strict hiding, old chap,' said Willie. 'Women can be tricky. In my experience it's better just to keep well out of the way until everything has blown over. For all I know she's got private detectives queuing up outside every shop in the county.'

Trevor sighed. 'OK. I'll go.' He looked at Willie. 'How many times have you been divorced?' he asked.

'So far, exactly one less than the number of times I've been married,' replied Willie with a grin.

* * *

Trevor walked the two miles to the village shop with a light shopping bag and a heavy heart. But it was a beautiful, warm, summer's day. The bees were buzzing, the butterflies were fluttering and the birds were singing their hearts out in the trees. Trevor was so accustomed to sunshine at the golf club that he had almost forgotten that there were any alternatives. On his way he saw the assistant greenkeeper on his tractor. He waved to him.

'Excuse me,' said Trevor, when the tractor driver had switched off the engine. 'But are you twins?'

The tractor driver frowned. 'Twins?'

'You and your sister?'

'Oh!' The tractor driver seemed flustered. 'Yes. Sort of.' Trevor could see that he was blushing. The boy started up the tractor and hurried off, leaving behind his usual cloud of grass cuttings.

Trevor watched buzzards circling high over the cornfields. He paused for a few moments on a small stone bridge and watched a heron catch a small trout with one swift dart of its beak. And he thought a lot about the good golf shot he had played on his last outing with Mr Schmidt.

By the time Trevor returned to the caravan he had a light heart and a heavy shopping basket. The world seemed a decidedly decent place.

And then he stepped into the caravan.

There was a sudden scuffling at the far end of the caravan and Trevor got a brief glimpse of a well-turned breast, a plump, white buttock and two short and rather hairy legs.

'I say, old fellow, you really should knock!' said Willie, clearly the owner of the short and hairy legs. 'You had us worried for a moment.' He didn't seem to be wearing anything other than his shirt.

The unmistakable owner of the other two items, a petite, raven-haired woman whom Trevor had never seen before, peeped out from behind a lilac jumper which she had been holding up as a screen and giggled nervously. There was a small silver brooch pinned to the front of the jumper.

'I thought you had to practise!' said Trevor, putting the shopping down.

'I *have* been practising!' insisted Willie.

The owner of the raven hair, the plump buttock and the lilac jumper giggled again and playfully hit Willie on the arm with her fist.

'This is Hortense,' said Willie, pulling down his shirt a couple of essential inches. 'Hortense this is Trevor.' He stood up and peered into the shopping basket. 'Did you remember the tomato ketchup?'

Hortense giggled again and held out a very tiny hand. She wore rings on her fingers and a thick gold bracelet around her wrist.

'Hello, Hortense,' said Trevor, taking her outstretched fingers and shaking her hand.

'Hello, Trevor,' said Hortense. 'We thought you were Spencer.'

Willie was busy taking items out of the shopping basket. 'You've forgotten the tomato ketchup, haven't you?'

'Spencer?' said Trevor. He looked at Willie. 'Who's Spencer? They hadn't got any.'

'They hadn't got any tomato ketchup! What sort of shop did you go to? Spencer is Hortense's husband.'

'Oh. Is he a member?' asked Trevor.

'A member?'

'Of the golf club?'

'Who?'

'Spencer.'

'Oh yes,' replied Hortense. 'That's how Willie and I met.'

'I popped over to the bar for a drink and the telephone was ringing,' explained Willie. 'There was no one else there apart from the barman and he didn't look as if he was about to answer it so I did. It was Hortense.'

'I was ringing Spencer to remind him to be home early tonight,' explained Hortense. 'We're going to a dinner tonight,' she added. 'It's the annual dinner and dance of the Carpet Traders' Association and Spencer is chairman.'

'We just got chatting,' said Willie.

'You're not married to Spencer Prendergast by any chance, are you?'

'Yes! That's right!' said Hortense. She leant forward confidentially. 'Spencer is a very important person in the golf club,' she told Trevor.

'Trevor owns the golf club,' said Willie, dryly.

'Oh, good heavens, do you?' said Hortense, with a giggle. 'You must be really, really important!'

'Oh, no,' began Trevor. 'You see...'

'I say,' said Hortense, 'you won't say anything to Spencer, will you?'

'Of course not!' replied Trevor.

'Spencer can be just the teeniest bit jealous sometimes,' explained Hortense. 'But Willie sounded very lonely on the telephone,' said Hortense, looking at her companion.

'I was lonely,' said Willie, looking at Hortense. 'Until we met.'

'Isn't he a darling?' asked Hortense.

'Oh, absolutely,' agreed Trevor.

'I came over to cheer him up,' said Hortense. She leant forward, as though pretending that Willie wasn't there. 'He told me about his marital troubles,' she mouthed.

'You certainly cheered me up!' said Willie. He put his arm around her and kissed her.

'The break up has devastated him, you know!' mouthed Hortense to Trevor.

'Yes, so I gather,' said Trevor.

'He asked me if I'd like to play a round with him!' said Hortense. She looked at Willie and punched him again. 'I said he was a very naughty boy.' She giggled.

'Yes' said Trevor, 'Willie can be a very naughty boy, can't you Willie?' Trevor shot a glance at his friend. 'I think perhaps I should just pop along to the practise ground and knock a few balls about,' he added.

'Great idea!' said Willie. 'I'll see you out there later.' He suddenly remembered something and looked around the caravan. 'Oh, by the way, a packet came for you.'

'A packet? For me?'

'There it is!' said Willie, pointing. 'On the draining board.'

Trevor took a couple of steps forward and picked up the packet. His name was scrawled in capital letters but he nevertheless recognised the writing. With the packet in one hand he picked up his golf bag and headed back towards the door.

'Bye!' cried Hortense. 'I'll try and cheer him up a bit more for you.'

'Goodbye!' said Trevor, struggling with the door. 'I'm sure you'll manage to do that.'

When he got outside Trevor opened the packet and tipped the contents out onto his hand. The packet contained a bracelet, a brooch, a ring, three letters, two postcards and a dozen colour photographs in a white envelope. There was also a letter from Sylvia. It didn't take long to read.

Dear Trevor,
I am returning the things you gave me and everything I have which reminds me of you. There isn't much. My mother has taken the sweater you bought me last Christmas to the Oxfam shop.
Yours sincerely
Sylvia Instow

Trevor looked at the stuff in his hand. Sylvia was right. There wasn't much. He remembered the song: 'Breaking up is hard to do'. He thought how wrong it was. Breaking up didn't seem very hard at all. He felt nothing but relief. He dropped the letters and photographs into a nearby dustbin and slipped the jewellery into his pocket. Then, after taking two steps forward, he stopped, turned, took the jewellery out of his pocket and dropped that into the bin too. It hadn't been expensive. Trevor realised that he felt happier than he had for a long time, and for a moment or two he felt rather guilty.

* * *

Trevor spent the afternoon on the practice ground.

'You be patient and the good shots will arrive,' said Mr Schmidt as Trevor stabbed his seven iron into the ground six inches behind the ball. ' You must relax.'

'I am relaxed,' insisted Trevor, through gritted teeth. 'I am relaxed.' He repeated this phrase silently to himself as though it were a magic prayer. He had an awful feeling that worrying about relaxing was making him more tense.

'Try to keep your head and to play through the ball,' said Mr Schmidt, as Trevor played an air shot.

'Do those really count?'

'Pardon?'

'Do I really have to count a shot if I miss the ball completely?'

'Of course!'

'It doesn't seem fair,' protested Trevor, standing back from his ball for a moment. 'If a marksman doesn't pull the trigger it doesn't count as a shot fired. In cricket if a bowler loses his stride and doesn't bowl the ball it doesn't count anything on the score.'

'Cricket! Pah!' said Mr Schmidt. 'You English and your cricket.'

'I still don't think it's really fair,' muttered Trevor. He swung again. This time his club hit the ball which squirted off to the right, though it never rose more than a foot above the ground.

'I seem to be getting worse instead of better,' he moaned. 'I haven't hit a decent shot for ages.'

'That is usual,' said Mr Schmidt.

'To get worse?'

'Yes.'

'Why?'

'When you know nothing the game seems easy,' explained Mr Schmidt. 'It is when you know more and discover that there is even more that you do not know that it becomes difficult.'

'Then maybe I shouldn't be taking lessons at all,' said Trevor glumly but logically. He pulled another ball towards him, kept his head still, his elbow straight and his eye fixed firmly on the ball. Then he swung. The ball shot off to the left.

'But then you will never any better get!'

'But I'm not getting better!' countered Trevor. 'I'm getting worse!'

'You must be patient!' said Mr Schmidt, getting rather excited. 'Try to imagine that your hips are a circle in the air and your club is a paintbrush.'

Trevor muttered a silent curse and pulled another ball towards him. This time the ball, smitten by his imaginary paintbrush, flew sixty feet straight up into the air and landed a few yards in front of him.

'You see this is a good sign!' said Mr Schmidt, enthusiastically.

'What on earth do you mean?' asked Trevor. 'How can it be a good sign? I never know where the ball is going to go!'

'This is good!' insisted Mr Schmidt. 'You have yet not acquired any bad habits or any constant faults.'

'Not *yet*?'

'Oh, all golfers have bad habits. It is the nature of the game. But we do not know what yours will be.'

'And that is good?'

'Oh yes!' said Mr Schmidt emphatically. 'The faults you develop may be very small, little teeny, weeny ones! You may a great golfer become.'

'Really?'

'Really!'

Trevor beamed. 'Oh,' he said. 'That's cheered me up a bit.' He pulled another ball towards him, swung and hit it hard. But he hit across the ball and put so much spin on it that although it started off going straight ahead it suddenly veered sharply to the right and ended up in the deep rough on the right-hand side of the practice ground. He looked across at Mr Schmidt. 'That's the second one I've hit to the right,' he said. 'That doesn't mean that there's a pattern does it? There isn't one particular fault coming through, is there?'

'No!' said the golf professional certainly. 'Certainly not! You are still no better than you ought to be. You are blowing hot and cold and doing everything wrong.'

'Oh, good,' said Trevor, as he watched a ball skim across the grass like a flat stone skimming across a smooth surfaced pond. 'That's reassuring.'

CHAPTER TWELVE

Time was running out for Trevor. He had to satisfy his uncle's two requirements; first, to play a round in fewer than 100 strokes and, second, to beat a pair of golfers from the bank. He had been religiously practising every day and had encountered rather more disappointment than elation during his hours of practice. Nothing seemed to be getting easier, though even Trevor had to admit that the number of strokes he required to complete a hole was very gradually decreasing. Even so, there was very little time left. He had to attempt his uncle's first challenge.

'I've asked the professional to come round with me this afternoon,' he said to Willie as he ate lunch and Willie ate a late breakfast. 'I'm going to try and break 100. The bank is sending along an observer.'

'You'll do it easily!' said Willie, taking the lid off his sandwich and pouring brown sauce onto curly and slightly burnt strips of bacon. He took a bite out of the sandwich.

'Willie,' said Trevor wearily. 'If I break 100 it'll be a miracle.'

'Oh, don't be silly!' said Willie, with half a bacon sandwich crammed into his mouth. 'You'll do it easily!'

'I hope so,' said Trevor. 'I do hope so.' He felt his new responsibility keenly and was well aware that the lives of a lot of people were resting on his back. He paused. 'I say, Willie, would you make up the four with us?'

Willie swallowed, washed down his mouthful of bacon sandwich with half a mugful of tea and raised an eyebrow. 'This afternoon?'

'I'd appreciate it,' said Trevor.

A statuesque blonde squeezed out of the tiny shower room

and struggled to hide her nakedness in a towel which was quite inadequate for the purpose. She tried to wrap the towel around her body but the two ends were a good nine inches apart.

'Do you want some breakfast before you go?' asked Willie. The blonde pouted. 'Do I have to go?'

'I'm afraid so, darling!' said Willie. 'Trevor has just reminded me that I promised to play golf with him this afternoon.'

'Oh, Willie!' protested the blonde. 'Stay and play with me!'

'I'd love to, darling!' said Willie. He shrugged his shoulders. 'But...!'

Thirty minutes later the blonde wiggled her way towards a Mercedes coupe, turning to wave a hand to Willie and to blow him a kiss.

* * *

'Thanks for coming, Willie,' said Trevor, as the two of them headed for the professional's caravan to collect Mr Schmidt and the representative from the bank. 'I appreciate it.'

'Don't mention it,' said Willie. 'I could do with a bit of a rest.'

Trevor, who had never known anyone like Willie, and wasn't at all sure that there *was* anyone else like Willie, pushed open the door to the professional's caravan and led the way into the shop. A tall, cadaverous-looking man in a bright red sweater and a pair of plaid trousers was standing by the counter signing a credit card slip. He wore the most amazing cap Trevor had every seen; a cross between a deerstalker, a french beret and a flat cap.

'This is Victor Barclay,' said Gunther Schmidt, introducing the stranger. 'He vice-president is of a bank; the Mettleham...,' he paused and looked to Mr Barclay for help.

'The Mettleham Banking Corporation,' said Mr Barclay, hesitating for a moment and then holding out a limp, pink hand. Trevor and Willie both shook it.

'I must come back here when you have your closing down sale,' said the banker to the professional.

Mr Schmidt looked puzzled. 'My closing down sale? What is

this?' He looked at Trevor for help. Trevor, as puzzled as the professional was, shrugged.

'You won't want a golf shop here when our bulldozers are busy preparing the ground for our industrial estate,' said Mr Barclay, with a thin smile. 'Maybe you'd like to talk to our people about taking a lease on a small factory unit. You could perhaps make golf tees.'

'A factory?' roared Mr Schmidt. 'I am a golf professional not a tee maker!'

'Of course you are,' said Mr Barclay, smirking.

'What a very nice piece of headgear,' said Willie, nodding towards the banker's hat in an attempt to defuse the situation. 'Most unusual, Was it your father's?'

'My father's?'

'I just assumed that it must be something that had been handed down in your family,' said Willie.

'No,' said the banker, puzzled. He raised his eyes as though trying to examine his headgear. The hat made him look a complete plonker.

'It suits you,' said Willie.

* * *

Fifteen minutes later the four of them were standing on the first tee, and Trevor was about to play the most important round of golf of his life.

'Just remember what I told you and everything will he fine and dindy,' said Mr Schmidt to Trevor. 'Keep your eyes on the ball and your head still while you move it, keep your elbow straight until you bend it and do not forget the knees!'

'Dindy?' whispered Willie. 'What's dindy?'

'Dandy,' Trevor whispered back. 'I think he means dandy.'

'Oh,' said Willie. He frowned. 'And what does that mean?'

Trevor thought for a moment. 'I don't know,' he admitted.

The professional stabbed a tee into the ground, balanced a ball on it, pulled his driver out of his bag and used the latter to send the former two hundred and seventy five yards down the centre of the fairway. The banker stabbed a tee into the ground, balanced a ball on it, pulled a three wood out of his bag and used the latter to send the former two hundred and twenty yards down the left-hand side of the fairway. Willie stabbed a tee into the ground, balanced a ball on it, pulled a driver out of his bag and used the latter to send the former three hundred yards down the right-hand side of the fairway. His ball finished up in the light rough. Trevor looked around nervously, as though hoping that there might be someone else to play.

'Come on,' whispered the professional. 'Show us what you can do!'

Trevor took a tee from the pocket on the side of his golf bag and tried to push it into the ground. The tee bent as it hit a small stone. He took out another tee, found a softer piece of ground and stuck it in. Then he took out a ball, balanced it on the tee and paused.

'Good stuff so far,' said Willie, trying to relax his friend. The professional stared at Willie as if he was completely mad. 'Thanks,' said Trevor, wryly. He reached out towards his golf bag and grasped the head of his driver.

'Why not use an iron,' suggested Willie quietly.

'A driver!' said the professional firmly.

'That's a two stroke penalty,' said the Mr Barclay.

The other three looked at him.

'Rule 8,' said the banker. 'If a player accepts advice which might influence his choice of club there is a two stroke penalty.'

'Oh come on!' said Willie. 'It wasn't really advice!'

'Two stroke penalty,' said Mr Barclay firmly. He made a mark on his card.

Trevor looked at Willie. Willie, scowling, shrugged. Trevor pulled out his driver, took a practice swing and then started his swing. At the top of his back swing Mr Barclay suddenly coughed. Trevor, disturbed by the noise, jerked uncontrollably and sent the ball skidding four or five yards off the left-hand edge of the tee. The ball came to rest deep in a clump of thick, coarse grass. It was unplayable. Trevor felt sweat beginning to run down his spine.

'Oh dear!' said Mr Barclay. 'I am sorry. I hope I didn't put you off!'

'The left knee!' hissed the professional. 'You forgot to bring your left knee round. And you must make a big circle with your hips.'

Trevor looked down and saw, with some relief, that his knee was where he had left it.

'That's another two stroke penalty,' said Mr Barclay. 'Advice from another player.' He made another note on his card.

'Well, at least it's gone in the right direction,' said Willie. 'I once managed to drive a ball that ended up eighty yards behind the tee. The bloke whose ankle it bounced off wasn't too pleased.' He paused. 'It takes great skill to hit a ball backwards,' he added, reflectively.

'What shall I do now?' asked Trevor, who wasn't in the mood for funny stories.

'You will have to take another ball off the tee,' said the banker with a big smile. 'You are now playing seven.'

'Seven!' groaned Trevor. He looked around. The professional, who looked very sad, nodded his agreement.

Suddenly, without warning, Willie fell to his knees, grasped his stomach and groaned in pain.

'What on earth's the matter?' asked Trevor, anxiously.

'Just my old trouble,' said Willie bravely. 'I've got some of my pills in the caravan,' he said, bent almost double. Bravely he stood up and started to shuffle off the tee. Instinctively, Trevor helped him.

'What is this?' demanded Mr Barclay as the two of them left the tee. 'Where do you think you are going?'

'The doctor said that if I take my pills the moment the pain starts I should be OK,' said Willie through clenched teeth, stopping and resting on his trolley. 'Otherwise...'

'What about the game?' demanded the banker, striding after them. 'Your attempt to break 100?' he said to Trevor's back.

'I'm sorry,' apologised Trevor, turning his head. 'I've got to go with my friend. I'll be back as soon as I can.'

'Shouldn't be more than half an hour,' said Willie. 'One way or another,' he added.

'Perhaps we could start again then?' asked Trevor.

'But we've already started!' insisted Mr Barclay. 'You've taken seven and you aren't off the tee yet.'

'I'm sorry,' said Trevor. 'But surely you don't expect me to let my friend go back to the caravan alone?'

'Tomorrow maybe back you could come?' suggested Mr Schmidt.

'I can't just take whole days away from the bank!' said the Mr Barclay.

'I'll be OK when I've had my pills,' said Willie weakly. 'Maybe we could abandon that start and have another go in half an hour's time?'

The banker scowled. 'I suppose so,' he agreed at last.

When they got back to the caravan Trevor helped Willie up the steps. 'You sit down,' he said as he started to hunt around. 'Where are they?' he asked, suddenly realising that he didn't have the foggiest idea where to look.

'Where are what?' asked Willie, sitting on one of the bench seats.

'Your pills, of course!' Trevor stared at Willie. 'Are you all right?' he asked, for Willie was no longer crouching double.

'I'm fine, thanks,' said Willie, grinning broadly. 'Marvellous recovery!' He rubbed his stomach.

Trevor stared at him, opened his mouth and then shut it again. 'There wasn't anything the matter with you, was there?'

'Well that banker was making me feel a little nauseous,' said Willie.

'But there wasn't any pain at all was there?'

Willie shrugged. 'It depends on how you define pain.'

'I bet there aren't even any pills, are there?'

'I think there's a box of indigestion tablets in my bag somewhere,' said Willie. 'Come on, Trevor. If I hadn't done something you'd have started off trying to go round in 92 not 99!'

Trevor stared at Willie and looked around as though frightened that someone might overhear. 'But ... leaving the tee like that ... it wasn't exactly according to the rules was it?'

'We didn't break any rules,' said Willie. 'We just abandoned that round and we'll start another one in half an hour's time.'

Trevor scratched his head.

'That empty suit from the bank isn't going to do you any favours,' said Willie. 'He wants you to fail just as much as you want to win. He coughed deliberately while you were taking your first shot. It wasn't against the rules but it wasn't exactly playing the game in the proper spirit, was it? And then all that stuff about a two stroke penalty...!'

Trevor thought about it and nodded. 'You're right,' he said. 'He's obviously prepared to do anything to make sure that the bank gets the golf course.'

'One other thing: can you have a word with Gunther Schmidt and get him to sit out the next attempt,' said Willie.

'Oh dear,' said Trevor. 'Really? He'll be terribly disappointed.'

'He'll cost you the match if you don't,' warned Willie. 'He won't be able to resist offering you advice. That's what he does for a living.'

Trevor thought about it for a moment. 'I suppose you're right,' he agreed. He couldn't imagine Mr Schmidt playing a hole of golf without offering advice to everyone within earshot.

'By the time you get to the first green you'll have a score of at least 200 against your name in penalties alone,' said Willie. 'You won't stand a chance.'

'Mr Schmidt gives everyone advice,' said Trevor. 'He can't help it.'

'I know,' agreed Willie. 'But no one else's score matters. Your score does. Remember, you aren't playing against the banker. All you've got to do is break 100.'

Trevor stood up. 'You're right,' he agreed, moving towards the door. 'You stay there and look ill for a few minutes while I have a word with him.'

Much to Trevor's surprise the professional understood. 'You

are right,' he sighed. 'I talk too much. I am a lot of chiefs and not enough Indians.'

'It isn't that I mind at all,' said Trevor. 'I'm very grateful to you for your help. I wish you could be there advising me. It's just...'

'I know, I know!' said the professional. 'The rules, the rules. You do not have to beat the bushes.' He sounded strangely Jewish, a trick that isn't easy for a man with an accent like Goebbels. He reached out and patted Trevor on the shoulder. 'Good luck!' he said intently. He looked around, as though to make sure that no one was listening. 'And make sure you bend your knees otherwise your game will come apart.'

'I will,' promised Trevor. He shook hands with the professional and walked slowly back towards the caravan to collect Willie.

'Mr Dukinfield!' he heard someone call. He turned and saw Captain Jarrold standing on the clubhouse steps waving to him.

Trevor hurried over. 'What is it?' he asked anxiously.

'There's someone on the telephone for you, sir,' said Captain Jarrold.

'Trevor,' said Trevor. 'Do call me Trevor.'

'There's someone on the telephone for you, Trevor,' said Captain Jarrold rather uncomfortably.

'Oh dear,' said Trevor. 'I really can't. Not at the moment. Do you know who it is?'

'It's someone from the national press, sir, er Trevor,' said Captain Jarrold. 'She did give her name but I'm afraid I can't remember it. I think she said she was from the Daily Globe.'

'Would you tell her I've emigrated?' asked Trevor.

Captain Jarrold frowned. 'Are you thinking of emigrating, sir?'

But Trevor had disappeared back into his caravan.

'Ye Gods, man, what the hell have you got in this bag?' demanded Willie, meeting Trevor just inside the caravan door and handing him his bag. 'Do you really need all these clubs?'

'Mr Schmidt said I would,' replied Trevor.

'You won't need that,' said Willie, taking out Trevor's

number one wood and standing it up in the corner of the caravan. 'Nor that,' he added, removing the number two wood. 'Nor these,' he went on, putting Trevor's number one and two irons next to the two woods. 'Most golfers would play much better if they took their woods out of their bags and used them as bean sticks.'

'What on earth am I going to use to drive with?' asked Trevor. 'The bag?'

'Use a number three or four wood or, better still, a three iron,' said Willie. 'How often do you hit a drive three hundred yards up the centre of the fairway?'

Trevor stared at him.

'How often?'

Trevor shrugged and looked uncomfortable. 'Well ...' he mumbled.

'Never?' suggested Willie.

'More or less,' admitted Trevor reluctantly. 'Roughly.'

'Exactly,' said Willie. 'If you've going to go round in under 100 you've got to play percentage golf – playing safe shots whenever you can. Imagine you're playing a hole that is three hundred and fifty yards. You have brilliant luck and instead of going into the trees on the left or the rough on the right your drive goes two hundred and twenty yards straight down the middle of the fairway. You've got a second shot of a hundred and thirty yards. Could you put that shot close to the pin?'

'Of course not!'

'Could you put it on the green?'

'Sometimes,' said Trevor. 'Not often,' he admitted. 'I'd be happy to try and get it close to the green.'

'So you'd be happy if you got on the green in three?'

'Oh yes!'

'Right. Now, if you drive one hundred and eighty yards with your three iron – a shot that you are much more likely to be able to make – you should still be able to reach the green in three. Right?'

Trevor frowned. 'Yes. I suppose so.'

'So using a wood from the tee doesn't help you much, even on the rare occasions when you connect properly?'

'I suppose not.'

'Imagine that you're playing a two hundred yard par three. Could you hit the green with a wood from the tee?'

Trevor laughed. 'No. Hardly ever.'

'You'd probably end up in a bunker or in a clump of bushes?'

Trevor thought about his answer for a moment. 'Yes,' he admitted.

'If you used a three iron from the tee what would happen?'

'I'd almost certainly be short of the green.'

'Yes. But where would your ball be?'

'Oh, there's a good chance that it would be on the fairway.'

'So you'd have a fairly straightforward second shot to the green?'

'I see what you mean' said Trevor.

'Now, what other clubs do you usually make a mess of?'

'That pitching wedge,' said Trevor. 'I don't know whether it's the club or me. But I hate it.'

'Fair enough, we'll leave it behind,' said Willie.

'But Mr Schmidt says I'll never be any good with it if I don't use it,' said Trevor.

'And he's absolutely right,' said Willie. 'But this isn't a practice round. This is for real. What about your middle irons?'

'Oh, I get on OK with those,' said Trevor. 'Well, except for the four iron. I always seem to fluff my shots when I play with a four iron.'

Willie took Trevor's four iron out of his bag. 'Right,' he said. 'That's better. 'Now we've just got the clubs you know you can play with.' He smiled. 'The bad news is that you can't blame your clubs if you aren't playing well, can you?'

'No,' agreed Trevor sadly.

Willie stopped as though suddenly struck by a thought. 'You hadn't ever met that banker before, had you?'

'No.'

'We missed a good opportunity there,' said Willie, rather sadly.

'What do you mean?'

'Since they don't know what you look like I could have played the round for you.'

Trevor stared at him. 'But that would have been downright dishonest!' he protested.

'You're right,' sighed Willie, though clearly with some regret. He jumped out of the caravan and marched off towards the first tee with Trevor striding along behind him.

* * *

The three of them stood on the first tee again.

'Are you sure you're going to be all right now?' the banker asked Willie, his voice dripping with sarcasm.

'Oh yes, I think so,' said Willie. 'Thank you very much for your concern,' he added politely.

'And your professional definitely isn't joining us?'

'No, he suddenly remembered that he's got another engagement,' said Trevor.

'What a pity,' said Mr Barclay, rather coldly. 'I'm sure we would have all benefited from his advice.'

Willie stepped forward, stuck a tee into the ground, balanced a ball on the tee and took his driver out of his bag. A few seconds later the ball, which had headed off apparently straight down the fairway, was circling around to the left. A few seconds after that it was crashing into a small copse.

'I wish I could do that,' thought Trevor, who was still enough of a novice to be impressed by length more than accuracy. 'Well played!' he said. Willie, who was rather proud of the shot, for he had spent many months perfecting his deliberate hook, said nothing audible but seemed to mumble something under his breath.

The banker played next. His ball landed right in the middle of the fairway two hundred and fifty yards away.

'I was going to suggest that we had a little side bet,' said Willie. 'Just the two of us.' He shrugged. 'But I think you're going to be too good for me.'

The banker looked at him.

'Just to make things a bit more interesting,' said Willie.

'I suppose you're angling for odds?' sneered Mr Barclay, if a man in a ridiculous hat can sneer.

'Odds?' asked Willie, as though he'd never heard the word before.

'What's your handicap?' asked the banker.

'I haven't got an official handicap,' admitted Willie. He leaned over towards the banker and spoke confidentially. 'But some days I can play to 24.'

'A straight game and straight odds,' said the banker, whose handicap was nine. 'Medal play.'

'That's damned decent of you,' said Willie. 'Five hundred?'

Mr Barclay stared at him. 'Five hundred pounds?'

'Sorry,' said Willie with a shrug. 'I'm a bit strapped for cash at the moment. I could maybe manage seven hundred and fifty if you like.'

The banker, who had gone white, swallowed hard. 'No,' he said. 'Five hundred will be fine.'

Trevor, who had been listening to this exchange in disbelief opened his mouth to remind Willie that he didn't have a spare five pounds let alone a spare £500 but closed it and then used a three iron to put his first shot eighty yards down the middle of the fairway, just ahead of the ladies' first tee.

'Good shot!' said Willie, picking up his bag and heading off up the fairway. Trevor was quite pleased with it too. The view from the first tee was undoubtedly the most daunting on the course and his shot had missed a large patch of mixed gorse and heather.

'So,' said the banker, as he and Trevor followed in Willie's footsteps. 'Are you beginning to wish you'd taken the money when you inherited the golf club?'

'No,' said Trevor, quite firmly.

Mr Barclay, clearly surprised, looked at him.

'I like the club,' said Trevor. 'I've grown very attached to it.'

'That's rather a pity, isn't it?' said the banker.

'What do you mean?' asked Trevor.

'It won't be long before we'll have our bulldozers churning it all up.'

'Won't you feel guilty about destroying a wonderful golf course like this?'

'Not in the slightest,' said Mr Barclay. 'We'll make a lot of money out of it. Aren't you going to play your ball?'

'I beg your pardon?'

'You just passed your ball,' said the banker, stopping. He nodded back in the direction from which they'd come.

Trevor turned and looked. The top of his ball was just visible. He walked back to it. 'Someone has trodden on it!' he complained.

'Oh no, how terrible!' said Mr Barclay. 'Is it playable?'

Trevor looked at it. 'Just about,' he said, rather miserably. He felt sure that the banker had trodden on it deliberately but knew he couldn't prove anything. He selected a seven iron, choosing this club on the grounds that the blade was closest to that of a garden hoe, the tool which would really have been most appropriate. He then took an almighty swipe at the ball and moved both it and enough grass to turf a suburban lawn a yard or so along the fairway.

'Two,' said Mr Barclay. 'Not doing terribly well, are you?'

'I can count my own score,' said Trevor.

'I'm sure you can manage with the smaller numbers,' said the banker, rather smugly. 'But at the rate you're going you'll need a calculator before long.' He folded his arms and stared as Trevor tried to decide what club to use for his next shot. If there was one thing Trevor hated it was having someone watch him. He put the seven iron back into his bag and took out a three iron. Mr Barclay raised an eyebrow and pulled a face.

'What's the matter?' demanded Trevor.

'What do you mean?'

'Why are you looking like that?'

'Oh don't mind me,' said the banker, whose obvious attempts to suppress a snigger had resulted in the production of a very clearly defined smirk. 'Don't mind me at all.'

Trevor, trying hard to concentrate on the ball and to ignore the smirking banker, took careful aim, kept his head steady, brought the club head down in a perfect arc and hit the ball with enough force to send it across half a dozen counties.

Unfortunately, the result was a disappointment. The ball, rebellious and inconsiderate thing that it was, skidded and jumped and bounced and travelled about twenty yards in a diagonal direction.

'You're certainly making progress,' said Mr Barclay condescendingly. He looked at his watch. 'I could perhaps pop back to the clubhouse. I could have a cup of tea while I'm waiting to play my next shot.'

Trevor felt himself turning red, though he wasn't sure whether the colour was inspired by anger or embarrassment.

'How are you doing?' asked Willie, running up and wheezing slightly from his exertions.

'Terrible,' replied Trevor, gloomily.

'I think we'll hire your friend to help us with the earth moving,' said the banker. 'He digs bigger holes than any workman I've ever seen.'

'I'm pleased to say that I found my ball!' announced Willie. 'I'll have to take a drop, of course, but at least I don't need to play another tee shot.'

The banker looked at him disbelievingly. 'You found your ball!'

'Yes! Lucky wasn't it?'

The banker scowled. 'Are you sure it was your ball?'

'Absolutely!' said Willie. 'A Horton 2. Do you want to come and watch me take the drop?' Trevor who knew that Willie had driven off with a Pilton 45 held his breath but the banker said nothing. For a moment Mr Barclay didn't seem to know what to do; whether to stay and continue to try to put Trevor off his game or to go and keep an eye on Willie. For the first time Trevor realised why Willie had initiated the bet with the banker.

In the end the banker, probably deciding that he could trust Trevor to make a mess of his round by himself, followed Willie back across the fairway. Without the banker distracting him and ruining his fragile confidence Trevor succeeded in putting his ball on the short plateau, only about a hundred and eighty yards from the pin. His next shot, also with a three iron, landed at the bottom of the fairway, had a lucky bounce over the stream and ran onto the front edge of the green. Three putts meant that Trevor had completed the first hole in eight strokes – four over par. It wasn't a good beginning but it wasn't quite the disaster it could have been. Willie and the banker halved the hole in five.

* * *

'What the hell are you going to do if you lose?' Trevor whispered to Willie as they walked to the second tee. The banker had gone on ahead.

'What on earth makes you think I'm going to lose?' asked Willie.

'You're playing for £500!' Trevor reminded him. 'And you haven't got £500!' he added, quite unnecessarily.

'This guy cheats,' said Willie quietly. 'No cheat is going to beat me at golf.'

'How can you be so sure?'

'Because I cheat better than anyone else,' said Willie firmly. 'Besides, if I hadn't got the guy involved in a wager he'd spend every minute trying to put you off. This way he'll be busy trying to keep an eye on me and worrying about his own game.'

'I say!' said Mr Barclay, leaving his trolley by the side of the second tee and climbing up to take a look down towards the green. 'This is going to be quite a challenge!'

'I'm glad you like it!' said Trevor.

'I meant to our bulldozers,' said the banker. 'But I hope you've got plenty of balls with you!' He reached into his bag and pulled out a nine iron.

'Pardon?' said Trevor, frowning.

Mr Barclay nodded towards the thick patch of gorse which lay between the tee and the green. 'A chap of your ability should be able to fill that with balls,' he said. He dropped his ball down onto the grassy tee, took aim and carefully pitched the ball up into the air. It went so high it seemed to hang in mid air for a moment before plummeting down to land on the green.

'Not bad,' said the banker. He stepped aside for Willie to take his shot. 'Still using the Horton 2?' he asked. He bent down and looked at Willie's ball as he spoke. 'Fiver says you can't get inside my shot,' he said.

'Done!' said Willie, without hesitation.

When it was Trevor's turn to play his tee shot he stepped into position, put his ball on a tee to reduce his chances of just fluffing it into the gorse, took aim with a seven iron and watched in delight as his ball landed high on the bank at the back of the green. He didn't mind being over the back of the green on this hole. He knew that if he left the second green with nothing worse than a four on his card he would have done well.

'That's a fiver you owe me,' said the banker a minute or two later.

'Take it out of the £500 you'll owe me at the end of the round,' answered Willie.

CHAPTER THIRTEEN

Trevor did take four on the second hole, and with the banker's interest divided between himself and Willie he played with steadily increasing confidence.

Two hours later, when the three of them stood on the 15th tee, Trevor had taken 80 shots and Willie had taken just two shots more than Mr Barclay. Trevor had to complete the final four holes of the course in 19 strokes or less. It wasn't an easy target; but it was possible.

The main hazard on the 15th hole is the stream. It is quite wide and runs straight across the fairway at a distance of about two hundred and twenty yards from the tee. A ball which pitches short of it is far more likely to bounce into it (or, at least, into the bulrushes and water irises which grow along the banks on either side) than to bounce over it. To be sure of clearing the stream a player really needs to be confident that he can hit a drive which will carry at least two hundred and thirty yards from the tee.

Willie knew he could make this shot easily, Mr Barclay thought he might be able to and Trevor was quietly confident that he not only couldn't carry the stream but that he couldn't even reach the water, however cleanly he hit his drive. Since golf is, like all other sports, a game which is very largely played in the mind, Willie's shot cleared the stream and landed around a hundred yards from the green, the banker's tee shot landed about ten yards short of the stream and bounced straight into the water and Trevor's shot, which travelled only about a hundred and fifty yards (which doesn't sound a lot but which was perfectly acceptable as far as Trevor was concerned) ended up around seventy yards short of the hazard.

Trevor cleared the stream with a lofted five iron shot which landed about a hundred and ten yards away from the green. Just to be on the safe side the banker had played a second shot from the tee which was just as well since his first ball wasn't anywhere to be found. His second tee shot was, quite sensibly but perhaps a touch overcautiously, played with a four iron. It landed a good forty yards short of the stream, and around two hundred yards short of the putting surface. It was hardly surprising that his next shot still didn't reach the green. This meant that he had played four shots on a par four hole and still wasn't ready to start using his putter.

Seeing a chance to claw back his deficit, Willie played a beautifully delicate seven iron approach shot. His ball landed on the front edge of the green on the third bounce, ran across the green and stopped no more than twelve feet from the pin. Willie was now on the green in two shots and in an excellent position to take the lead.

Trevor, only too well aware that he really needed to put his next shot safely onto the green, watched with dismay as his ball, hit perfectly straight but badly aimed, pitched straight into one of the horseshoe-shaped bunkers at the side of the green.

The banker, looking remarkably happy despite his own predicament, played a very nicely judged little chip shot which ran on and on, threatened the pin and eventually ended up no more than four feet past the hole.

Trevor, his mouth dry and his hands clammy with sweat, walked up to the bunker and stared at his ball in dismay. The last golfer to land in the bunker had left the rake lying in the sand and Trevor's ball was lying up against the handle. Trevor didn't know enough about the rules to know whether he was allowed to move the rake or his ball. Either way the shot looked nigh on impossible as the banks of the bunker were over three feet high.

'Don't worry about it,' said a voice. 'Just remember we can always come back out tomorrow if you don't break 100 today.'

Trevor looked up and smiled thinly at Willie. 'Thanks,' he said. He felt in his heart that he had played as well as he could and that if he didn't break 100 on this round then he wouldn't be able to do it tomorrow.

'What was that?' demanded Mr Barclay, who had been out of earshot. 'Was that advice?'

'I was just asking my friend if he'd come out with me tonight to help spend your £500,' said Willie.

The banker immediately went rather red and scowled at them both.

'You do have the cash, don't you?' said Willie.

'You haven't won yet,' muttered Mr Barclay, through clenched teeth. 'Not by a long chalk.'

'Does anyone know the rule about rakes in bunkers?' asked Trevor. 'Can I move that thing or do I have to play my ball where it lies?'

'It's an impediment,' said the banker.

'It certainly is,' agreed Trevor.

'It's not an impediment,' said Willie quickly. 'It's an obstruction.'

'What does it matter what we call it?' asked Trevor, in desperation. 'It's a rake!' he said. 'But can I move it?'

'You can if it's an obstruction,' said Willie. 'But not if it's an impediment. A rake is an obstruction.'

'It's an impediment,' said the banker. 'You've got to play the ball as it lies.'

'Don't talk rubbish!' said Willie. 'He can move the damned thing out of the way.' He bent down to examine the ball and the rake more closely. 'They aren't touching,' he said to Trevor. 'You can move the rake.'

Trevor stepped forward and started to bend down to move the rake.

'If you move it there's a two stroke penalty!' shrieked the banker.

Trevor looked across at Willie.

'Move it,' said Willie.

'Leave it alone,' said Mr Barclay firmly.

'Trust me,' said Willie. 'Rule 24.'

Trevor realised that he was sweating.

'We ought to ask the club secretary for a ruling,' said the banker.

'Maybe we should ask,' said Trevor, hesitantly. 'I can't afford to lose two strokes.'

Willie sighed. The banker looked very pleased with himself.

'He's just trying to put you off,' said Willie. 'If we fetch the secretary it'll be dark by the time we finish.'

'I think we should,' said Trevor.

'I'll go and fetch Wing Commander Trout,' offered the banker.

'You stay here with me,' said Willie, reluctantly accepting the situation. 'Trevor, you go. But be as quick as you can.'

* * *

It took Trevor fifteen minutes to get back to the clubhouse and ten minutes to find Wing Commander Trout. It then took the secretary seven minutes to find a copy of the Rules of Golf and it took Trevor and Wing Commander Trout twenty two minutes to walk back to the 15th green. By the time they got there it was beginning to go dark.

'Where on earth have you been?' demanded Willie, as they appeared out of the gloaming.

'I was as quick as I could!' protested Trevor, who was still slightly breathless after his exertions.

'What's your ruling?' asked the banker, pointing to the offending rake. 'Is it an impediment or an obstruction?'

'It's a loose obstruction,' said Wing Commander Trout immediately. 'Rule 24.' He opened his rule book and read out the relevant paragraph.

Willie bent down, carefully picked up the rake and tossed it onto the grass by the side of the bunker. 'There you are,' he said to Trevor. 'Play your shot!'

'If I were you ...' began the secretary.

'Shut up!' screamed Trevor and Willie at the same moment. The secretary looked at them both as if they'd gone mad.

'Sorry,' apologised Trevor. 'Rule 8.'

The secretary looked puzzled. 'Rule 8?'

'Advice from anyone except a player's own partner or caddie incurs a two stroke penalty,' explained Willie.

'Good heavens!' said Wing Commander Trout. 'You are taking this seriously!'

'Thank our friend here,' said Willie, inclining a head in the banker's direction.

'Oh,' said the secretary. 'I see.' He turned to Willie. 'How's he doing?' he enquired in a whisper.

'He'll do it,' said Willie. 'He'll do it.'

The banker snorted. Trevor, sand iron in hand, gulped noisily.

'He'll break 100,' insisted Willie.

Trevor climbed into the bunker.

'I don't think I can watch,' murmured Wing Commander Trout to Willie. He turned and hurried away back down to the clubhouse.

Trevor climbed out of the bunker again and stared at his ball.

'There is a time limit on shots,' said Mr Barclay.

'Shut up,' said Willie. 'You've just delayed things by an hour.'

'How many shots have I had?' asked Trevor.

'Three,' answered the banker immediately.

'And this is a par four?'

'Yes.'

Trevor had been secretly thinking of playing backwards out of the bunker and then chipping up onto the green off the fairway. But he didn't have enough shots left. He knew that if he took more than six then his chances of breaking 100 were well and truly gone. He had to try to get the ball out of the bunker and up onto the green in a single shot. Not only that – but he had to get the ball as close to the hole as possible.

He walked back into the bunker.

'Good luck,' murmured Willie.

'Very difficult shot,' said the banker. 'Very difficult indeed. So easy to hit the ball into the side of the bunker from where you are lying.'

'You can do it,' said Willie.

Trevor, trying to close his mind to all this, gripped his sand iron and tried to visualise the ball flying up out of the bunker, landing on the green and rolling steadily up towards the flag.

He aimed at a spot about an inch behind his ball, closed his eyes and played the shot.

'Terrific shot!' he heard Willie cry. 'Marvellous. Brilliant. Gary Player couldn't have done better.'

Trevor opened his eyes in time to see his ball come to a halt no more than two yards from the pin.

The banker said nothing.

Willie finished the hole with two putts for a par four. The banker holed his putt for a two over par six. And although his ball bobbled about before eventually dropping into the hole from the far side, Trevor sank his putt to complete the hole in a quite remarkable five shots.

The banker and Willie were now all square.

And Trevor had taken 85 shots with three holes to play.

* * *

The 16th hole is widely regarded as one of the most difficult on the course. If you hit a decent tee shot then the hole holds few terrors. But even quite low handicap players often feel satisfied if they leave the green with no more than a four on their cards.

Theoretically the hole is a fairly simple par three. The distance from the mens' tee to the centre of the green is a fraction over two hundred yards and the green itself is quite large and flat. There are no bunkers and no trees guarding the green.

What makes the hole particularly tricky is the twin combination of a stream running in front of the green and a thick circle of bushes around the back of the green. Most long handicap players automatically either take too big a club or hit the ball too hard in an attempt to make sure that they clear the stream. All too often the result is that their shots clear the stream *and* the green, and their balls are lost forever in the bushes. Captain Jarrold once spent a whole Saturday sitting in a deckchair beside the 16th tee and reported afterwards that nearly half the golfers who played the hole had to play a second tee shot because their first had landed in one of the two hazards.

Willie changed clubs twice before settling on a three iron. But, wary of hitting through the green, he underhit and could only stand and watch as his ball landed straight in the stream. The banker, not bothering to hide a broad grin, watched with delight as his ball pitched on the front of the green and rolled on to within fifteen feet of the pin. After much heart searching Trevor decided that he would play what he knew that Willie would describe a percentage shot. He used a five iron and his ball landed forty yards short of the stream.

'Chicken,' muttered Mr Barclay.

'Sensible shot!' said Willie to his friend.

As he walked off the tee Trevor knew that even if he was to play a round in even par he would never feel under more pressure. He suspected that even if he was playing for the Open Championship the tension could not be any greater. He felt proud of himself for facing the pressure successfully; pleased that he hadn't cracked. He used a nine iron for his second shot and decided to aim at the right-hand side of the green which was slightly deeper than the rest of the putting surface.

It may have been overconfidence or it may have been carelessness, or maybe his knees didn't move properly or perhaps his head moved a fraction of an inch because he was so eager to see the result of his shot. Whatever the cause, the shot was one of the worst he had played during the whole round.

As the ball, hit only with the bottom of the club head, rolled and bounced and skipped across the fairway Trevor thought for a brief moment that it was going to make it across the stream. But it didn't. It disappeared into the water without a splash and with hardly a ripple. It was a nightmare shot which Trevor would see a thousand times.

'Jolly good shot,' murmured the banker.

And that was a mistake.

For at that moment, which should have been the lowest moment of his life, Trevor vowed to himself that come what may the bulldozers would never flatten the Butterbury Ford Golf Club. Instead of being demoralised by his terrible shot he felt his determination renewed. He took hold of his trolley and strode forward to the stream.

With the aid of his eight and nine irons he managed to drag his ball out of the bank onto the nearside bank of the stream. Willie had already rescued his own ball. The two of them were doomed to exceed par because of the penalties they had accumulated (though theoretically Willie could still make a par if he chipped straight into the hole).

Willie's chip pitched on the back edge of the green and just ran off into the slightly longer fringe of grass which circled the green. Willie knew that, whereas the banker was likely to be able to complete the hole in par, he was going to have his work cut out to get down in five.

Trevor's chip, hit low and hard, and travelling far too fast, hit the flagstick on its second bounce and dropped straight into the hole. Trevor had finished the hole in a one over par four and now had ten strokes in which to complete the last two holes.

Predictably, the banker completed the hole in three.

Willie took five and was now two strokes behind.

* * *

The banker's tee shot on the 17th was perfect; long, straight and as close as was possible to the rough on the right-hand side of the fairway. When his ball finally stopped rolling the banker was in a perfect position to play a long second shot to the green.

Trevor, who used a three wood, sliced his tee shot. His ball landed in thick rough on the right-hand side of the fairway. He consoled himself with the thought that it could have been worse. If he'd hooked the shot the ball would have landed in gorse and heather. And if he had driven the ball further a sliced tee shot would have put him in Poacher's Lake. If he had a decent lie he would, he thought, still stand a chance of reaching the green in three. Although his fluke at the 16th had kept him in with a chance to break 100 he couldn't afford to make any more mistakes.

Willie, playing last, and still angry with himself for landing in the stream on the 16th, wound himself up and hit his tee shot with great venom. The ball travelled over two hundred and fifty yards before it even hit the ground and rolled another fifty or sixty yards before it stopped. It finally came to rest in the light rough on the left-hand side of the fairway. It was now so dark that Willie couldn't see his ball.

Trevor's second shot was (with the possible exception of the fluke at the 16th) one of the best shots of his round. His lie wasn't as bad as it might have been and the ball was sitting up very well in the long grass. Knowing that he had to get close to the green with his next shot he threw caution to the wind and took a four wood from his bag. His brave shot sent the ball clattering through the low bushes which studded the rough and scampering down and across the fairway. It finally came to rest no more than forty yards from the green. It was the first time he had ever played a wood from rough grass and he felt very pleased with himself.

Mr Barclay played a perfect second shot, curling very slightly to the left, and his ball landed on the green, bounced once and stopped quickly a yard from the back of the putting surface.

Willie knew that if he was going to stand a chance he had to hit the green with his next shot. Using a sand wedge he lifted the ball out of the rough and high over the trio of huge oak trees which stood between him and the green. The ball went so high that Willie had plenty of time to drop his club and run out sideways to see where it landed. To his absolute delight his ball landed right in the middle of the green, just a few yards from the pin. He knew that if he could hole the putt he would probably walk onto the last tee just one stroke behind the banker.

Trevor's third shot was almost as good as his second. His ball landed a yard in front of the green, bounced twice and then rolled gently forwards until it came to a rest six or seven feet from the pin. He had one putt for a par four.

Mr Barclay putted first. He misjudged both the pace of the

green and the borrow and his ball ended up five feet away from the hole.

Willie's third shot and first putt was more successful. He just missed a birdie; his ball ending up no more than six inches away from the hole.

The banker missed his second putt and scored five; Trevor holed out in one, took a par four and halved the hole with Willie.

* * *

It was so dark when they left the 17th green that the three combatants found it difficult to find their way to the 18th tee.

'This is quite absurd,' said Mr Barclay, as they all stood on the 18th tee and stared out into the darkness of the night. 'We can't possibly play in this!'

'Are you conceding?' Willie asked him.

'No!' replied the banker instantly. 'I certainly am not.'

'Are you game to carry on?' Willie asked Trevor.

'Yes,' replied Trevor. 'Absolutely.' He knew that he had to complete the final hole in six in order to complete a round of 99. He didn't want to have to wait until the following morning to complete his round.

'It's all your fault that we're playing in the dark,' said Willie to the banker. 'Trevor and I are willing to carry on.'

'My fault! How do you make that out?'

'You were the one who insisted that we get a ruling on that rake in the bunker at the 15th,' Willie pointed out.

Mr Barclay sighed and muttered something inaudible.

Willie pulled his driver out of his bag, took a tee out of his trouser pocket, stepped forward and stuck the tee in the ground.

'It's his honour,' said the banker, nodding towards Trevor.

Trevor was surprised. 'Mine?'

'You two halved the last hole but he beat you on the previous hole,' explained the banker.

Rather to Trevor's surprise Willie didn't argue with the

banker. Instead he simply picked up his tee and stepped back to allow Trevor to take the honour.

'Oh,' said Trevor, with a gulp. He had been hoping to follow Willie's direction from the tee. He really had very little idea where the green was. And he had little room for error. He took a three iron out of his bag, put a ball on a tee, took a practice swing, and then hit the ball into the darkness. The ball was lost from sight the moment it left the tee.

Much to Trevor's surprise when Willie stepped onto the tee he took a stance at an acute angle to the two tee markers. He was clearly aiming out to the right of the hole. Trevor was surprised because he strongly suspected that if Willie's ball went straight it would either land in thick rough or in the stream at the bottom of the hill. Trevor was also surprised that Willie was using a driver. He knew that the sensible, percentage shot would be an iron shot played down the hill towards the stream which ran across the middle of the fairway. And he knew that when it really mattered Willie always played the percentage shot. But Trevor suspected that Willie knew what he was doing so he said nothing.

The banker had clearly been watching Willie carefully. He too took a driver from his bag. And he too took a stance which meant that he was aiming way out to the right.

'I'm glad you went first,' said Mr Barclay, putting his driver back into his bag with a self-satisfied little smirk. 'I wouldn't have known to aim out over there.'

'I hope you held back on the shot and put a lot of hook into it,' said Willie.

Even in the semi-darkness it was possible to see the banker lose colour. 'What do you mean?'

'If you played that shot straight you've lost your ball,' said Willie with a grin.

The banker opened and shut his mouth several times without anything coming out. 'What a filthy, dirty, contemptible trick!' he managed eventually.' Willie shrugged, winked at Trevor and taking hold of his trolley handle walked off into the pitch black darkness in search of his ball. Trevor followed him.

'Wait!' called the banker. Willie and Trevor both turned. 'I'm going to play a second ball,' said the banker. The two friends stopped and moved to one side out of the way. Mr Barclay pulled a six iron out of his bag and played a gentle shot straight down the fairway. Willie turned to Trevor and grinned.

Five minutes later, however, it was the banker's turn to grin when Willie couldn't find his ball. It had been a clever idea to trick the banker into playing down the wrong line and Willie had executed the shot perfectly. His ball had flown straight for a hundred and fifty yards and had then hooked in viciously. It had ended up roughly in the middle of the fairway, a comfortable fifty yards short of the stream.

Part of Willie's downfall undoubtedly lay in the fact that because he had spent a good deal of time helping Trevor look for his ball he had become quite disorientated. By the time Willie had found Trevor's ball neither of them had any idea how far from the tee they were. The slope of the fairway told them that they had not yet reached the stream, and told them the direction of the green, but that was all.

'I'll have to play another ball from the tee,' said Willie miserably. 'That means I'll have to take an extra penalty for not playing a provisional ball.' He sounded really fed up. Trevor had never seen him so down hearted. 'I'd just drop another ball,' he confessed quietly, 'but that damned banker has taken to checking my ball and I've played my last Horton 2.'

'I can't find my ball,' Willie shouted out into the darkness. 'I'm going back to the tee.'

The banker's voice came out of the darkness somewhere behind them. 'That means you'll be playing your fourth shot.'

'I realise that,' Willie shouted back, rather crossly. 'I can count.'

'Just checking that you knew the rules,' shouted the banker. He sounded obscenely triumphant and full of self satisfaction. 'You'll no doubt be pleased to hear that I found my second ball. I've just played another nice little six iron shot down the hill.'

'Great,' murmured Willie to himself. He pulled a driver out of his bag.

'Is that sensible?' asked Trevor, in a whisper. 'Shouldn't you play safe with an iron?'

'I'd like to but I can't,' whispered Willie. 'I was a shot behind when we left the 17th green. I've got to win this hole.' He marched back up the hill, as miserable as a fat man on a diet, head bowed, while the banker and Trevor left their trolleys marking their balls and moved out to stand at the side of the fairway. A minute or two later they heard the face of Willie's driver collide with the ball and then, high overhead, the sound of the dimpled missile flying through the night sky.

The splash as the ball landed straight in the stream at the bottom of the hill may not have been audible back on the tee but it could certainly be heard where Trevor was standing.

* * *

When the three of them finally stood together on the 18th green Trevor had, much to his surprise and delight, taken just three shots. He had undoubtedly been helped enormously by the fact that Willie had spent much time helping him look for and find his ball. He was the only one of the three who had suffered no penalty strokes. The banker, who had lost two balls, had taken nine strokes to reach the green. By the time he had reached a point where he could take his putter out of his bag Willie had lost three balls and had taken the same number of strokes. He was, therefore, still one stroke behind Mr Barclay.

It was now so dark that even on the green the three players could hardly see one another; they certainly couldn't see one another's balls.

Trevor's ball was on the front, right-hand corner of the green, about twenty-five feet away from the pin. Willie's, which had reached the putting surface after a beautifully played and quite spectacular, long iron shot from down near the stream, was right at the back of the green, about thirty feet from the pin. The banker's ball, about eighteen feet from the pin, was the closest of the three to the flag. After much discussion these distances were agreed and it was decided that Willie should putt first.

Willie knew that he had to go for the hole. If he was to stand a chance of winning the hole and squaring or winning the match he had to get down in two putts at most. The main problem he faced was neither the fact that the speed of the green was difficult to judge now that dew was beginning to form nor the fact that the borrows of the green were impossible to read in the darkness, but the fact that from where his ball lay he could not see the hole.

Under the circumstances he should have probably been pleased that his ball ended up no more than three feet past the hole. If he holed his remaining putt he would complete the hole in eleven strokes.

Trevor's first putt ended up about the same distance away from the hole as Willie's. He knew now that he had two shots to finish the hole in order to satisfy the first of his uncle's stipulations.

When it was the banker's turn to play he took a lighter out of his pocket, lit it and placed it down on the ground a couple of feet behind the hole. He looked up and smiled at Willie. 'You see,' he said smugly, 'when it comes down to it you're just not clever enough!' He then played a very nice shot and left his ball no more than two feet from the hole.

'Shall I finish it off?' he asked, picking up his lighter, closing it and slipping it into his pocket.

'If you like,' said Willie. He didn't seem as miserable as Trevor expected him to be.

Mr Barclay duly put his ball into the hole, picked it up and stood back. 'I think you'll find that's £500 you owe me,' he said. 'No,' he said, suddenly holding up a hand. '£505! I almost forgot our small bet on the first.' He held out a hand. 'Have you got the cash on you?'

'Don't be so hasty!' said Willie. 'I haven't finished my round yet.'

'There isn't a lot of point,' said the banker. 'You can't beat my score.'

'Oh yes I can,' said Willie. 'You haven't added on your penalty points yet.'

Mr Barclay stared at him and frowned. 'What the hell do you mean?' he asked. 'I lost two balls and I've counted two penalty strokes.'

'Plus two penalty strokes on the green,' said Willie quickly.

The banker peered at him through the darkness. 'What for?'

'The lighter,' explained Willie. 'Rule 8.'

The banker, suddenly realising that something was seriously wrong, took a pace or two forwards. He was still holding his putter but his grip had changed so that he almost seemed to be holding it as a weapon. 'What are you talking about?'

'Using an object or person to indicate line of putt while playing a stroke,' said Willie. 'Rule 8.2. Penalty two strokes. If I hole this putt I've won by one stroke and you owe me £495.'

Mr Barclay blanched. He was so white he looked like a ghost. 'It was only there so that I could see,' he protested. But there was no venom in his voice and Trevor knew that his heart wasn't in the protest.

'The lighter was directly behind the hole,' Willie reminded him. 'It clearly helped you judge the line of your putt. The fact that it was lit is almost irrelevant. There would still have been a penalty if you hadn't lit it.'

For a moment the banker didn't say anything.

'You've still got to sink your putt,' he said at last. 'If you miss then the match is halved and you don't win anything.'

Willie looked down at his ball and then looked at Trevor's. He turned to Trevor. 'Whose ball is closest?'

'I think they're both about the same distance away,' said Trevor.

'Do you want to go first?' Willie asked him.

'I don't mind,' said Trevor. 'You go first,' he said a moment later. 'I'll wait.' He would have happily waited a lifetime.

Willie bent over his ball, took aim and knocked it straight into the hole.

'Well played!' said Trevor. 'Good shot!'

'That's £500 you owe me!' said Willie to the banker. 'No! Sorry! £495!'

'Will a cheque do?' asked Mr Barclay. 'I'm afraid I don't carry that much cash.'

'Fine,' said Willie, rather to Trevor's surprise. 'Your turn,' Willie murmured to his friend. 'Good luck,' he added.

Trevor stepped forward and stared long and hard at his ball and the hole. He sat down on his haunches and squinted along the line of the shot he needed to make. He stood up, took a deep breath, swallowed hard and stepped up to his ball. He bent over the ball, wrapped his fingers around the shaft of his putter and concentrated hard. He tried to see the ball moving forwards slowly in a perfectly straight line and then dropping down into the hole. He held his breath to keep his body still, took his arms back, stopped for a tiny fraction of a second at the top of his backswing and then brought his club down onto his ball.

It was Willie who spoke first, as Trevor's ball rattled into the hole. 'Congratulations!'

Trevor had taken five shots on the final hole and had completed his round in 98 strokes, just one less than he needed to go round in to meet the conditions of his uncle's will. 'I shouldn't start celebrating just yet,' the banker warned Trevor, handing Willie a cheque. 'Butterbury Ford Golf Club isn't out of the woods yet.'

The three of them stumbled along the gravel path back towards the lights of the clubhouse. There was loud cheering when Trevor and Willie entered the building and announced the news. Captain Jarrold greeted him like a long lost friend. 'I'm so glad you decided not to emigrate,' he said, looking genuinely relieved. 'By the way, that young lady from the Daily Globe rang again. She left a number for you to call.' He fished in his pocket, took out a grubby envelope and, after examining it, handed it to Trevor.

'Thank you,' sighed Trevor. 'Let me buy you a drink.'

Captain Jarrold obediently headed for the bar at a canter. Willie was already there trying, without any success, to persuade Jake the barman to cash his cheque. Trevor screwed up the old envelope without looking at it and dropped it into an ashtray on the nearest table.

* * *

Four hours later Willie and Trevor were walking back to their caravan when they heard what sounded like a woman crying.

'Is someone there?' Willie shouted into the darkness. The club had only got one outside light fitting. It contained a single 100 watt bulb which was economical but of little practical value.

The crying stopped.

'Hello?' called Trevor.

The silence seemed to grow louder the more they listened.

'I'm sure I heard crying,' whispered Willie.

'I did too,' whispered Trevor back. 'It's OK!' he shouted. 'We want to help you?'

Silence.

'I think it came from over there!' said Willie.

'Where?' asked Trevor.

'Here!' replied Willie, half a second before tripping up over something and falling flat on his face.

'Are you all right?' asked Trevor, peering into the blackness.

'My car won't start,' said a voice which Trevor knew did not belong to Willie unless his fall had caused him serious physical harm.

'No, I'm bloody well not all right,' said a voice which did belong to Willie. 'I've broken my arm, my leg and my neck.'

About ten yards away someone switched on a torch. The beam flicked around until it found Willie.

'Thanks!' said Trevor. 'Hold it there, will you!'

The torch holder kept the beam steady and moved a little closer.

Trevor bent down. 'Don't move!' he told Willie. 'Stay there and I'll get an ambulance.'

'I don't want a bloody ambulance!' said Willie, rather crossly.

'But if you've got broken bones ...,' said Trevor.

'I haven't really broken anything,' said Willie impatiently. He sighed. 'I just want some bloody sympathy.'

'Oh,' said Trevor, not sounding very sympathetic.

'I'm sorry about all the trouble you're having,' said the owner of the torch. The torch beam moved closer.

'Did you say you'd got a car here?'

'Yes.'

'Can't you turn the headlights on so that we can see?'

'That's the problem. The car won't start. I think the battery is flat. It was foggy this morning. I must have left my headlights switched on.'

'Are you a club member?' Trevor heard himself asking. Captain Jarrold would have been proud of him.

'No. I'm a visitor. I was passing and thought I'd just pop over and have a look around. My brother plays a lot of golf. If I see a course I think he might like I always get the details.'

'How long have you been out here?'

'I don't know. Hours.'

'Why didn't you pop into the clubhouse and telephone for help?'

'I would have done but, well, I was frightened out of my wits in the dark so I decided to stay with the car. That's what they always tell you to do, isn't it?'

'I suppose it is,' said Trevor. 'But I don't think they mean you have to stay with the car if you're in a car park.'

'Is there anywhere round here where I could stay the night? Even if I get the car started I'll still have to find a room.'

'Where do you live?'

'London.'

'You could stay with us,' said Willie, who seemed to have made a remarkable recovery. 'Couldn't she?'

'I suppose so,' said Trevor.

They took the stranded motorist back to their caravan and made up a bed for her on the couch.

CHAPTER FOURTEEN

It was another gloriously sunny morning. Trevor, dressed in a pair of old fashioned khaki shorts and a white T shirt, was sitting on the top step of the caravan basking in the early morning sunshine. The shorts came down just below his knees and the T shirt had the faded portrait of a cartoon character on the front. He had woken early, got up and tiptoed out of the caravan at dawn.

He was just about to go back into the caravan and make himself some breakfast when the postman, whose van Trevor had watched arrive in front of the clubhouse a few moments earlier, walked across in his direction. He was carrying a single white envelope.

'Mr Dukinfield?' asked the postman.

Trevor nodded. 'That's me.' He felt his heart beating faster and wondered why his letters were never the ones which got lost. He hated getting mail. It always meant that he had to do something.

'Letter for you,' said the postman, handing Trevor the envelope. Relieved of his burden he removed his cap and wiped his forehead with a large, red handkerchief.

'Thank you,' said Trevor.

'Going to be another warm one,' said the postman.

'Yes,' agreed Trevor.

'I expect the water board will declare a drought soon.'

'Yes,' said Trevor. 'I expect they will.'

The postman put his cap back on and waved a hand. 'Must get on.'

'Yes. Right,' said Trevor. 'Cheerio.'

'Cheerio.'

Trevor watched the postman walk back into his van, climb into the driver's seat, start the engine and drive off to continue his round. For a moment Trevor couldn't help envying him. It seemed a simple, honest way to live. Get up in the morning. Go to work. Drive around delivering people's letters. Go home. Forget about work and enjoy yourself.

There was a sudden noise behind him as the caravan door swung out and hit Trevor in the back. Trevor yelped and leapt forwards, lost his footing and fell sideways onto the hard baked ground. He swore. The letter flew from his hand and fluttered down to earth a few feet away.

'Oh dear!' said a woman somewhere behind him. 'I'm sorry. I didn't know you were there!' He felt a woman's soft hand on his shoulder. He turned round. He had never seen the woman properly the night before, though he recognised her voice well enough.

She was in her early thirties, had shoulder length jet black hair, sharp features and a lot of laughter lines around her eyes and mouth. Her eyes were kind and full of concern. Trevor noticed that she was wearing one of his shirts which she must have taken from one of the caravan's tiny cupboards. He didn't mind at all. In fact he felt a small thrill and was pleased that she'd chosen one of his shirts rather than one of Willie's. She had rolled the sleeves half way up her forearms but hadn't fastened all the buttons and Trevor had an idea that it was the only item of clothing she wore. Embarrassed he lowered his eyes and looked away.

'Are you all right?' she asked.

'Yes, thanks,' said Trevor. 'I'm fine.' His shoulder hurt where the caravan door had hit it and he had grazed his right knee badly on a stone when he had fallen but he was English.

'I am sorry,' apologised the woman again. 'I'm Megan,' she said. When she smiled the skin around her eyes wrinkled. She held out a hand. 'Thanks for taking me in last night.'

'Trevor,' said Trevor, touching her finger tips. He scrambled to his feet. 'That's OK,' he said. 'We couldn't leave you out there in the cold.'

'It was very kind of you,' said the woman. She must have been aware that the shirt she was wearing didn't hide much but she didn't seem to mind.

'I just popped out to see if there was any milk,' explained the woman. 'For a cup of tea,' she added. She had a slim, athletic, well-tanned body.

'I'm afraid there isn't any,' said Trevor, swallowing hard. Despite living with Willie he still wasn't used to having conversations with attractive, half clothed women. 'I'm afraid we ran out of milk yesterday afternoon.'

'Do you think there will be any in the clubhouse?'

'There might be,' said Trevor, frowning, and wondering how to warn her about Jake the barman.

'I'll go and see if they'll lend us a cupful!' said Megan. She tossed her head and threw her hair back revealing long, dangling silver earrings. She had perfect teeth which sparkled in the sunshine. 'It's going to be a lovely day!' she said, heading off towards the clubhouse. 'Back in a minute!'

When she got to the gravel car park in front of the clubhouse she walked cautiously, like a swimmer on a pebbly beach. Trevor felt he ought to call after her and warn her about Jake but he didn't really know what to say. He was about to go back into the caravan to make himself some breakfast when he noticed the envelope he had dropped when he had fallen from the step. He picked it up and examined it carefully. His name and address had been typed, and instead of a proper stamp the envelope had been franked by one of those machines which big firms use when sending out their mail. He turned the envelope over. There was no sender's name. He pushed his thumb under the flap, tore the envelope open and pulled out the letter. It was from his solicitor.

Dear Mr Dukinfield,

I am informed by Mr Victor Barclay Jr, vice-president of The Mettleham Banking Corporation that you have successfully satisfied the first stipulation made by your late uncle.

As executor of your uncle's will it is now my responsibility to remind you that you have five days left in which to satisfy the second stipulation: that you and another member of the Butterbury Ford Golf Club should play a match against two representatives of the bank: the contest to be decided by the match play rules of golf.

Official handicaps will be taken into consideration with each team's handicap considered to be the total of its two members.

If you and your partner should win this match then you will become sole legal owner of the freehold to the Butterbury Ford Golf Club, including the clubhouse and all its associated buildings.

If you and your partner should lose this match then the Golf Club, including the clubhouse and all its associated buildings, will become the property of The Mettleham Banking Corporation, to do with as they see fit subject to satisfying planning permission requirements and building regulations according to Code 67b of the Local Authority Planning Act (1967).

If the match is drawn then extra holes shall be played and the first team to take a clear one hole lead shall be deemed to be the winning team. Finally, I must also inform you that your uncle stipulated that your partner should be a member of the club, should be an amateur golfer with a handicap no lower than your own and should have been born within twenty five miles of Pettigrew Towers. The representatives of the bank must be full time employees of the bank.

Yours faithfully,
Twist, Kibble and Fenshaw

Trevor sat down on the grass and read the letter several times. Clearly, his first task was to find a partner for this all-important match. He dearly wished his uncle had not included the clause about his partner being born within twenty five miles of Pettigrew Towers and having a lower handicap than his own. He would have felt confident with Willie by his side, for whatever his faults (and it wasn't difficult to think of faults when you thought of Willie) he had that unique blend of qualities which are usually summed up in the phrase 'street wise'. Still, he knew there was no point in worrying about that. Willie had been born in Newcastle and you can't get a lot further from Pettigrew Towers than Newcastle.

'Would you like me to make you breakfast?'

Trevor looked up and turned round. Megan was holding an unopened bottle of milk, a fresh packet of bacon and a large loaf of bread.

'Where on earth did you get all that from?' he asked.

'Jake,' said Megan. She smiled. 'He's nice, isn't he? Would you like a cup of tea to start with?'

'Er, yes, thank you,' said Trevor, so shocked at hearing of Jake's generosity that he found it difficult to reply. 'That would be very nice.'

Megan bent over. 'Not bad news I hope?'

Trevor stared at her uncomprehendingly. 'I'm sorry?'

'The letter.'

'Oh!' Trevor looked down at the letter. 'No. It's from my solicitors.'

'Ugh!' said Megan, making a face. 'I hate solicitors.' She shuddered involuntarily, as though suddenly cold. She put the milk, the bread and the bacon down on the caravan step, sat down beside him and put a hand on his arm. 'You're not in some sort of trouble, are you?'

'Oh, no!' said Trevor. 'It's nothing like that.' He handed Megan the letter and proceeded to tell her everything about his uncle, the will and the golf club. He was surprised at how easy it was to talk to her.

'I'll go and make the tea,' she said at last. She touched Trevor lightly on the shoulder and disappeared into the caravan.

* * *

Forty five minutes later, with a nice cup of tea and two crispy bacon sandwiches inside him, Trevor said a temporary goodbye to Willie and Megan and headed off towards the clubhouse to try to find a partner prepared to shoulder the burden of playing eighteen holes of golf for the future of the Butterbury Ford Golf Club.

On his way across to the clubhouse he saw a scruffy looking fellow in jeans and a fishing vest leaning against the wall. The man was messing around with an expensive looking camera as though he didn't really understand how it worked. He pointed the camera at Trevor, grinned and pressed a button. Trevor heard a whirring noise and a series of clicks.

'Morning!' said the stranger.

'Good morning!' replied Trevor.

'Just trying it out,' said the man, raising the camera again. There was the same whirring noise.

'It looks very complicated,' said Trevor.

'Yes,' said the man. 'It does, doesn't it?' He hauled himself away from the wall and wandered off.

Even though it was still early in the morning and Trevor hadn't seen anyone enter the clubhouse there were half a dozen men sitting around in easy chairs.

Ever since he had first arrived at the Butterbury Ford Golf Club Trevor had had a suspicion that some of the members never went home at all but stayed in their chairs all night. As usual Captain Jarrold was one of the members settled comfortably in one of the faded red leather armchairs. He had his hands folded across his stomach and his eyes were closed.

'Good morning,' said Trevor brightly, collapsing into a chair beside the captain. The seat had broken springs and Trevor cautiously adjusted his buttocks to avoid serious injury.

Captain Jarrold opened his eyes and scowled until he saw who it was who had spoken. 'Good morning, sir!' he said, touching his right temple with his right forefinger and pushing himself up in his chair. 'How are you today, sir?'

'I'm fine, thank you,' replied Trevor. 'I wish you wouldn't call me sir,' he added.

'Very well, sir,' said Captain Jarrold, firmly.

'I had a letter from my solicitors this morning,' said Trevor. 'I've got to find someone to play with me against the bank.'

Captain Jarrold picked up a cup of milky coffee which was resting precariously on the arm of his chair. He carefully used a crested teaspoon to remove a layer of skin from the top of the coffee. He put the discarded skin into his saucer and then sipped noisily from the cup. A small piece of brown skin clung to his tobacco stained military moustache. He sighed contentedly, before putting his cup back down into its saucer.

'Can you think of anyone suitable?' asked Trevor. 'It's got to be someone born locally with a handicap no lower than 24 I'm afraid. What about you? Would you play?' he asked.

'Me, sir?' demanded Captain Jarrold.

'You must have fought some pretty fierce campaigns in your time,' said Trevor. 'What's your handicap? I suppose it's too low.'

'Oh yes, sir!' agreed Captain Jarrold immediately. 'I've fought some fierce campaigns all right! You can count on that, sir!'

'You must know a thing or two about the tactics and strategies of winning!'

'Certainly do, sir!' agreed the Captain, nodding furiously.

'Well, what about it?' asked Trevor. 'Would you be my partner?'

Captain Jarrold stared at Trevor as though he had asked him to marry him. 'Play golf?' he asked.

'Well, yes,' said Trevor, puzzled. 'Golf.'

'Never played the game,' said Captain Jarrold, furiously shaking his head. 'Damned silly game as far as I can see.'

Trevor was surprised to discover that Captain Jarrold, stalwart member of the club though he was, had never touched a golf club in his life.

*   *   *

As the day went by Trevor gradually realised that finding a partner for the big match was going to be more difficult than he had originally anticipated.

When he had set off after breakfast, on his search for a companion to stand shoulder to shoulder with him in defence of the golf club, he had rather imagined that he would be able to choose a partner from among a clutch of enthusiastic volunteers. He had, in his innocence, expected to be overwhelmed, even embarrassed by offers of support.

By the end of the afternoon he realised that he would be lucky to find anyone at all willing to play with him.

'Not me, thanks,' said Elvis Ramsbottom, the committee member and chiropodist. 'I wouldn't want that sort of responsibility.'

'There isn't any responsibility!' said Trevor. 'You just have to do your best!'

The laugh that Elvis laughed was hollow. 'Have you any idea what'll happen to anyone who misses a putt and hands the club to the bank?'

'What?' asked Trevor, who had no idea what would happen to anyone unfortunate enough to miss a putt and hand the club to the bank.

'He'll be blackballed!' said Elvis, shuddering at the very thought of it. 'Ostracised! Thrown out of the club! They'll have his guts for garters.'

'But there won't be a club!' explained Trevor. 'If we lose the match the bank will own the club. No one will be able to do anything to you.'

'Bah!' said Elvis scornfully. 'That won't stop 'em!' He paused. 'Anyway,' he said. 'I don't want to go down in history as the man who lost Butterbury Ford Golf Club.'

* * *

By the end of the day Trevor was submerged in gloom.

He had spoken to every high handicap player he could find in the clubhouse and although they had all had different and often imaginative excuses they had all said 'no'. Word soon got around that he was looking for a partner for the golf match to save the club and by the afternoon people were making fairly obvious attempts to avoid him. When he walked into the bar members would rush out into the locker room. When he walked into the locker room they would rush into the tiny washroom. Eventually, he had begun to feel about as welcome in the clubhouse as a butcher at a vegetarian society meeting.

Shoulders slumped, heart heavy and spirit weakened he

trudged back to the caravan, convinced that he was going to lose the match by default. He could understand the other members not wanting to play in such an important match. Given the choice he would have probably said 'no' too. But this didn't help. He still felt depressed, downhearted and as full of beans as a nauseated parrot. He opened the caravan door and stumbled in to try and cheer himself up with a nice cup of tea. As he entered he wondered if Megan would be there. The prospect cheered him up.

Willie was sitting on the bench seat. A young blonde was sitting on his lap. Willie had his arm around her shoulders. Her undoubted physical charms were inadequately hidden beneath a pair of cut off jeans and a cut off T shirt. She looked as though she bought her clothes from a tailor who used a chainsaw instead of scissors. A half empty bottle of white wine and two glasses stood on the table in front of them.

'Hello!' said Willie. 'This is Muriel.'

'Hello Muriel,' said Trevor, wondering what happened to Megan. He had liked Megan.

'Willie is going to help me with my homework,' said the blonde. She smiled and giggled. 'I'm doing technical drawing, French and social studies at college,' she told Trevor. 'But I'm not very good at academic work.'

'Willie will be able to help you,' said Trevor. 'He's very good at technical drawing, French and social studies.'

The blonde brightened. 'Is he?' she asked. She then squealed her delight. It was not an endearing sound. Willie lowered his eyes and looked embarrassed. 'Pop into the clubhouse and ask the barman to lend us another glass,' he whispered.

The blonde looked at him and frowned. 'We've got two glasses,' she said.

'But my friend might like a glass of wine,' said Willie, inclining his head in Trevor's direction.

'Oh yes!' said Muriel. She put a hand over her mouth. 'Silly me!' she said.

'Don't bother on my behalf,' said Trevor.

'No bother,' said Willie. He wriggled around so that the

blonde was dislodged from his lap. She squeezed out from behind the table and stood up. She was taller and thinner than she had appeared when sitting down.

'I won't be more than a minute or two,' she said, smiling at the two men. She giggled again and then left.

'What happened to Megan?' asked Trevor, when she had gone. 'She was nice.'

'Yes,' said Willie. 'She said she had to go to work.'

'Work?'

'Yes. I thought it sounded a bit dismal.'

'What does she do?'

'I haven't the foggiest.'

'She got her car mended all right then.'

'Must have done.'

'Where on earth did you find Muriel?'

'She came with the bread man,' explained Willie. 'She's helping him on his round so that she can earn some money to help herself through college.'

Trevor filled the kettle, lit the gas and put the kettle on top of the calor flame. 'Do you want a cup of tea?'

'No thanks. You look as though you've had a bad day.'

'I have.'

'Did you find anyone to partner you in the match?'

Trevor shook his head, reached up and took a mug out of the tiny cupboard above the stove.

'No one?'

'They were all too frightened of what would happen if we lose.' He took a tea bag from a small packet and dropped it into the mug. 'Where's the milk?'

'I think it's all gone. So what are you going to do?'

Trevor sighed and shrugged. 'I haven't the faintest idea,' he admitted. 'Where's all the milk gone?' he asked. 'Megan brought a full bottle this morning!'

'Muriel made us both milk shakes,' said Willie, explaining but not apologising.

'I hate tea without milk,' said Trevor miserably. He turned the gas off. 'I think I'll go out and try to find a bottle,' he sighed.

He didn't want to be in the caravan when Muriel returned. It wasn't that he didn't like her. It was just that she was too jolly. He didn't feel like being around anyone quite so jolly.

When he stepped out of the caravan the scruffy stranger in the jeans and fishing vest was trying out his camera on Muriel. She seemed to enjoy posing.

'Excuse me, have you got a moment?' called the stranger.

Trevor looked around. There was no one else within earshot. 'Me?'

'I don't suppose you'd help me, would you? Your colouring is quite different to this young lady's. If I could take a photo of the two of you together it would help me test the camera.'

Trevor didn't particularly like having his photograph taken but the stranger was clearly having great difficulty with his camera. He wandered over towards Muriel who suddenly clapped her hands as a thought entered her head.

'Oh, can I get my friend Willie?' she asked the photographer. 'You could take a picture of us all together!'

The photographer shrugged. 'Why not?'

Muriel ran across to the caravan, opened the door and emerged a moment or two later with Willie in tow. Willie was glowering and clearly unenthusiastic. With some reluctance he posed with Trevor and Muriel for half a dozen photographs.

'Thanks!' said the photographer, when he'd finished. 'I'll pop some prints in the post to you.' He walked across to a brand new silver BMW, climbed in and roared off in a cloud of dust and gravel.

'Who was that?' asked Willie.

'A friend of Trevor's,' said Muriel.

'I don't know him,' said Trevor. 'He's been around all day taking snaps. I think he was just testing out a new camera.'

'You don't know him!' cried Willie, turning and staring at the rapidly disappearing BMW. 'What do you mean, you don't know him!'

Trevor thought about this for a moment. 'I don't know him,' he explained at last. He couldn't think of any other way to put it.

'Do you know who that was?' demanded Willie, by now almost hysterical.

'No,' said Trevor. 'I've just told you...!'

'I'll tell you who it was,' said Willie. 'It was a private detective. He must have been hired by my wife!'

Muriel giggled. 'Oh, golly gosh!' she said. 'A private detective! How exciting.'

'It isn't exciting at all,' moaned Willie. 'It's bloody disastrous. When my wife sees those photos she'll know where I am.' He groaned. 'And with you with your arm around me!' he added, glowering at Muriel.

Muriel frowned and pouted at the same time. 'Well, if you knew he was a private detective why did you pose for the photographs?' she asked him.

Willie, speechless, stamped off back to the caravan.

'Do you think I've upset him?' asked Muriel. 'Was it something I said?'

'I should pop back home for now,' said Trevor kindly. 'I think that perhaps today's tutorial is over.'

CHAPTER FIFTEEN

'I'm sorry to bother you,' said Trevor. 'But do you think you could lend me some milk?'

After leaving Willie he had walked around the golf course for hours and hours. It was now dark and he was tired and cold and just wanted to sit down and rest. But he didn't want to go back to his own caravan just yet.

'Of course I can, dear,' said Mrs Weatherby, for it was upon her door that Trevor had chosen to knock. She opened the door rather quickly and Trevor, stepping backwards to get out of the way, once again fell down a set of caravan steps. For the second time that day he lay sprawled, bruised and breathless on the hard, sun-baked grass.

'Oh dear!' said Mrs Weatherby. She clambered down her caravan steps as fast as her varicose veins would carry her and bent down beside Trevor. 'Are you all right, dear?'

'Yes, thank you,' said Trevor, not sure whether to rub his shoulder, his elbow or his knee. He tried to stand up but his right knee felt sore and painful and he fell over again.

'Oh dear me!' said Mrs Weatherby. 'Are you injured?'

'Just a little,' said Trevor, taking Mrs Weatherby's outstretched hand and cautiously standing up again. 'I think I've done something to my knee.'

'You'd better come in and sit down,' said Mrs Weatherby. 'Do you want me to fetch a doctor?'

'Oh no,' said Trevor. 'I don't think it's that bad.'

'I've got some oil of wintergreen,' said Mrs Weatherby, with a comforting smile. 'That'll make it feel better.'

'Thank you,' said Trevor, gratefully following Mrs Weatherby up the steps, along the narrow passageway through the caravan's tiny kitchen and into the small living area. Mrs Weatherby's caravan, was, in its design at least, exactly like the one Trevor and Willie were sharing. It had a tiny kitchen and the world's smallest shower room and toilet in what was really nothing much more than a cupboard. There was the small bedroom with bunks at one end and the tiny living room at the other. The big difference between Trevor's caravan and Mrs Weatherby's caravan was that Mrs Weatherby had realised that it is much easier to live in a small space if you are tidy. The caravan was spick and span and as neat as a newsreader's suit.

She led the way into the living room and stood to one side. Sitting at the table, dressed in a pair of baggy, blue and white striped pyjamas was what looked like Mrs Weatherby's son Charlie. Trevor could only see the top of Charlie's head and without his baseball cap his hair looked much longer and much lighter in colour. Trevor looked around wondering where the prettier of Mrs Weatherby's twins was.

'This is Charlie,' said Mrs Weatherby.

'Hello, Charlie!' said Trevor.

'Hello!' said Charlie, turning round.

Trevor had quite a surprise. Charlie wasn't a boy. There was absolutely no doubt whatsoever that Charlie was not a boy. Charlie was the girl Trevor had seen walking towards the first tee.

'Do sit down,' said Mrs Weatherby to Trevor. 'Would you like a little drink of something?'

Trevor squeezed past Mrs Weatherby and sat down on the couch on the other side of the table from Charlie. 'Thank you,' he said. 'That would be very nice.' He opened his mouth and started to say something. Then he shut it again.

'What would you like?' asked Mrs Weatherby.

'Yes, please!' replied Trevor.

'I think we've got a little whisky left.'

'Thank you,' said Trevor, whose mouth was operating without any reference to his brain.

Mrs Weatherby shuffled back towards the kitchen area.

'I thought you were your brother,' said Trevor.

'I haven't got a brother,' said Charlie.

Trevor opened his mouth and shut it again. 'Then who...?' Suddenly he realised. 'It's you, isn't it? There's only you? You're a girl?'

Charlie nodded.

'So, why do you pretend to be a boy when you drive the tractor?' asked Trevor.

'It was my fault,' said Mrs Weatherby. She put a bottle of Johnnie Walker whisky down in front of Trevor and then put a glass alongside it. 'Help yourself. And rub some of this on your knee.' She handed him a bottle of oil of wintergreen.

'Isn't anyone else having a drink?'

'Not for me,' said Mrs Weatherby with a shudder. 'I can't stand the stuff.'

'I'll have one, please,' said Charlie.

'You're not old enough, my girl!' said Mrs Weatherby.

'Oh, mum!'

Mrs Weatherby turned to Trevor. 'Sixteen!' she said. 'At sixteen they think they're old!' Nevertheless she started to get up to go and fetch another glass.

'I'll go,' said Charlie quickly, jumping to her feet.

Trevor took the top off the oil of wintergreen bottle, poured a little of the liquid onto his fingers and rubbed it onto his leg. It smelt wonderful.

'When I first got the job in the professional's shop I asked if there were any other jobs available,' Mrs Weatherby explained. 'They told me that they had a vacancy for an assistant groundsman but that the secretary would only hire male staff for work outside.'

'Are they allowed to do that?' asked Trevor, frowning. He finished rubbing the oil into the skin around his knee and looked around for something to wipe his fingers on.

'I don't know whether it's allowed or not,' said Mrs Weatherby with a shrug. 'But that's what they told me. When I told them that Charlie would be coming with me they said that he could apply for the job. They just assumed that Charlie was a boy.' She handed him a paper tissue. 'Here you are, dear,' she said. 'For your fingers.'

Trevor wiped his fingers and then put the top back on the oil of wintergreen bottle. Charlie came back with a glass and a small jug of water. She poured a small whisky for herself and a large one for Trevor and then added water to her own glass. She took a sip of the mixture and pulled a face.

'Don't you like it?' asked Trevor, adding a smaller amount of water to his own glass.

Charlie shook her head.

'So after you'd pretended to be a boy to get the job you had to continue with the pretence afterwards!'

Charlie nodded. 'I like it here,' she said. She took another sip from the whisky and grimaced again. She pushed the glass towards Trevor.

'And Charlie is your real name?'

'Yes. It's short for Charlotte. Will you drink that for me?'

'That's nice.' Trevor tipped the contents of Charlie's glass into his own.

'She's taught herself to play golf while she's been here,' said Mrs Weatherby proudly. She got up and walked to the other end of the caravan where she started folding a pile of clean laundry, putting towels, blouses and underwear onto their respective shelves in a long, thin cupboard.

Charlie looked at her mother. 'I'm still not very good,' she said modestly. Trevor got the impression that she wished her mother hadn't said anything about her playing golf. 'You won't tell anyone will you?'

Trevor frowned. 'Why not?' he asked.

'Because as an assistant greenkeeper I'm not allowed to play golf,' she replied.

'It's all a bit complicated, isn't it?' said Trevor. 'You can only keep your job by being a boy. But you can only play golf if you're not a greenkeeper.'

Charlie grinned. 'I suppose it is a bit complicated.'

'I'm going to bed,' said Mrs Weatherby. 'I'll leave you two alone to talk about golf.' Trevor and Charlie said goodnight to her.

'Have you heard about this match I've got to play against two bankers?' asked Trevor.

Charlie nodded. 'When is it?'

'Tomorrow,' answered Trevor.

'Oh, dear,' said Charlie. 'Who's your partner?'

'That's the problem,' said Trevor. 'I haven't got anyone.' He looked across at Charlie. 'Where were you born?' he asked.

'In the village,' replied Charlie. 'I've always lived here.'

'Do you have a handicap?'

'Yes. I joined as a junior member and got a handicap three weeks ago.'

'What is it?'

'Twenty eight. I told you I wasn't very good.' She hesitated, as though she wanted to say something else.

'I don't suppose you would...?'

Charlie looked at Trevor as though he'd just asked her to form a Government. 'Me? Play in the most important golf match ever played at...? Oh no!' she cried, horrified. She shook her head. 'Oh, no! I couldn't! Really! I couldn't!'

Trevor nodded. 'OK.' he said, unable to hide his disappointment.

'Anyway,' said Charlie, grasping at straws to confirm her inability to play in the all important match. 'I've got to work. I'm cutting the fairways tomorrow morning.'

'I think perhaps the fairway cutting ought to be postponed,' said Trevor. 'With the match...'

Charlie thought for a moment. 'Oh, yes. I suppose so,' she agreed. They were both silent for a moment or two. 'Anyway I don't expect the rules allow you to have a lady partner,' she went on. 'I don't think your uncle was very keen on lady golfers.'

'I don't think he ever even considered it a possibility,' said Trevor. 'I'm pretty sure it doesn't say anything in the rules about the sex of my partner.'

'I'm sure you'll be able to find someone better than me,' said Charlie.

'No one wants to take the risk,' said Trevor. 'I think I'm going to have to forfeit the match.'

'You can't do that!' cried Charlie. 'If you forfeit the match you'll lose the club!'

Trevor nodded. 'Yes, I know.' he said glumly. 'But I really don't have any choice.' Trevor stood up and blew his nose. 'I'd better go,' he said. He felt maudlin. He turned to look back at Charlie. 'Good night,' he said.

'Good night,' said Charlie.

'I've enjoyed our chat.'

'Even though I don't want to play in the match tomorrow?'

'Even though you don't want to play in the match tomorrow,' said Trevor, trying to smile. He reached out to offer Charlie his hand. She reached up and they shook hands rather formally.

Charlie looked down and spoke very quietly, so quietly that Trevor had to strain to hear her. 'Would you really like me to play?'

'Yes.'

'You really can't find anyone else?'

'No.'

'And if I don't play you'll lose the club anyway?'

'Yes.'

'What time do I have to be on the first tee tomorrow?"

Slowly it dawned on Trevor, who was very tired, that Charlie was agreeing to partner him.

'You'll play?'

'Yes.'

'That's wonderful!' cried Trevor.

'What time does the match start?'

'Eleven o'clock. See you then.'

'Eleven o'clock on the first tee.'

'That's right,' replied Trevor, who suddenly realised that Charlie was still gripping his hand tightly.

'I'm glad you asked me,' said Charlie, still clinging to Trevor's hand.

'I'm really glad you're playing. So, I'll see you tomorrow at eleven then,' repeated Trevor, trying to extricate his hand from Charlie's grip without being too obvious. He edged towards the caravan door.

'I hope I don't let you down.' Charlie gazed up at him with what Trevor thought was a decidedly dreamy look in her eyes.

Although Trevor was not what you could call a 'man of the world' he did know enough to realise that Charlie's behaviour was not simply a case of neighbourly friendliness.

Charlie looked down and swallowed. 'I know this might sound silly, but I've been watching you learn to play. I've seen nearly all your lessons with Mr Schmidt.' She started to blush. 'I'm really proud of you, you know, the way you stuck at it...,' her voice trailed off with embarrassment.

Trevor didn't reply, not being sure exactly how to handle what was rapidly becoming a very difficult situation for him. He did not have much experience of 16 year old girls who had crushes on him. In fact, his experience of such things was approximately zero.

Trevor felt his face redden. He liked Charlie. He didn't want to upset her by rebuffing her attempts at romance, but he certainly didn't want to escalate the problem by appearing to encourage her affections. So Trevor did what most men do best in moments of romantic crisis. He changed the subject.

'Well, I'd better be off to bed now. Got to get plenty of rest before the big day.' Trevor knew his voice was just that bit too jolly to sound entirely natural. He managed to prize his hand from Charlie's grasp and edge through the door and down the caravan steps.

'I suppose we had better get to bed,' replied Charlie. Now it was her turn to blush as she realised what she had said. 'I think what you're doing is absolutely marvellous.'

'Better wait and see what happens before you pay me too many compliments,' said Trevor as he retreated slowly towards the safety of his own caravan. 'See you tomorrow.'

He felt rather bad about brushing Charlie off so brusquely. He comforted himself with the thought that in a few years time Charlie would be fighting off boyfriends ten deep.

* * *

When Trevor got back to his own caravan Muriel had disappeared and Megan was back. She and Willie were sitting watching an old black and white movie on a small, portable television set that Trevor had never seen before. For the first time since Willie and Trevor had been living there all the curtains were drawn.

'Hello!' said Megan, looking up. She seemed genuinely pleased to see Trevor.

Willie, who was cowering in a corner looked relieved when he saw who it was. 'That photographer isn't still around, is he?'

'I don't think so,' said Trevor. 'Anyway its dark.'

'They have flashes and infra red gadgets. They can take photographs in the dark these days.'

'I've heard they can take photographs through curtains,' said Megan. 'They use cameras that are activated by body heat.'

Alarmed, Willie crouched down below window level. 'Is that true?'

'No,' smiled Megan. 'Stop being silly! I made it up.'

'Don't joke about it!' said Willie. 'This is serious.' Gingerly he raised his head. 'Where have you been? he asked Trevor suddenly.

'You're limping,' said Megan. 'Have you hurt your leg?' She reached forwards and turned off the television set.

'It's nothing,' said Trevor, with a shrug. 'I fell over. It's just a bit sore.'

'Did you find anyone?' asked Willie.

'Oh you poor thing!' said Megan, touching him gently on the arm. She touched him lightly, as a cat will sometimes do. Trevor liked the way she touched him.

'Anyone for what?'

'For tomorrow. A partner for the match.'

'Oh. Yes. Where did the TV set come from?'

'Great! Who? Megan borrowed it from Jake when she went over to get some more milk.'

'I forgot about the milk,' said Trevor, deciding not to tell about the incident with Charlie. 'I was going to bring some back with me but I got chatting with Charlie. Jake lent it to you? Did he give you more milk as well?'

'Yes. Charlie? Who is Charlie?'

'Mrs Weatherby's daughter,' explained Trevor.

'Charlie is a girl?' said Megan.

'Charlie is short for Charlotte,' said Trevor.

'Do you want a caddie?' asked Willie.

'A caddie?' Trevor frowned. 'What sort of caddie?'

'For the match tomorrow! A 'Carry your bag, sir?' sort of caddie.'

'Yes, please!' answered Trevor immediately. 'That would be terrific.' Then he paused and thought for a moment. 'But won't it be dangerous? If you give me advice I'll be penalised, won't I?'

Willie shook his head. 'Not if I'm your caddie,' he said. 'Rule 8. A player can ask for and accept advice from his caddie.'

'Great!' grinned Trevor. 'That would be good.'

'I'll wear dark glasses and buy some of those terrible clothes from the professional's shop. No one will ever recognise me.'

'What on earth is he talking about?' Megan asked Trevor, with a laugh.

'I think he's still worried about his wife finding him,' said Trevor.

'The Porsche!' said Willie. 'I'll have to hide it somewhere!' He stood up and headed for the door. 'Where can I put it?'

Trevor thought for a moment. 'There isn't anywhere round here,' he said. 'Perhaps you could drive it into the village and park it in the pub car park?'

'Good idea!' said Willie, rushing off and either not realising or not caring that this would mean a walk of several miles back to the caravan in the dark.

* * *

'I'm glad you came back,' said Trevor as they sat together and watched Casablanca on the small black and white television set.

'Yes,' said Megan. 'I wanted to see you again.'

They watched in silence for another ten minutes or so.

'Are you and Willie ...?' asked Trevor. He felt himself blushing. He had become accustomed to the idea that if Willie and a woman spent any time together they would almost inevitably end up as lovers.

'What?' asked Megan, two minutes after that. 'Am I and Willie what?' She suddenly realised what Trevor meant. 'Me and Willie?' She laughed out loud. 'What a terrible thought!'

Another minute and a half went by.

'It was none of my business,' said Trevor, at last.

They sat and watched another three minutes of the film.

'It's just that I wondered...,' said Trevor. 'If you aren't... if you aren't committed then maybe we could go out to the cinema or to a meal somewhere.' He paused. 'Sometime,' he added. 'Perhaps. If you'd like to, of course.'

Megan didn't speak. She seemed engrossed in the film. The silence seemed to last a long time. Everything seemed to be happening very slowly on the screen.

'I'm sorry,' said Trevor. 'I shouldn't have asked.'

'I'd love to go out with you,' said Megan, speaking at the same moment. 'I really would.' She paused.

'But ...,' said Trevor, with a sigh.

'It isn't a 'but',' said Megan. 'At least, not the sort of 'but' you're thinking of.'

Trevor didn't say anything.

'There's something I've got to tell you,' said Megan.

'Oh.' said Trevor. 'You're married.'

'No,' said Megan. 'Well, I was. But that was a long time ago. No I'm not married.' She paused and stared at the screen. 'It's worse than that.'

Trevor waited. He couldn't think of anything worse.

'Do you remember that telephone call you had from the Daily Globe?' Megan asked him, suddenly and unexpectedly.

Trevor frowned. He remembered the call, or rather the calls, but he didn't understand the relevance of what Megan was saying. 'Yes?'

'You spoke to someone on the phone. You wouldn't let her interview you. Do you remember?'

'Yes. Of course.'

'That was me.'

'You're a reporter?'

'Yes.'

'For the Daily Globe?'

'Yes.'

'Is that why you came here? For your story?'

'Yes.'

'Thank you for telling me,' said Trevor, his voice laden with sarcasm.

'There's more, I'm afraid. You won't like it. I don't think you'll want to take me out when I've told you.'

'Do you want to go out with me?'

'Yes. But wait until you've heard what I have to tell you.'

'You want to do the interview, don't you? That's OK. I don't mind now I know it's you.'

'It's worse than that,' said Megan. Her voice was very quiet now. Trevor could hardly hear her. He reached forward and turned the television off. 'What do you mean? Worse?'

'I've already written the story,' said Megan. 'It'll be in tomorrow's paper.'

Trevor frowned. 'But how?'

'You told me everything I needed to know,' said Megan.

'When we were just talking? This morning?'

Megan didn't look at him but just nodded.

'You were interviewing me?'

'Yes.'

Trevor was silent for a moment. 'The photographer? The chap in the fishing vest. Was he from the Globe?'

'Yes. Geoff's one of our best photographers. When I left here this morning I went into the village, wrote my story in the pub and then dictated it over the telephone.'

'You're very good,' said Trevor. 'I never suspected for a moment.'

'I'm sorry,' said Megan. 'I've never felt bad about a story

before. But I feel bad this time. The trouble is that I really do like you.'

'I think it's a good thing that I abandoned a career in journalism,' said Trevor. 'I would never have made it.'

Megan stood up, picked up her bag and started to move towards the door.

Trevor looked up. 'Where are you going?'

Megan shrugged. 'I'm just going,' she said. 'I'm sorry,' she said again. 'I really am.'

'What have you said about me in the article? Is it nice?'

Megan blushed. 'Yes,' she said quietly. 'It's nice.'

'But I don't understand. I thought it was only naughty vicars and kiss-and-tell blondes who got this treatment. Why should you go to all this trouble to write a nice story about a me and a golf club?'

'The editor loved the story,' explained Megan simply. 'When the editor loves a story you do what it takes to get it. You don't try to explain that the star of the piece won't talk to you.'

Trevor thought back to his few days in Fleet Street and remembered that, even at his lowly level in journalism, excuses about lost stories were not usually met with either enthusiasm or understanding.

'Please don't go,' said Trevor.

Megan looked at him.

'Please,' said Trevor. He started to laugh.

Megan frowned. 'What are you laughing for?'

'Willie,' he said suddenly. 'I was just thinking. Willie has got to walk all the way back from the village because he thinks your photographer was a private detective working for his wife.'

Megan smiled.

'Poor old Willie!' said Trevor.

'Do you really want me to stay?'

'Really,' said Trevor. 'Definitely. Anyway, your car probably won't start.'

'Ouch,' said Megan. 'That hurt.'

Trevor looked at her. 'What did you do? Just disconnect a lead?'

Megan nodded. Trevor thought he might have detected a hint of a blush.

'Please stay.'

'Turn the TV on,' said Megan. 'Let's watch the end of Casablanca. It always makes me cry.'

CHAPTER SIXTEEN

Megan was still asleep and Trevor was waking up with a cup of tea and some gentle Mozart on the radio when there was a gentle tapping on the caravan door. Trevor put down his cup and limped to the door. His knee now felt very stiff. He unfastened the tiny brass catch and carefully opened the top half of the caravan door to see who it was.

Elvis Ramsbottom was standing on the grass at the bottom of the steps. He looked as though he had just played the shot of his life and then discovered that he had played the wrong ball. 'I'm sorry to bother you,' he said.

'You look terrible, Elvis!' Trevor opened the lower half of the door and stepped outside.

'I haven't slept a wink,' confessed the chiropodist. 'I've been worrying all night.' He shuffled his feet and looked down at the ground. He reminded Trevor of a small boy staring at the carpet in a headmaster's study. 'I feel bad about refusing to play in this match.'

'That's OK,' said Trevor. 'I understand.'

'No,' said Elvis firmly. 'It's not OK.' He swallowed hard. 'I'll play.'

'It's all right,' said Trevor. He opened the bottom half of the door and stepped onto the top step. 'I've got someone to partner me.' He stepped down onto the grass. His knee was very stiff and walking wasn't easy.

'I don't want to do it,' said Elvis, glumly. 'God knows, I don't know what I'll do with myself if we lose. But . . . ,' he looked up at Trevor, 'what did you say?'

'You don't have to play,' said Trevor. 'But thanks for offering. I really appreciate it.'

Elvis grinned broadly. 'I don't have to play? That's marvellous!' The slump had gone out of his shoulders. He looked like a man reborn.

'Thanks again for offering,' said Trevor.

'Eleven o'clock start, isn't it?'

Trevor nodded.

'Do you mind if I come and watch?'

'No! Of course not.'

'Great!' said Elvis. 'I think one or two other members might want to come along too. I'll pass the word around in case anyone is interested.' He turned and started to walk away then turned back. 'Good luck!' he said. He walked back to the caravan door and held out his hand. 'Good luck!' he said again. He clasped Trevor's hand with both his hands. 'Good luck!' he said, for the third time.

'Thank you,' said Trevor. He winced as Elvis squeezed his hand rather tightly.

'I'll be right there with you,' said Elvis. 'You can do it.'

'Thanks,' said Trevor. He gently prised Elvis's fingers from around his hand. 'Thank you very much.'

'Oh, I nearly forgot,' said Elvis, 'congratulations on that story in today's Globe. Nice picture too!'

'I haven't seen it yet,' said Trevor. 'Is it OK?'

'Wonderful!' said Elvis. 'Sounds as if you had the reporter eating out of your hand.' He reached behind his back and pulled a folded up newspaper out of his back trouser pocket. 'Here you are,' he said, trying to smooth out of some of the creases and then handing the paper to Trevor.

'Thanks' said Trevor, accepting the offered newspaper. 'Thanks very much.' As he was clambering back up the steps he heard a car squealing to a halt a few yards away. Turning round he saw Willie climbing out of a battered old Ford which had a small red and white plastic sign stuck on its roof. The sign, which was broken, said simply: TAX.

'Where on earth have you been?' asked Trevor, standing and waiting for Willie to walk over to the caravan.

'I couldn't find anyone sober enough to drive me back last

night,' said Willie. He didn't look as though he had slept very much.

'You could have walked,' suggested Trevor.

'Walk! It's miles!'

'Where did you stay? In the pub?'

'No, I didn't think that was a good idea since the Porsche was parked there. A woman who runs an antique shop took me home with her.' Willie yawned. 'You haven't seen that detective chappie again, have you?'

Trevor shook his head. 'He wasn't a detective,' he said. 'He was a photographer.'

Willie looked puzzled. 'What do you mean, he was a photographer? I know he was a photographer. He had a camera. What matters is what he does with the photographs he took.'

'He's a photographer for the Daily Globe,' said Trevor. He opened the newspaper Elvis had given him and flicked through the pages. Megan's story, accompanied by a huge photograph of him, took up the whole of page nine.

'Why didn't you tell me he was from the Globe?'

'I didn't know he was from the Globe until after you'd gone,' sad Trevor. 'Anyway, your photo isn't in the paper.'

'What do you mean, my photo isn't in the paper?'

'Look' said Trevor, showing Willie the page. 'Just me.'

'What?' demanded Willie, grabbing the newspaper. 'What do you mean, no photograph of me?'

'I thought you didn't want your photograph in the paper?'

'Well, I didn't!' said Willie. 'But I don't like being snubbed.'

He seemed quite put out about it. 'Anyway, I'm beginning to wish Brenda would hurry up and find me. I'm getting too old for all this chasing about. And to be honest I'm getting fed up of being all squashed up in your damned caravan.'

Trevor led the way into the caravan and found Megan standing just inside the door. Once again she was wearing one of his shirts though she hadn't had time to fasten the buttons at the front.

'Hello!' he said. 'You're awake.'

'Yes.' said Megan. 'Hello.' She kissed him and put both her

arms around his neck. Trevor put one hand round her back and one hand on her bare bottom.

'Did I hear Willie say he wished that Brenda would find him?' Megan asked in a whisper.

'Yes,' whispered Trevor back. 'It would give us a bit more privacy if she did, too.'

'Good god, Trevor!' said Willie, standing on the caravan steps. 'You're a fast worker! And what on earth have you two found to get all lovey-dovey about at this time in the morning.'

Trevor felt himself blushing.

'I'll get dressed,' whispered Megan. 'Is that this morning's Globe?'

'Yes,' said Trevor. 'Elvis brought it. Thank you. It's a super story.'

'You can thank me properly later,' said Megan. She kissed him again and then disappeared back into the bedroom.

* * *

The kettle, filled with just enough water to make a mug of tea, was starting to boil, and four strips of best Danish bacon were sizzling under the grill when Trevor heard another tap on the caravan door. He walked across and, again, opened the top half of the door.

Victor Dussenberg was standing there. Compared to him, Elvis Ramsbottom had looked like a pools winner attending the cheque presentation ceremony.

'Nice morning isn't it,' said Trevor, feeling it his duty to try to cheer Victor Dussenberg up. 'Looks as though it could be quite sunny later.'

Mr Dussenberg shook his head. 'It'll rain,' he prophesied miserably.

'Oh,' said Trevor. 'What makes you think that?'

'The frogs were noisy last night.'

'Right,' nodded Trevor. 'Of course.'

'I'll play,' said Mr Dussenberg, with a sigh.

'It's ...,' began Trevor.

Victor Dussenberg held up a hand. 'No,' he said firmly, 'I've thought about it and I can't let you or the club down. I'll play.'

'It's OK,' said Trevor. 'You don't have to.'

'No, I'll play,' insisted Mr Dussenberg. 'I've thought about it and I've made up my mind.'

Trevor smiled at him. 'No, really,' he said. 'There's no need.'

'What do you mean?' Victor Dussenberg seemed puzzled. 'You're playing this match against the bankers today aren't you?'

'Yes, but there's no need for you to play now.'

'You've got someone else?' Mr Dussenberg's tone had changed.

'Yes.'

'What's wrong with me? I can hit the ball as far as anyone in the club!' Mr Dussenberg sounded quite belligerent.

'I know. I appreciate that. But someone else has agreed to play.'

'So what you're saying is that you don't need me?'

'I'm very grateful to you for offering,' said Trevor.

'Well is he as good as I am?' demanded Mr Dussenberg.

'It isn't a question of how good anyone is,' said Trevor, soothingly.

'Well, it seems a bloody funny way to go about things,' said Mr Dussenberg, rather angrily. 'One minute you ask me to play and the next you say you don't want me.' He scowled at Trevor. 'If that's the way you want it then that's fine by me. But don't complain when you lose.' He turned and stalked off.

'I'm very grateful to you for offering,' shouted Trevor. 'It was kind of you.' He turned and went back into the caravan. The bacon was burning and the caravan was full of steam from the boiling kettle. He moved as quickly as he could to the stove and turned off the gas. The air was full of a sharp, acrid, metallic smell and when Trevor lifted up the kettle he realised that it had boiled dry. The bottom of the kettle was blackened and a small hole was clearly visible. He put the kettle down and pulled out the grill pan.

Suddenly there was a noise from the other end of the

caravan. Trevor turned to see what it was. Dimly, through the steam, he could see Willie burst out of the tiny shower room and hurry towards him. Willie was stark naked.

'Are we on fire?' Willie shouted.

'No, it's OK,' said Trevor. 'I've burnt some bacon, that's all.' In his right hand he held the grill pan which contained the blackened remains of the essential ingredient for his bacon sandwiches.

Willie wrapped a towel around his right hand and picked up the kettle. 'This doesn't look as if it's going to be much good!' he said, examining its black bottom and looking at the hole.

'What on earth is going on?' asked Megan, poking her head around the bedroom door.

Trevor explained.

'I'll go and borrow another kettle as soon as I'm dressed,' Megan said immediately. Willie, who was naked and who had turned to look in Megan's direction, modestly turned away again and grunted something that no one could understand. Behind his back Megan opened the bedroom door wide and winked at Trevor. She was wearing one flimsy piece of underwear below the waist and nothing but a rather concerned look above it. She slipped back into the bedroom to carry on getting dressed. She hadn't been gone for two seconds before the caravan front door opened. 'Do you know there's something burning in there?' called a voice which Trevor did not immediately recognise.

Willie, not knowing who was opening the door, lowered his hands to protect his modesty. As he did so he forgot that in his right hand he was holding a very hot kettle.

He screamed as the kettle touched a very delicate part of his anatomy, dropped the kettle and then screamed again as the kettle landed on his bare foot.

'Hello!' said Bert Grubb, poking his head into the caravan. 'Shall I call the fire brigade?'

'No, thanks!' said Trevor. 'Everything is under control!' This was clearly a lie for Willie, who was now crying, was trying to hold two parts of his anatomy which were some distance apart.

'Ambulance?' suggested Bert, stepping into the caravan and walking over to see what was happening.

'No, thanks!' said Trevor.

'What on earth is going on?' asked Megan, opening the bedroom door again. She was now decent but still not fully dressed and Bert Grubb's eyes very nearly popped out of his head when he caught sight of her.

'You don't want me to dial 999 at all?' asked Bert Grubb, when he had regained control of his breathing. He sounded very disappointed when both Trevor and Willie said 'No'. He'd never had a chance to dial 999 before.

'Everything is OK,' insisted Trevor, holding up a reassuring hand. 'Really!' he insisted. He took a step forward without bothering to look where he was walking and trod on the hot kettle which Willie had dropped. He too started to scream, and as he started to dance a rather ungainly little jig he dropped the grill pan. The grill pan fell on Willie's leg and Willie, still holding onto his lightly roasted wedding tackle, and now having three sore spots to comfort, joined in the impromptu jig.

'Are you sure you don't want an ambulance?' asked Bert Grubb.

'I'll go and borrow another kettle from Jake,' said Megan, reappearing yet again, this time dressed. 'What on earth are you two doing down there? This is no time to be dancing.' Then she saw what Willie was clutching. 'You haven't damaged anything important have you?' she asked, trying hard not to laugh.

'It'll probably be all right,' said Willie, speaking through clenched teeth. 'I need a nurse.'

'I'll get a fresh kettle,' said Megan firmly. 'You two need a nice cup of tea.'

'I just came to let you know that I'd be playing with you this morning,' said Mr Grubb. 'I thought about it during the night and decided that I had a responsibility to the club.'

Trevor staggered over to one of the bench seats and sat down. It was half past eight and there was just two and a half hours to go before the match that would decide his future.

* * *

There was quite a crowd around the first tee. Trevor had never before seen so many small, embroidered giraffes gathered together in one place. The club secretary was there, of course. And so was Captain Jarrold. The Dussenbergs both looked very smart. Mr Dussenberg, who had a low irritancy threshold but a quick recovery time, waved a hand and smiled sweetly. The club professional, Mr Schmidt, was there too. He was wearing a green jumper, a pair of sky blue plus fours, brown and white shoes with multi-coloured laces and the inevitable Tam O'Shanter. The jumper, in addition to the obligatory giraffe, had a picture of a golfer sewn onto the front.

'Strewth!' said Trevor, quietly, looking around and nodding at many familiar faces. 'There must be a hundred people here!' He was desperately looking for Charlie but he couldn't see her anywhere. He realised he should have agreed to meet her at her caravan. He took his bag from his shoulder and lay it on the ground. At Willie's suggestion Trevor was once again playing with a depleted bag of clubs.

Both Trevor and Willie were limping. Trevor now had a burnt foot as well as a sore knee. Willie had burns on both legs and a burn in a private place which made him walk like a cowboy who has spent too long in the saddle. Megan had filled his underpants with a large quantity of cotton wool, though where she had got this from only she knew. The cotton wool gave him what can only be described as an improbable looking walk. Megan said he would have been a great success at a hen party and Willie looked rather pleased with himself until she muttered something about how disappointed they would be when they discovered the truth.

'My cotton wool is slipping,' whispered Willie who was wearing a bright blue jumper, a pair of red and green plaid trousers, a purple and yellow Tam O'Shanter and a pair of dark glasses. The jumper, trousers and Tam O'Shanter all bore tiny embroidered giraffes. 'I'm going to have to go back and take some of it out.' He hurried back towards the caravan.

The bankers were there already, of course. They weren't the sort of men ever to be late for anything if money was involved.

Mr Barclay had forsaken the colourful costume he had bought from Mr Schmidt's shop and looked far more comfortable in a very ordinary and undistinguished brown cap which someone had covered with a thin layer of plastic, presumably as some sort of waterproofing, a beige anorak, zipped almost to the throat, over what appeared to be a light beige polo necked sweater, dark beige trousers with an almost invisible check pattern and a pair of brown, rubberised golfing shoes.

The man standing beside Mr Barclay was slightly older and slightly plumper and didn't look to have Mr Barclay's natural sense of fun. He too was dressed in a beige anorak, zipped almost to the throat, over what appeared to be a light beige polo necked sweater. He too wore dark beige trousers with an almost invisible check pattern and a pair of brown, rubberised golfing shoes. His cap was also covered in a thin layer of plastic. The two of them looked like a pair of non-identical twins dressed by a mother with an underpowered imagination and a penchant for beige. Trevor, who was wearing a thin pair of Mr Schmidt's summer golfing trousers and a thin golf shirt decided that they must both be rather thin-blooded and pessimistic individuals.

Both men had their hands resting on the handles of battery-powered trollies, and even without counting Trevor knew that both beige, imitation leather golf bags were packed with the full complement of 14 clubs. These were not, thought Trevor, the sort of men who would choose to do anything light-heartedly.

'This is Mr Lloyd,' said Mr Barclay, introducing his colleague. 'Mr Lloyd is associate vice-president at The Mettleham Banking Corporation and senior vice-president of our associate bank, Mettleham Global Banking Corporation.' He paused to let this important information sink in. 'Mr Lloyd is in charge of Corporate Liability Relations and Public Affairs,' Mr Barclay added.

'And this is my daughter,' said Mr Lloyd, introducing a short but extremely curvaceous woman in her late twenties. She had piercing blue eyes, a button nose, perfectly capped teeth and a bust which cocked a snook at gravity. She was wearing a low cut, figure-hugging blue and white silk dress which displayed an alarming amount of cleavage, a pair of blue stiletto-heeled shoes and a small, flimsy and entirely functionless hat. She looked as if she was dressed more for a wedding than a golf match. 'She's come along to learn a little about the game,' he added.

Just then Willie appeared, having removed half a pound of cotton wool from his trousers.

'Willie!' cried the banker's buxom daughter. 'You bastard!

Willie, who, possibly because of the dark glasses he was wearing, hadn't seen the girl in the blue dress up until that moment, didn't flinch. Trevor was very impressed.

'Brenda!' he said, giving the banker's daughter one of his widest smiles. 'What are you doing here?' He looked around as though trying to decide whether or not he could escape. He apparently decided that he couldn't. 'How did you find me?' he asked, widening the smile still further. 'Do you like the new golfing gear?'

'I came with Daddy because I was bored. We're flying over to Frankfurt later,' answered Brenda. 'After he's played a match with this Mr Dukinfield.' She nodded in Trevor's direction. 'Daddy's bank is going to turn this golf club into something more profitable,' she said. 'And you look a complete and utter prat.'

'Oh, I say ...,' began Trevor, protesting not at the honest description of his friend but at Brenda's outspoken assumption that he and Charlie were about to lose their golf match.

'Have you had private detectives following me?' demanded Willie.

'No!' said Brenda. 'I have not! Why should I? I didn't care whether I ever saw you again.'

'Can I just say that I object to the assumption that my partner and I are going to lose this match,' said Trevor.

'Oh, do be quiet Trevor,' said Willie.

'Please be quiet,' said Brenda, rather imperiously.

'So what are you doing here?' demanded Willie.

'Why shouldn't I be here?' demanded Brenda. She turned

and flounced away and stared at nothing in particular with great intensity.

'Is that *the* Brenda?' Trevor whispered to Willie, when Brenda was out of earshot. 'Your wife?'

'Yes' said Willie. 'Isn't she wonderful? And this is Mr Lloyd, her father,' he added, bravely ignoring the banker's impressive glower. Trevor decided that Mr Lloyd could probably win medals for his glowering. He could certainly have glowered for England.

'Don't speak to me you ... you ...,' spluttered Mr Lloyd in Willie's direction.

'Come on, dad, can't we just let bygones be bygones and forget that little incident?' said Willie, far too reasonably for Mr Lloyd's liking.

'Little incident! It might have been a little incident for you. It certainly wasn't for the bank. You know how much money we lost, don't you?'

Willie nodded, winking slyly at Trevor and clearly not taking things at all seriously.

'And it was all your bloody fault. You couldn't possibly lose to the Japanese man, could you? Oh, no, not you Willie,' continued Brenda's father. 'For the sake of one round of golf and your bloody pride you had to go and win.'

'But it was a cracking round, wasn't it!' replied Willie, starting to grin. 'And it wasn't *your* money that was lost, was it, dad. It did really belong to the bank, or had you forgotten?'

'That's hardly the point,' said Mr Lloyd, still glowering impressively. 'It still goes on my record. It might as well have been my money. And stop calling me dad!' He was clearly infuriated by Willie's lack of concern and rather flippant manner.

Trevor decided the time had come to intervene.

'Hello,' he said, with a rather timid smile. He held out a hand. 'I'm Trevor.' Mr Lloyd looked at Trevor's hand as though he had never seen anything like it before. Trevor withdrew his hand and examined it carefully, checking that he had not suddenly acquired any particularly unpleasant skin diseases.

'You're Dukinfield?' asked Mr Lloyd. He managed to phrase

the question in such a way that Trevor instinctively felt guilty and wondered if he ought, perhaps, to have a solicitor present before answering. The banker repeated his question.

'Er, yes,' admitted Trevor. 'I'm Trevor Dukinfield.'

'And where is your partner?' asked Mr Lloyd, 'I assume it isn't him?' he added, indicating Willie and managing to fill the word 'him' with enough venom to poison an army.

'Oh no,' said Trevor. 'Willie wasn't born in the area. He isn't eligible.'

'He's the most ineligible man I've ever met,' snorted Mr Lloyd.

'I'm Trevor's caddie,' explained Willie.

'Caddie?' said Mr Lloyd, doing a fair imitation of Edith Evans playing Lady Bracknell in Oscar Wilde's 'The Importance of Being Earnest'. He turned to his colleague. 'Is that allowed Mr Barclay?'

'I'm not, er, sure, Mr Lloyd,' confessed Mr Barclay, rather nervously. Mr Lloyd was clearly his senior. Mr Barclay unzipped his anorak and took a piece of paper out from an inside pocket. It was, Trevor guessed, a copy of his uncle's will. The banker studied this carefully for a few moments before looking up. 'It doesn't seem to say anything about caddies here, Mr Lloyd,' he admitted at last. He folded the paper, put it back into his pocket and zipped up his anorak again.

'Hrmph!' said Mr Lloyd, who clearly didn't approve of this omission.

Mr Barclay stared at them both in turn. 'So,' he said at last, 'who *is* your partner?'

Trevor who had been looking everywhere for Charlie suddenly spotted her. She was wearing a pair of dark green trousers and a matching sweater. She looked very professional. Megan, wearing a white, pleated tennis skirt, a white tennis shirt and white ankle socks was walking alongside her. She looked, Trevor thought, like an angel. Megan was pulling a trolley which presumably carried Charlie's clubs.

'There!' Trevor said, gleefully, pointing in Charlie's direction. 'There's my partner!'

The two bankers turned their heads and followed Trevor's outstretched arm with their eyes. 'Where?' demanded Mr Lloyd.

'There!' insisted Trevor.

'But those are women!' said Mr Lloyd, perceptively.

'One of them is your partner?' said Mr Barclay, his voice heavily laced with disbelief and disapproval.

'The one on the left,' said Trevor.

'The one on the right is her caddie,' said Willie.

'This is preposterous!' said Mr Lloyd, who would have stamped his foot if his gout hadn't been playing up. 'Is this allowed?'

Mr Barclay unzipped his anorak, took out his copy of the will and studied it again. 'It doesn't seem to say anything here about women,' he said.

'There you are!' said Mr Lloyd firmly. 'It doesn't say you can have a woman playing with you.'

'It doesn't say I can't,' Trevor pointed out.

The two bankers moved away just as Charlie and Megan joined Trevor and Willie. 'Hello, Charlie!' said Trevor. 'Thanks for coming.'

Charlie smiled nervously but didn't speak.

The two bankers returned and Mr Barclay cleared his throat. 'We have studied your uncle's will,' he said to Trevor, 'and we admit that your choice of partner is not outside the rules he outlined. We therefore have no objection. We assume that your partner satisfies your uncle's requirements about being a locally born member of the club?'

'Absolutely!' said Trevor.

'We will, of course, be playing this game according to the strict rules of golf,' said Mr Barclay. 'Is that understood?'

'Yes,' said Trevor, feeling rather weak. He looked at Willie who knew the rules much better than he did.

'Any deviations from the rules and any infringements will be penalised. Is that understood?'

'Yes,' agreed Trevor, swallowing a lump the size of a large golf ball which had mysteriously appeared in his throat.

'Then shall we start the match, gentlemen?' said Mr Barclay.

He looked confused. 'Er, and, er, ladies,' he added. He looked at his watch. 'It is seventeen minutes past eleven and Mr Lloyd has to be in Frankfurt tonight.'

Mr Lloyd and Mr Barclay, Willie, Charlie and Megan all walked briskly to the first tee where their arrival was met with loud cheers of approval. Trevor, limping, arrived a few moments behind them. His arrival attracted by far the greatest cheers.

Brenda, Willie's estranged wife, struggled to bring up the rear as she tottered along on her decidedly unsuitable footwear.

'Come on, Brenda, do keep up!' said Mr Lloyd.

'Oh, don't be rotten to her!' said Willie. 'She's only got short legs.'

'Pig!' shouted Brenda, rushing over and hitting Willie on the chest with her handbag. When she ran her entire superstructure wobbled and shook like two very large jellies.

'Oooh, I love it when you're all angry!' said Willie, laughing.

CHAPTER SEVENTEEN

When Trevor's uncle had thought up the idea of the golf match he had decreed that it should be played according to the rules acknowledged by the Royal and Ancient Golf Club of St Andrews and the United States Golf Association. Recognising that his nephew, not being an experienced golfer, would be at a severe disadvantage unless some sort of handicapping system was used, he had outlined some joyfully simple handicapping rules in his will.

Trevor had a handicap of 24. Charlie had a handicap of 28. Mr Barclay had a handicap of 9 and Mr Lloyd had a handicap of 7. According to Uncle Pettigrew's rules Trevor and Charlie received one free stroke on every hole.

All Trevor and Charlie had to do to win a hole was for one of them to finish the hole in the same score as the best of their opponents – the handicapping would do the rest. Halved holes were to be ignored. If the match was drawn after eighteen holes then the two sides would play a game of sudden death play off – starting again at the first tee.

* * *

Mr Lloyd, having the lowest handicap of the four players, took the red leatherette cover off the head of his graphite-shafted driver, unwrapped a brand new, uncuttable ball and walked onto the first tee. He had little charisma, less presence and no sense of occasion, and the throng of members which had collected around the first tee seemed disappointed when he simply put his ball onto a tee, took one practice swing and then hit his ball a good two hundred and fifty yards down the centre of the fairway. They hadn't come to watch an exhibition they had come to watch a golf match, and there were many among the crowd who rather suspected that the whole contest might well be over on the tenth green.

Mr Barclay was equally clinical in his approach. His ball landed about twenty yards to the left of Mr Lloyd's and, thanks to a lucky bounce, finished up some thirty yards further on.

When it was Trevor's turn to limp forward and step onto the tee, clutching his trusty three iron in one hand and one of Mr Schmidt's 50 pence top of the range 'groundsman specials' in the other, the cheers and shouts of support were deafening. Trevor found the experience daunting and rather intimidating. He smiled weakly and tried to remember whether he was supposed to keep his knees steady and his head bent or his knees bent and his head steady.

It was perhaps through nervousness that he topped his first shot. It travelled just over seventy yards and narrowly missed a foolhardy phalanx of spectators who, misled by the excellence displayed by the two bankers, had started to creep down the edge of the fairway in anticipation of Trevor's maiden shot.

'Never mind!' said Willie. 'At least you've hit it in the right direction – and you're on the fairway!'

Trevor smiled weakly and wondered whether he was doomed to play the whole round with a battalion of heavy-booted butterflies clog dancing around in his stomach.

Willie put Trevor's three iron back into his bag and set off towards the ladies' tee. Charlie and Megan had already begun to walk in that direction.

'Where are you going?' demanded Mr Lloyd.

'To the ladies' tee,' replied Willie, clearly surprised that anyone should ask.

'Mr Dukinfield's partner has to play from the mens' tee,' said Mr Lloyd.

Willie laughed. 'Don't be silly!' he said. 'Charlie may have a boy's name but you can see for yourself she's a girl.'

'It's in the will,' said Mr Lloyd.

Willie stopped laughing and the smile melted from his face at the mention of the word 'will'. He called to Megan to wait a moment. Trevor felt a cold chill in the pit of his stomach. He shuddered involuntarily and the butterflies lay down and kept quite still.

'Read it to him, Mr Barclay,' said Mr Lloyd.

Mr Barclay unzipped his anorak and took out his favourite reading matter. It didn't take him more than a moment to find the relevant clause. He obviously knew the will by heart. 'All players will tee off from the yellow (ordinary) mens' tees,' he read.

'But that was just put in because Trevor's uncle didn't want the match to be played from the white match tees,' protested Willie. 'He obviously didn't intend Charlie to play from the mens' tees.'

'How do you know?' asked Mr Lloyd.

'Well, of course he didn't!' said Willie. 'It's just that he didn't realise that Trevor's partner would be a girl.'

'I'm afraid that since Mr Dukinfield's uncle is no longer with us it isn't possible to find out exactly what he did not or did not intend,' said Mr Lloyd. 'What we do have is his will – and that, used in conjunction with the rules of golf, is what we are playing by. You did agree to that didn't you?'

'Well, yes,' said Willie. 'But be reasonable!'

Mr Barclay stared at him as if he'd suggested that they all try nude parachute jumping.

'I'm afraid you're going to have to play from the mens' tees,' said Willie to Charlie with a sigh. The club secretary exchanged glances with Captain Jarrold and frowned. There was much angry whispering among the collected members.

Charlie looked at Trevor, then looked at Megan, then looked at Willie and then looked down the fairway.

'You're bound to hit it further than I did!' said Trevor, attempting to be cheerful.

'It seems such a long way from here,' said Charlie quietly, taking her driver from Megan.

'Don't let them get to you!' Trevor heard Megan murmur. 'That's what they want!'

Charlie put her ball on a tee and hit it over a hundred and fifty yards down the left of the fairway. It was a cracking shot. If she had played from the women's tee her ball would have been almost level with Mr Lloyd's ball. She and Trevor were pleased but Mr Barclay and Mr Lloyd, standing smugly at the side of the tee, also looked very pleased.

'I think we can get the bulldozers down here this afternoon, Mr Lloyd,' said Mr Barclay.

'I think you're right, Mr Barclay,' said Mr Lloyd, rubbing his hands together gleefully.

* * *

By the time they reached the green both Trevor and Charlie were feeling deeply depressed, and the travelling gallery of supporters and spectators had sunk into a moody silence. Trevor, who had hit his second shot into the thick rough on the left, had taken eight shots. Charlie, who had hit two superb long iron shots, had fallen slightly short of the green with her fourth shot, had hit her fifth into a bunker and had taken a total six shots to reach the putting surface. Mr Lloyd had taken three shots and Mr Barclay had taken four shots to reach the green. Mr Lloyd's ball was twenty feet closer to the pin than Charlie's. It was Charlie's turn to putt first. She hit the ball quite hard, realising that there was no point at all in leaving her ball close to the hole since it was, to say the least, rather unlikely that Mr Lloyd would take more than three putts.

She missed the hole by two inches and her ball ended up six feet past the cup. In the end the putt didn't matter. Mr Lloyd needed just two putts to finish the hole.

'There's one good thing,' said Willie.

'What's that?' asked Trevor, whose knee was hurting quite a lot and who couldn't think of anything at all to be cheerful about.

'It's match play,' said Willie. 'We may be one hole down but we start afresh at the second.'

* * *

But the second hole was no better than the first, and nor was the third. The fourth was a disaster. Trevor lost two balls, Charlie lost one and the two bankers won the hole by four clear shots, even with their handicap of a stroke a hole. The spectators were becoming increasingly gloomy, and if there had been a competition to find the number of long faces in one place the Butterbury Ford Golf Club would have won it by many a jowl.

Charlie could hit the ball straight enough but the disadvantage of having to play from the men's tees meant that for her every hole was a real challenge. To make matters worse she found that she was constantly playing from an unusual position on the fairway. Her knowledge of the course had become quite useless, and it was as though she was playing it for the first time.

Even using a three iron Trevor often managed to hit the ball quite a distance from the tee, but whether it was because he was trying too hard or was simply nervous he was having tremendous difficulty in keeping the ball on the fairway. For the first two holes he hooked the ball. For the second two he acquired a vicious slice. If there hadn't been a large, enthusiastic and unashamedly partisan gallery to help him look for his ball the five minute rule, strictly adhered to by the bankers, would have meant that he would have lost even more balls than he did.

The rot stopped at the fifth hole. And it was Charlie who helped restore some semblance of pride and hope to the home side.

The fifth hole is the longest hole on the course and was, therefore, probably the hole that those supporting Trevor and Charlie least expected them to win.

Inspired, no doubt, by the awesome Poacher's Lake which lies in front of the fifth tee the two bankers, playing first, both hit their drives with extra venom. Although they cleared the lake easily both of them managed to miss the wide fairway on the other side. Mr Lloyd's ball drifted left into thick heather. Mr Barclay pushed his ball out to the right where it landed in a small beechwood copse. Both men sensibly played provisional balls which landed safely over the water and on the fairway.

Trevor hit his usual three iron tee shot and watched with delight as his ball landed on the left-hand side of the fairway around thirty yards the other side of the lake. Charlie, seeing that her partner had successfully cleared the lake, decided to play a riskier shot. She used her driver and put her tee shot straight across the lake and a hundred yards down the middle of the fairway. It was a glorious shot which the gallery cheered with great enthusiasm. They hadn't had much else to get excited about.

No one in the gallery seemed too keen to help the two bankers find their balls.

'I say,' called Mr Barclay to the nearest group of spectators. 'Give me a hand, will you?' He was standing in the middle of the beechwood copse and had absolutely no idea where his ball had landed.

'It's full of brambles in there!' complained Elvis Ramsbottom who had, at the third hole, quite happily crawled on his hands and knees through brambles to find Trevor's ball, not even complaining when he had knelt on an ants' nest.

'Come on, you chaps,' called Mr Lloyd, up to his waist in heather and gorse. 'Get stuck in! Twenty pence to the fellow who finds my ball.' He tried to accompany this none too generous offer with a smile, but his facial muscles, unaccustomed to this sort of manoeuvre, found the effort too much for them and the result was a rather startling grimace which frightened Mrs Dussenberg so much that she needed a nip from Mr Schmidt's hip flask.

'Sorry! I've got blood pressure,' answered Captain Jarrold, without troubling to explain the significance of the confession.

'Watch out for the snakes!' shouted Elvis.

'Come on Brenda!' called Willie, to his wife. She was tottering along fifty yards behind the rest of the spectators. 'Help your Dad find his ball. Don't worry about the snakes.'

'Shut up!' replied Brenda. 'Anything you've got to say you can say through my solicitor.'

Willie just laughed.

Muttering something inaudible, Mr Lloyd abandoned his search and played his replacement ball. He was so cross that he hurried his shot and sent the ball flying diagonally across the fairway. It landed, with a loud clattering, in among the same beech trees that had already swallowed up Mr Barclay's first drive.

By the time they reached the green Mr Lloyd had already taken seven shots while Mr Barclay, after an extraordinary shot with a hickory-shafted brassie from an unpromising looking lie on the fairway, had taken five. Trevor and Charlie had played the hole almost perfectly. Trevor, playing safely, had taken another four iron shots to reach the green and so, with his handicap, had a clear shot over Mr Barclay. Charlie, throwing all caution to the winds, had reached the green with her third shot and was three shots ahead of Mr Barclay. When Trevor almost holed a long, curling putt, leaving the ball no more than two inches from the hole, it meant that Mr Lloyd was out of contention and Mr Barclay had to hole his long putt to halve the hole. Much to the relief of the spectators Charlie put the whole thing beyond question by completing the hole in two putts.

The bankers' lead had now been cut to four holes and there were thirteen left to play.

'I think that bad knee is helping your game!' said Willie, as they walked to the next tee.

Puzzled, Trevor stared at him.

'It's a bit stiffer than usual,' Willie explained. 'It's helping your swing.'

'Thank God for that. I need all the help I can get. Perhaps I should fall down and twist the other one' said Trevor.

* * *

The sixth hole, one of the shortest on the course, was a hole which Charlie and Trevor really had to win. It was here that Trevor had scored his never-to-be-forgotten hole in three (by now very nearly an even more unforgettable hole in one) when playing his first ever round of golf with Mr Schmidt. As he stepped onto the tee he felt a sudden and welcome flutter of confidence.

'You have to win this hole,' whispered Willie as he and Trevor climbed up onto the tee. 'A half isn't good enough. And you have to assume that one of the bankers will get at least a three. There's a good chance that one of them will get a birdie two. That means that both of you are going to have to play for the green. It isn't any good playing short and safe, thinking that a four, net three, will win you the hole. I don't think it will.'

Trevor swallowed hard. 'Will you have a word with Charlie?' he asked.

'I can't,' replied Willie. 'The rules say a player can only accept advice from a partner or caddie. I'm not Charlie's caddie.' He winked. 'But you can talk to her.'

Trevor walked over to where Charlie and Megan were standing.

'How are you feeling?' he asked Charlie.

She swallowed, licked her lips and smiled thinly. 'I've never been so nervous in my life,' she confessed, touching his arm gently with her hand. Trevor did his best to ignore her touch but felt his face redden.

'Willie thinks we should both play for the green on this hole,' said Trevor quickly. He explained why.

'I don't think I can reach the green unless I use my driver,' said Charlie. 'Not from the men's tee.' She smiled at him nervously and removed her hand to pull a driver from her bag. The gathered crowd of spectators, heartened by the win at the fifth hole, gasped at Charlie's audacity and then quietened as she prepared herself to drive off. You could have heard a tee drop on a fresh molehill.

For the first few moments after the ball left Charlie's club face Trevor thought that all was going to be well. Indeed, for a second or so he thought that Charlie's shot was going to be perfect. It flew very low and very straight and was undoubtedly heading straight for the green. But when the ball landed and kicked forward he knew it was going too fast and would go too far. The sixth green isn't visible from the tee but a score of so of spectators had rushed ahead and their silence said it all. Charlie's ball had landed on the green on its second bounce but because its trajectory was so low it had failed to slow down at all. It had flown through the rhododendron bushes and disappeared down the hill at the back of the green. The waiting crowd rushed after it but there was no chance that they would ever find it. Standing on the tee Charlie had watched her ball's progress with a mounting sense of horror and frustration. She knew what was going to happen but also knew that there was nothing she could do about it.

Trevor stepped onto the tee knowing that their chance of success on this hole was now in his hands. He hesitated for a brief moment, tempted to play a safe shot down the middle of the fairway.

'Go for it!' whispered Willie as he tried to decide what to do.

Making a conscious effort not to grip his club too hard, swing too fast or hit the cover off the ball, Trevor closed his eyes and tried to recreate the shot he had played when he had beaten the professional.

The ball flew from Trevor's club and soared high into the air straight down the middle of the fairway. It seemed to hang in the air for minutes before plummeting to earth. It then bounced twice and slowly disappeared from sight as it rolled over the edge of the bank leading down to the green. The crowd might have seen this success, and cheered loudly at their hero's courage had they not been struggling through the rhododendron bushes in search of Charlie's ball. But back on the tee the players and caddies did not know this, and the silence depressed Trevor and Charlie and their two caddies.

'It must have gone through the green,' said Willie sadly. 'You'd better play a second.'

'Never mind,' said Megan. 'At least you had a go.' She put her arm around Trevor and gave him a big hug.

The two bankers were cheered by Trevor's apparent failure. The silent reception his shot had received did not depress them one little bit.

'I think we can afford to play this one rather conservatively, Mr Barclay,' said Mr Lloyd.

'I agree, Mr Lloyd,' said Mr Barclay, who would have agreed if Mr Lloyd had suggested that they play their shots standing on their heads in buckets of yoghurt.

So both bankers played rather limp and tentative little approach shots which stayed on the fairway and did not roll down onto the green. Certain that Trevor and Charlie, who would be playing three from the tee, would each take at least four shots they were confident that they would, at the very least, halve the hole.

Their confidence soared to unprecedented heights when Trevor and Charlie played their second, precautionary shots.

Charlie's second shot from the tee crashed into the trees on the left of the fairway, bounced out and dropped into thick uncut grass where it lay virtually unplayable. Trevor's second shot may well have hit the same tree, it certainly hit a tree in the same part of the wood. It too dropped into what subsequently proved to be an unplayable lie.

As it happened, of course, none of this mattered one jot because Trevor's first shot had, in fact, rolled down onto the green and come to rest no more than four feet from the hole. Elvis Ramsbottom, who had stayed behind at the tee with the players, ran down the course to report that Trevor's first ball had not, after all, gone through the green. This news was met with resounding cheers from the rest of the gallery, many of who had some considerable difficulty in dragging themselves back up the hillside and through the rhododendron bushes.

'Don't go for the birdie,' said Willie, when the two bankers had played their approach shots onto the green. 'Just try to leave your ball as close to the hole as you can. Imagine that the hole is a yard across.' Willie knew that a three, net two, would certainly win a point. There was no point at all in Trevor trying for a heroic finish and risking sending the ball several feet past the hole.

Faithfully obeying instructions Trevor played cautiously and watched in astonishment as his ball went straight into the hole for a quite spectacular birdie.

Trevor and Charlie had won two holes in a row and were now just two holes behind the bankers.

'Are we nearly finished yet?' demanded Brenda. 'I'm tired. How much longer is this going to go on for?' She shot a menacing look at Willie who winked at Trevor and grinned back at his estranged wife.

* * *

Trevor scored a five, net four, at the seventh and halved the hole with Mr Lloyd. Charlie scored a six net five at the eighth and halved the hole with Mr Barclay. The ninth hole was won by Mr Lloyd, who got a very good birdie, and so Trevor and Charlie finished the first half of the course three holes behind the bankers.

Trevor stood on the tenth tee waiting while Mr Lloyd rummaged in his bag and noticed that Willie, standing a few yards behind them, was whispering something in Megan's ear.

Mr Lloyd, having produced yet another packet of brand new balls tore into the cellophane impatiently. He apparently liked to play with a new ball on every hole. The flimsy box broke open, and although the banker caught hold of one ball two fell onto the ground. Megan stepped forward and quickly picked them up. She stood right in front of him, holding out her hand with the two balls resting on her palm. 'Your balls, Mr Lloyd,' she said, with her brightest smile. Mr Lloyd looked at her as though for the first time. 'Thank you, er ...,' he stuttered.

'Megan,' said Megan.

'Thank you, Megan,' said the banker, blushing. He reached out for the two balls, fumbled with them, nearly dropped one and then eventually took them and dropped them into the opened pocket on his golf bag.

'What a strong man you are,' murmured Megan, reaching out and touching the banker's arm. 'You do hit the ball a long way, don't you?'

'Do you think so?' asked the banker.

'Oh yes,' whispered Megan breathlessly.

Mr Lloyd looked at the tee marker, checked the distance of the hole and pulled a three iron out of his bag. As he settled into his stance he looked up at Megan. She smiled at him and winked. He blushed, swung and, desperate to impress her, hit the ball as hard as he could. It landed right at the very back of the green and rolled straight into one of the huge pot bunkers from which escape is almost impossible. There was a huge cry of delight from the crowd standing at the back of the green. Megan turned and smiled at Willie. The mastermind behind this little piece of deceit grinned back at her.

Trevor moved closer to Willie. 'Wasn't that a bit below the belt?' he asked.

'Match play isn't about playing well,' replied Willie. 'It's about playing better than your opponent. And there are only two ways to do that: either you have to score less than he does or you have to make sure that he scores more than you do.'

Mr Barclay, playing next and playing under pressure, swung a little too cautiously and put far too much back spin on his ball. It landed on the front edge of the green, spun back and then rolled down the long hill. It ended up sixty yards short of the putting surface.

Trevor and Charlie now had an excellent chance to claw back a hole.

Trevor stepped forward and balanced his ball on a tee. As usual he teed the ball up high. He felt more confident of getting the ball into the air when the ball was high up to start with.

'Play short and try to roll it up onto the green,' said Willie, as Trevor took a club from his bag.

'Short?' Trevor sounded surprised.

Willie nodded. 'You can probably win this hole with a four, net three. You can almost certainly win it with a three, net two. Don't try to do anything too heroic. If you go for the green and slide off the back edge you're lost. Put the ball on a low tee, play a low, running shot and even if the ball doesn't reach the green the chances are that it will stay where it lands.'

Obediently, Trevor bent down and pushed his tee further into the ground. His tee shot landed ten yards shorter than Mr Barclay's and then skipped and bobbled up the fairway, ending up just eight or ten feet short of the putting surface. For a terrible moment Trevor thought it was going to roll backwards down the slope. But it didn't.

'Great shot!' said Willie, with a grin. 'Get Charlie to play a similar shot.'

Trevor passed Willie's instructions on to Charlie.

Charlie's shot, played with a four wood, did even better. It pitched about the same place as Trevor's but finished up on the front of the green no more than nine or ten feet from the pin.

'Terrific!' shouted Willie, who could not contain his excitement. He punched the air with delight. The spectators went wild.

Mr Barclay, playing his second shot from the fairway, hit a high nine iron shot which landed twelve feet to the left of the pin, and either through luck or skill stopped almost exactly where it had landed.

Trevor chipped his ball onto the green but didn't hit it hard enough. He was a little disappointed when it ended up no closer than Mr Barclay's second shot.

With both Charlie and Trevor on the green there was little point in Mr Lloyd playing sideways out of the pot bunker. He made a brave attempt to clear the rim but failed. His ball buried itself into the soft sand about a foot below the slightly overhanging turf. He had to play his third shot sideways into the rough and his chances at the tenth were now gone.

Mr Barclay made a good effort to hole his putt but missed by two inches. He left himself a return putt of three feet. Trevor, trying to win the hole outright also sent his ball yards past the pin. In the end he five putted and cursed himself for not playing more sensibly.

But it didn't matter. Charlie's first putt ended up a foot from the hole. Her second putt clawed a hole back for the home team and meant that with eight holes to play the bankers were, once more, just two holes ahead.

'I always thought people played this game for fun,' said Trevor to Willie as they walked off the green and headed for the eleventh tee.

Willie looked at Trevor as if, for the first time, he doubted his friend's sanity.

*   *   *

The eleventh hole is probably the easiest hole on the course. The fairway is straight and flat and slightly downhill. The green is level and is protected by just three shallow bunkers. The distance from the mens' tee to the flag is around three hundred yards.

Charlie, who was accustomed to being able to hit her tee shot from the ladies' tee to within just a few dozen yards of the front edge of the green, took her driver from her bag and stepped onto the tee determined to hit the ball as hard as she could. She and Trevor knew that to win the hole outright one of them would probably have to complete the hole in a four, net three; even to halve the hole one of them would have to take a five net four.

But, as so often happens when any golfer tries to overhit a ball everything went just very slightly wrong. Instead of soaring straight and high down the middle of the fairway, as had been Charlie's intention, the ball curved quickly and viciously to the left, landing in a small patch of shrubs and saplings which ran along the side of the fairway.

'Play it safe,' urged Willie anxiously, handing Trevor his three iron. 'Just knock it down the middle. You should still be able to reach the green in two.'

Anxious to obey, and worried by the fact that Charlie's ball looked to be unplayable, Trevor played far too gentle a shot. His ball landed about a hundred and thirty yards from the tee, rolled and bounced another twenty or thirty yards and came to a halt only slightly more than half way to the green.

Mr Barclay and Mr Lloyd exchanged satisfied glances and

both succeeded in putting their drives in the middle of the fairway – considerably less than a hundred yards from the pin.

Charlie, having played another tee shot, half walked and half ran to find her ball. Much to her surprise it wasn't lost and it wasn't even unplayable. It was sitting up quite well in long, thick grass. The main problem was that the ball was very close to a small oak tree, and to get anywhere near to it Charlie had to back into two long and spindly branches. As she did so the branches inevitably bent backwards out of the way.

'Our hole!' said Mr Barclay immediately.

Charlie looked up, clearly confused.

'It's a penalty!' insisted Mr Barclay. He turned to his partner. 'Isn't that right, Mr Lloyd?'

'It certainly is,' said Mr Lloyd sternly. 'Moving or bending a branch while taking a stance is an offence under Rule 13. Two stroke penalty in stroke play and loss of hole in match play.'

Willie shook his head and took a rule book out of his back trouser pocket. 'If you study Rule 13 I think you'll find that it says that there is no penalty for backing into a branch or sapling if that is the only way to take a stance even if this bends the branch.' He flicked through the pages of the rule book, found the relevant page and then handed the book to Mr Lloyd.

The banker examined the book, went rather red, and then handed it to his partner without a word. Mr Barclay closed the small book and handed it back to Willie.

The two bankers stepped back to allow Charlie to take her shot.

But Charlie had been rather shaken by all this and she failed to hit the ball properly. Her ball bounced forwards a yard or so and buried itself even more deeply in the thick grass. It was quite unplayable and Charlie knew that her chances of winning or even halving the hole were gone.

Trevor was aware that the responsibility for winning the hole was now his.

'What shall I do?' he asked Willie.

'You've got to go for the green,' answered Willie immediately. 'Use your three iron again and give it a good clout.'

Trevor swallowed, bent over the ball, hesitated for a second or so and then hit one of the best shots of the round. The ball flew high and straight, pitched on the fairway just a few yards in front of the putting surface, rolled forwards across the green and came to rest in a pile of grass cuttings.

'That's OK,' said Willie. 'Grass cuttings count as Ground Under Repair. You can take relief from there without penalty. You can still win this hole.'

The two of them stood and watched as Mr Barclay and Mr Lloyd played their shots. Both of their balls landed safely on the green but both were twenty feet or more from the hole.

'You can still halve the hole,' said Willie, as they walked forward towards the green. 'They're unlikely to get down in less than two each. If you can get down in three we'll get a half.'

'Those two are the most hateful men I've ever met!' said Charlie, walking alongside them. She looked as if she was having to struggle not to cry.

'Hey!' said Trevor. 'It's only a game!'

The others looked at him and said nothing.

Trevor apologised.

They walked the rest of the distance to the green in silence.

'I'm afraid you've got a pretty tricky lie there!' said Mr Barclay with a smirk, as Trevor walked up towards his ball, which was virtually buried in grass cuttings.

'He can take relief from there,' said Willie. 'Grass cuttings count as Ground Under Repair.'

'Not if they aren't marked as such,' said Mr Barclay smugly.

'They are marked!' said Charlie indignantly. 'We always mark grass cuttings if we have to leave them.'

'They're not marked properly!' said Mr Barclay.

'But I can see the sign from here!' said Trevor. He pointed to a small metal Ground Under Repair marker.

'It doesn't say GUR,' Mr Barclay pointed out. 'It only says GU.' What he said was true. There was a jagged break where part of the metal sign had been broken off.

'That's because someone has broken off the bit with the R on it,' said Trevor. He bent down. 'Look!' he said, holding up the R.

Mr Barclay shrugged.

'I thought you agreed that we would play according to the strict rules of golf,' said Mr Lloyd.

'Well, yes,' agreed Trevor. 'But the grass cuttings are still marked.'

'They aren't marked GUR,' said Mr Barclay.

'You must play your ball from where it lies,' said Mr Lloyd.

'But I can't possibly play a shot from there!' protested Trevor.

The two bankers, knowing that this was true, said nothing.

'Come on, Trevor,' said Willie quietly, putting his arm around his friend's shoulders. 'They're right. Play the shot.'

'But how on earth can I play a shot out of there?'

'Play as it as though it was in thick sand,' suggested Willie, 'but use a seven iron.'

Trevor took the iron from Willie's outstretched hand.

'Hold it right at the bottom of the grip,' suggested Willie. 'Even though it's buried the ball is still two feet off the ground.'

Trevor made a brave attempt to play what was, in truth, a virtually unplayable shot. Even a skilled professional would have had difficulty in controlling the ball. Willie said afterwards that he thought Trevor had done well to get the ball out of the grass at all. The ball, caught by the heel of Trevor's club, flew out of the grass cuttings at quite a pace. It ran across the green with no intention of stopping and continued back down the fairway for another twenty yards. Trevor, having played three shots, knew that he had to get down in just two more to halve the hole. He played a good approach shot but was still fifteen or twenty feet from the hole and he had played four shots. When Mr Barclay put his long putt within six inches of the hole Trevor knew he had to sink the long putt to halve the hole. His ball missed by an inch and went six feet past the hole.

The bankers were now three holes ahead with seven holes to play. Things were not looking good for Trevor, Charlie and the Butterbury Ford Golf Club.

'I've laddered my tights!' screeched Brenda. She wheezed

noisily and then sneezed. 'And all this grass is giving me hay fever.'

'Well take your bloody tights off!' said Willie. 'And take those stupid shoes off too. And for God's sake stop moaning, woman.'

Brenda opened her mouth to deliver some sort of reply but clearly thought better of it. Instead, she turned her back on Willie, marched over to her father and began to complain to him.

But Mr Lloyd was too busy gloating to listen to his daughter and Brenda ended up standing alone looking rather forlorn, her high-heeled shoes sinking into the turf, as the rest of the crowd headed off for the next tee.

CHAPTER EIGHTEEN

'You've got to take chances,' said Willie to Trevor. They were both standing on the edge of the twelfth tee.

'I say,' said Mr Barclay, who was standing nearby, trying hard to overhear what Willie was saying. 'You do realise that it is against the rules for a player to take advice from a partner's caddie, don't you?'

'I'm not listening!' said Charlie, stepping quickly to one side.

'It's also against the rules for you to listen to what I'm saying,' said Willie.

Mr Barclay blushed slightly. 'I don't want your advice!' he said stiffly.

'Then I suggest you stop listening,' said Willie.

Mr Barclay stepped out of earshot and stood by the side of his banking companion.

'Those two will play safe now,' said Willie quietly, looking over his shoulder to make sure that neither of the bankers could hear him. 'They don't have to win holes. You do. Halving holes isn't good enough any more.'

'So one of us will have to get a five on this hole?'

'No!' said Willie, firmly but quietly. 'You'll have to do better than that. One of these guys is bound to get a four here. You or Charlie will have to get a four so that you can win the hole with a three.'

'But it's nearly three hundred and fifty yards!' said Trevor.

'You can cut at least fifty yards off that distance by playing your second shot straight across the lake,' said Willie.

Trevor stared out at the hole. Poachers' Lake, which ran along the left of the twelfth hole was broad and deep as well as long. And the green, which was long and fairly easy to hit if you approached it from the fairway, looked narrow and difficult to hit if approached from the other side of Poachers' Lake.

'We'll never do it!' said Trevor quietly.

'One of you might,' said Willie. 'If you play the hole the proper way you won't stand a chance. It'll take you three shots to reach the green and then your only chance of winning the hole will be to hole your putt. If you go across the water it'll be a more difficult shot but one of you could hit the green. Then you'll have two putts and winning will be a possibility.'

Trevor swallowed hard. 'OK!' he agreed. 'I'll try!'

'Tell Charlie,' said Willie. 'It's no good one of you taking the gamble. To make the risk worthwhile both of you have got to play across the water.'

Trevor limped across to where Charlie was standing. She listened carefully and then nodded.

'Are you giving your partner advice?' demanded Mr Barclay.

'He's perfectly entitled to advise his partner,' said Willie.

'But he's telling her what you told him,' protested the banker. 'Under Rule 8 a player can only take advice from his own caddie.'

'You don't know that,' said Willie. 'Not unless you were listening. And if you were listening then you're breaking Rule 8 as well because what you've heard might influence the way you play the hole.'

Mr Barclay opened his mouth to reply but thought better of it. He walked over to his trolley, took out his driver and played a safe and sensible shot down the centre of the fairway. Mr Lloyd did likewise. Both bankers could now reach the green in two.

Charlie pulled her tee shot slightly but it stayed on the fairway, and since she was planning to play across the lake the fact that her ball was on that side of the fairway was obviously an advantage. Trevor's tee shot didn't have the length of the shots played by the two bankers (he was, of course, playing with a three iron) but it did, at least, go straight and for that he was grateful.

Charlie was the first to play her second shot. The bankers

realised what she was planning to do the moment she settled into her stance.

'Risky shot!' said Mr Barclay, after drawing in his breath.

'Very dodgy!' agreed Mr Lloyd.

'The bastards are trying to put her off!' murmured Willie to Trevor.

'You can do it!' said Trevor. He looked across at the bankers. 'Encouragement not advice,' he said.

Charlie turned round, looked at Trevor and smiled.

'Come on, Charlie!' said Megan.

For a few moments Charlie's shot looked as though it was going to clear the lake. But then there was a telltale splash a yard or two short of the far bank.

'I thought it was a risky shot,' said Mr Barclay.

'Silly to try it,' said Mr Lloyd.

'Hard luck, Charlie,' said Megan.

'I'd better play another ball,' said Charlie.

Her second attempt was no more successful. Once again her ball landed straight in the lake.

'Sorry,' said Trevor. 'My fault.'

'No it wasn't,' said Charlie. Trevor noticed a defiance in her voice that he had never heard before. 'Could I have another ball, please?' she asked Megan.

Her third shot crossed the lake, pitched on the green and rolled slowly over it to land in a bunker.

'This ought to be the 13th,' said Charlie.

'That was rotten luck,' said Megan.

'Six shots and I'm still not on the green,' said Charlie glumly.

For a moment Trevor was tempted to play safe and chip the ball down the fairway so that he could reach the green with his third shot.

'No!' said Willie firmly when he realised what Trevor was planning to do. 'If you play safe then Charlie's efforts were all wasted. We knew there was a risk but there's no other way for you to play this hole. You've got to go for it.'

Trevor sighed. He trusted Willie.

'It's going to be all right!' said Megan, as his ball flew high over the lake.

'It could be brilliant!' said Willie. 'You've got enough height on that ball for it to stop dead where it lands. If you land on the green then you're in with a chance.'

'It's curving to the left,' said Trevor, shading his eyes with his right hand and watching his ball carefully.

'Only a fraction,' said Willie. 'It's going to be OK.'

The ball cleared the lake, landed on the green around fifteen feet away from the pin and stayed there.

'Brilliant!' said Willie. 'Brilliant!'

Charlie rushed over and hugged Trevor. Trevor tried not to show his embarrassment. He wasn't used to being hugged by young girls, especially not by young girls with a crush on him.

'Lucky shot,' muttered Mr Barclay.

The two bankers played good, safe iron shots onto the green. But Trevor only needed to hole out in two putts to win, and a few minutes later the bankers' lead had once again been reduced to two holes.

There were now only six left to play.

'Willie,' said Brenda, plaintively. 'My feet are sore. Will you carry me?'

'Do I look like a fork lift truck?' asked Willie.

* * *

The 13th hole is a nasty par five. Mr Lloyd won it with a six and it would be cruel to recall the way the others played the hole. Suffice it to say that between them they lost five balls. When they walked off the 13th green the bankers had restored their lead to three holes. And now there were just five holes left to play.

* * *

When the four players, the two caddies and the by now depressed and quiet crowd of club members walked towards the 14th tee the sky had begun to darken and there were already signs that it might rain.

'This is all we want,' said Captain Jarrold glumly. He looked around. 'Has anyone thought to bring an umbrella?'

No one answered but those spectators who had brought umbrellas with them hid them behind their legs.

'It'll hold off,' said Wing Commander Trout.

'No it won't,' said Elvis, who thought of himself as a bit of an expert on weather, and whose reputation as a forecaster had undoubtedly been enhanced by his ineradicable pessimism. British weather gives pessimists an undue advantage.

To everyone's surprise the two bankers both made a real mess of their tee shots. Mr Barclay hooked his ball slightly and it landed in the light rough on the left of the fairway. Mr Lloyd pushed his ball to the right and it too landed in light rough. Neither of them gained any advantage from the fact that the fairway was hard, close cropped and downhill.

'You should both be able to reach the green in two if you keep the ball low and play long, running shots,' said Willie. 'The fairway is hard and it's downhill most of the way.'

Trevor, playing first, was pleased with his drive. It travelled little more than a hundred and thirty yards before hitting the ground but it bounced and rolled and bounced and rolled for almost as far again and when it finally stopped Trevor beamed with delight for he too now believed that he might be able to reach the green in two.

Charlie pushed her drive out to the right and her ball landed in low cut rough. It wasn't a bad shot, but the rough meant that her ball didn't roll. She knew that she was going to have difficulty in reaching the green in one more shot.

Trevor's drive had ended up closest to the green.

Sadly, after they had all played their second shots the home side's slight advantage had evaporated. Trevor's attempt bobbed and rolled and bounced and finished up just short of a bunker to the left of the green. Mr Barclay's landed in the same bunker. Charlie's was still a long way from the green. But Mr Lloyd's landed on the fairway some fifty or sixty yards in front of the green and rolled downwards until it lay on the very front edge of the green.

'You can still win and you can certainly halve the hole,' said Willie as he and Trevor walked down the hill towards Trevor's ball. 'Just chip it over the bunker and two putts will almost certainly get you a half.' Charlie's third shot had rolled to the back of the green and was lying a yard or so behind the putting surface.

But Trevor's chip landed in the bunker instead of flying safely over it, and suddenly the bankers looked as if they were about to increase their lead to four holes with just four more to play. That would, of course, mean that Trevor and Charlie would have to win every hole just to stay in the game.

A superb recovery shot from the bunker left Trevor's ball twenty feet from the pin after four shots. Mr Barclay's bunker shot was less successful. He hit the ball right across the green and into another bunker. His recovery shot from the second bunker left him thirty feet from the pin.

Charlie, using a putter from the fringe around the green, put her fourth shot within six feet of the pin and earned herself a generous amount of applause from the crowd.

Everything now depended on Mr Lloyd, who, much to the crowd's delight, played an awful shot. He stubbed his putter on the ground and left his ball ten feet short of the hole. He had now taken three shots.

Trevor's fifth shot ended six inches from the hole. He putted out and had a six, net five to put on his card. Mr Lloyd's fourth shot ran well past the hole and ended up five feet away. Charlie's putt rattled firmly against the back of the hole. Much to her own surprise she had finished the hole in five shots.

Mr Lloyd now had to hole his putt to halve the hole. He bent over his ball, clearly concentrating hard, read the lie and struck it cleanly. His ball rolled around in a perfectly judged arc, slowing gently as it approached the edge of the hole. Everyone waited to hear the rattle as it dropped into the hole.

'Wonderful putt!' cried Mr Barclay, in admiration.

'Good shot!' said Trevor, rather sadly. He felt at that moment that his last chance of keeping the golf club had gone. He had enjoyed every moment of his time at the club. And he knew that it would take him a long time to get over losing it.

'It can't possibly stay out!' said Mr Lloyd, walking around his ball and waving at it with his putter. 'It's hanging right over the edge of the hole!'

Trevor watched in some surprise as Willie walked briskly across to where the club secretary was standing and whispered something to him. Wing Commander Trout immediately took his pocket watch out of his waistcoat pocket and studied it carefully.

'It's going in!' cried Mr Lloyd. 'Our hole I believe!' He was bent double over the ball, willing it to drop into the hole.

And drop it did.

'One stroke penalty,' said Willie clearly.

Mr Lloyd, who had started to reach down to pick his ball out of the hole, turned towards him. 'What the hell do you mean?' he demanded.

'One stroke penalty,' said Willie. 'You waited more than ten seconds with your ball on the edge of the hole.'

'Rule 16.2,' said Wing Commander Trout. 'If a player waits more than ten seconds to see if a ball on the edge of the hole is at rest and the ball subsequently falls in there is a one stroke penalty.'

'That's preposterous!' said Mr Lloyd. 'I've never heard of anything so bloody stupid in all my life.'

'Strict rules of golf,' said Willie.

'It wasn't ten seconds!' said Mr Lloyd.

'It was!' insisted Wing Commander Trout. 'It was fifteen seconds from the moment I started to time it.'

'Our hole,' said Willie firmly.

The bankers now led by two holes with four to play.

* * *

A stream runs across the fairway of the 15th hole. This stream was of little significance to Trevor or Charlie since both knew that they would be unlikely to reach it from the tee. But the stream, which lies around two hundred and twenty yards from the tee, was to play a vital part in the match.

Charlie and Trevor had both played safe shots well short of the stream, as had an unusually cautious Mr Barclay, when Mr Lloyd, clearly still angry, stepped onto the tee. He began by taking a vicious-looking practice swing which would have probably sent the ball into the next county if he had used it when playing the ball. His real swing was only slightly less aggressive.

It can probably be argued that there was some sense in the way he played the hole. After all his partner was lying safely on the fairway on the tee side of the stream. It was, perhaps, sensible for him to attempt to clear the stream with his drive and so give himself a chance to play a shorter iron shot into the heart of the green.

That may have been the theory.

In practice it proved to be something of a mistake.

Mr Lloyd's first drive landed ten yards short of the stream, bounced once and landed straight in the water. Mr Lloyd instantly announced his intention to play a provisional ball in case his first ball could not be found. This second ball also landed in the stream, though this time it landed full in the water.

When five minutes had elapsed and neither of Mr Lloyd's balls had been found the banker elected to play another ball from the bank on the tee side of the water hazard. He promptly topped the ball and sent it straight into the stream. Trevor and Charlie, both of whom had played decent shots to within thirty or forty yards of the green, exchanged glances as they struggled to contain their glee. Mr Barclay, whose second shot had narrowly missed the green and had rolled into one of the bunkers, looked worried.

It was at this point that Mr Lloyd's natural good humour and sense of goodwill towards all men deserted him. He threw his club straight into the stream and proceeded to curse everyone and everything around him. He cursed Trevor, Charlie, Willie and Megan. He cursed Mr Barclay. He cursed his clubs. He cursed his ball, the stream, the course designer and the ground-staff. And he cursed Willie again. He cursed with an ease and a fluency which would have been the envy of a do-it-yourselfer with a bruised thumb. Everyone within earshot was astonished at his command of the vernacular.

'I think you'd perhaps better give this hole a miss!' suggested Mr Barclay.

'I'll do no such thing!' shouted Mr Lloyd. 'I've started the damned hole and I'll bloody well finish it'

He fished another ball out of his bag, threw it onto the ground and proceeded to hit it hard into one of the tall elm trees which guarded the green. The ball fell out of the tree with a clatter and landed in the second of the two large, horseshoe shaped bunkers which protected the green. (Mr Barclay's ball was already in the other.)

'Damn!' cried Mr Lloyd, throwing his club down onto the ground furiously and storming off towards the green. A rather sad and embarrassed looking Mr Barclay followed, pulling both his and Mr Lloyd's trolley.

Mr Lloyd was clearly out of the reckoning when it came to deciding who was going to win the hole. And Mr Barclay was so shaken by his colleague's display of temper that he quite clearly found it difficult to concentrate on his game. He played a poor recovery shot from the bunker and had a forty foot putt for his par. Charlie and Trevor, on the other hand, played quite good approach shots and were both closer to the pin after just three shots. Mr Lloyd, determined to finish the hole, took three shots to get out of the bunker and sprayed the green with sand.

In the end Charlie won the hole with a five, net four. Trevor took a six, net five. Mr Barclay took a six. And Mr Lloyd admitted to a quite remarkable fourteen but was thought by some to have taken even more than that.

'Pity it's not stroke play,' said Willie to Mr Lloyd, as they left the green.

Mr Lloyd just glowered at him.

The bankers were now just one hole ahead with three to play. The match was more evenly poised than it had been for quite some time, and there were now those amongst the audience who were beginning to think that it just might be possible for Trevor and Charlie to win.

* * *

At the 16th Trevor and Mr Barclay halved the hole in three. Charlie took a five (net four) and Mr Lloyd, still furious after his problems at the 15th, lost yet another ball and was lucky to get away with a six.

This meant that they walked onto the 17th tee with the bankers still just one hole ahead. You could almost touch the tension, and the crowd of spectators was growing all the time as word filtered back to the club house that Trevor and Charlie were still in with a chance of winning. The rapidly darkening clouds overhead were now so close together that they seemed to be jostling for position to get the best view of the golf.

On a normal day the view from the 17th tee is breathtaking. But the sky was now so heavy with thunderclouds that it was as much as the players could do to see the fairway they were supposed to be aiming at.

Charlie played a long, straight drive. Trevor pulled his tee shot into the rough on the left of the fairway, thereby making his second shot more difficult. Mr Barclay played a good drive which travelled fifty or sixty yards further than either Charlie or Trevor had driven, and which ran along the right-hand edge of the fairway, leaving him in a perfect position for his second shot to the green. And Mr Lloyd, trying to hit his ball onto the green in one, lifted his head, overbalanced and produced a shot which skidded off the tee and travelled no more than thirty yards from the tee.

'Looks as though the pressure has got to you, dad,' said Willie, in a stage whisper, hissing in Mr Lloyd's direction.

'Don't talk such rubbish, you fool!' said Mr Lloyd angrily. 'I never succumb to pressure! And don't call me your 'dad'. I'm no 'dad' of yours, especially after what you've done to Brenda.'

Mr Lloyd slammed his driver back into his bag and pulled out his four iron.

'What the hell am I doing wrong?' he demanded, glowering at Trevor who happened to be walking alongside him as they left the tee together.

'Don't answer that!' said Willie immediately.

Trevor and Mr Lloyd looked at him.

'I'm surprised at you, Mr Lloyd,' said Willie, wagging a finger. 'Asking for advice from an opponent is a breach of the rules.'

'I wasn't asking for advice!' shouted Mr Lloyd. 'What would I want advice from him for?'

'Well, it sounded to me as if you were asking him for advice,' said Willie.

Mr Lloyd opened his mouth and tried to speak but no sound came out. He walked forward, stopped his trolley and hit at his ball without even stopping to take a proper stance.

'Slow down, Mr Lloyd!' said Mr Barclay, rather nervously. 'There's plenty of time.'

'When I want your damned advice I'll ask for it,' said Mr Lloyd, watching in frustration as his ball bounced and rolled along the ground. It travelled about sixty or seventy yards before it came to a gentle and undignified halt. Even Brenda, not the most considerate of people, attempted to calm her father, but she too was brushed aside brusquely as Mr Lloyd walked over to his trolley.

'Don't you push my wife out of the way,' shouted Willie, 'or else you'll have me to answer to!'

Mr Lloyd didn't even acknowledge Willie's threat, unlike Brenda whose face changed from miserable and moody to surprised and rather pleased. Whatever Willie's faults, and there were plenty, he was a gentleman and was certainly not going to see any lady manhandled by a bad-tempered old man, even if the lady in question was his wife. Brenda, clearly touched by this unexpected and chivalrous display, was attempting to walk over to her husband, but by the time she had unspeared her stiletto heels from the grass Willie and the rest of the crowd had set off down the fairway.

Charlie's second shot flew long and low and ended up no more than fifty yards short of the green. Trevor's second shot, from a difficult lie on the left-hand side of the fairway, crashed into a clump of trees near the end of the fairway. Mr Barclay's second shot curled to the right of the fairway and, much to everyone's astonishment, landed in Poachers' Lake. His fourth shot landed on the green, nine or ten feet from the pin. Mr Lloyd's third shot scampered up the fairway like a rabbit and stopped alongside Charlie's ball, fifty yards short of the green.

'We can win this one!' muttered Willie to Trevor. 'Just stay calm.'

Trevor's ball was unplayable in thick bracken. He played his fourth shot with an eight iron and watched with relief as it landed safely on the back of the green. As they walked onto the green the heavens opened and rain started to pour down.

By the time they had their putters in their hands Charlie, Trevor, Mr Barclay and Mr Lloyd were all soaked and shivering. A few moments later Mr Lloyd had a two foot putt for the hole and the match. As he crouched over his putt, rain buffeting his frail frame, Willie stepped forward with a huge, multicoloured umbrella which he had borrowed from Mr Dussenberg.

Mr Lloyd looked up, surprised. 'Thank you,' he said, assuming that a sense of family duty had, at last, got the better of his son-in-law.

Willie smiled at him.

Mr Lloyd played his shot. The ball rattled into the hole. The banker looked up, delighted with himself.

'Our hole,' said Willie firmly.

Mr Lloyd looked at him as if he had gone quite mad. 'What the hell do you mean?' he demanded. 'We won that one! It's our game!'

''Fraid not!' said Willie. 'You've lost the hole. Infringement of Rule 14.2.'

Mr Lloyd frowned and stared at him disbelievingly.

'Accepting protection from the elements whilst making a stroke,' explained Willie. 'Two stroke penalty in medal play. Loss of hole in match play.'

'You held the damned umbrella!' protested Mr Lloyd. 'I didn't ask for it.'

'You accepted it,' Willie pointed out. 'You lose the hole.'
Mr Lloyd stared at him in disbelief.

The two teams left the 17th green all square, and headed off towards the final tee.

'Your friend looks as though chips wouldn't melt in his mouth,' whispered Mr Schmidt as Trevor walked past him. 'But when the butter is on the table he knows how to fight fire with fire!'

'Oh yes,' smiled Trevor. 'He certainly does.' He looked heavenwards. 'It's certainly raining cats and dogs isn't it?'

Mr Schmidt looked up and squinted. 'It is?' he asked, frowning.

'It certainly is,' nodded Trevor, picking up his golf bag and heading for the next tee.

'I hope you win the match,' whispered Brenda to Trevor, having finally decided to admit defeat and remove her shoes. 'I knew my dad could be a bit unpleasant at times, but I had no idea he had such a nasty side to him. Anyway, his bank's got far too much money.' Her dress, sodden and clinging, stuck to her more than ample thighs. Trevor, though touched by her words of encouragement, thought she looked quite comical with her bare feet, wet hair and damp clothes outlining her rather chunky body.

*　*　*

As they stood on the 18th tee, with the sky as black as night and the rain pouring down and Willie struggling to control Mr Dussenberg's large multi-coloured umbrella, Mr Lloyd took several deep breaths and made a determined effort to calm himself, to concentrate and to play a more successful game. While Charlie drove off he glowered at her and repeatedly banged his ball against the face of his driver.

'Charlie's been great, hasn't she?' murmured Trevor to Megan.

'Do you want to make her really happy?' asked Megan. 'Really, really happy?'

Trevor looked at her and frowned. 'What do you mean?' He asked. He felt himself blushing, fearing the worst. He felt sure that Charlie must have told Megan about her feelings for him.

'There's something you could do that would really make her day.'

'I know, but look Megan, I really don't want to encourage her. She's only sixteen, you know. These things happen. She'll get over it soon enough.'

'Well, that's not a very nice attitude. What would it cost you? Especially after what she's done today. And why should she get over it, just because she's a young girl.'

Trevor was now feeling worried *and* puzzled.

'Look, I don't know why you're acting as some sort of matchmaker, but you can't play around with a young girl's feelings. Can't you remember what it was like to be sixteen?'

'I don't know what you're talking about,' replied Megan.

'Well, it seems odd to me,' said Trevor firmly. 'I thought you and I were, well, you know, together.'

'So did I.'

'So why are you trying to fix me up with Charlie?'

'What?'

'I'm not interested in Charlie. I wouldn't take advantage of a schoolgirl crush even if I wanted to, which I don't.'

'I should hope not!' said Megan. 'And you might do well to remember that she is not a schoolgirl. And she most definitely has not got a crush on you.'

'So why all the attention and admiration, then?' asked Trevor, with just a hint of sarcasm. He might not be all that experienced with women, but he knew when someone was flirting with him. Or he thought he did.

'She wants to be a golf professional!' said Megan, clearly gaining just the slightest bit of satisfaction from watching Trevor's ego slowly deflate.

* * *

Three minutes later the four players were marching down the

fairway in search of their balls. Now that Trevor knew the truth about Charlie's intentions he felt much more comfortable with her. Her smiles became friendly instead of threatening, her hand on his arm was reassuring instead of worrying. He wondered how he could have misunderstood her signals so thoroughly, and realised rather guiltily that he was just a little bit disappointed to discover that she didn't find him an irresistible hunk of manhood.

Charlie and Trevor had both hit safe shots down the centre of the fairway and well short of the stream which runs across the bottom of the valley. But the two bankers had clearly decided to try to finish the game quickly. Both players hit their drives so hard that their balls disappeared from view.

With Trevor's second shot safely over the stream and Charlie's first shot clearly visible just a few yards short of the water the spectators were becoming increasingly excited. An hour or so earlier most of them had been smothered in gloom. They had been convinced that Charlie and Trevor stood no chance of winning. Now, with everything to play for, their faith in their champions had been restored. As the two bankers marched towards the stream in search of their balls there was a constant buzz among the crowd as opinions were exchanged about the chances of a home side victory.

Mr Barclay was the first to find his ball, lying in the stream and quite unplayable. Gloomily, he fished it out with two short irons and dropped it on the bank.

Mr Lloyd had been more fortunate. His ball had come to rest six or seven yards the other side of the stream, level with Trevor's ball. The banker's excellent drive meant that he had succeeded in cancelling out Trevor's one stroke advantage.

A few minutes later, with the rain miraculously stopped but heavy rain clouds still hovering overhead, the four of them stood on the green.

Trevor had taken five shots and Charlie four. Mr Barclay and Mr Lloyd had each taken three. Trevor's ball was eighteen feet from the hole and it was his turn to putt first. Mr Barclay's ball was fourteen feet from the hole and it would be his turn to putt after Trevor.

Trevor hunched over the ball. His clothes were soaked and he had to make a real effort to stop himself shivering.

'This green is wet – it's going to be very much slower than the other greens,' said Willie, standing a yard behind him.

Trevor nodded and shook his head to try and clear the water from his eyes. Then he hit the ball; striking it considerably harder than he would have done just ten minutes earlier. As the ball rolled a small trail of spray marked its progress across the green. It stopped a good yard short of the hole. He had now taken six shots. The best he could hope for was a seven, net six.

Mr Barclay had been watching Trevor's shot with great interest to see just how much the rain had affected the green. He bent down and hit his ball. Although he clearly played it much harder than he would have done before the rainstorm, the ball still stopped four feet short of the hole. He had taken four and had a difficult putt for his par. Charlie then left her ball five feet short of the hole and it was Mr Lloyd's turn to putt. His ball missed the hole by three inches and rolled three feet past. He had taken four.

It was Charlie's turn again. She bent over her, licked her lips and hit her ball firmly. It went straight into the hole.

She had taken six, net five.

Now it was up to the two bankers. One of them had to hole a putt to halve the hole.

Mr Barclay missed first, leaving his ball a good six inches short of the hole.

And then Mr Lloyd missed too.

There was a moment of complete silence as the significance of the missed shot became clear. Charlie and Trevor had won the hole and the match and had saved Butterbury Ford Golf Club from the developers.

Trevor, forgetting his sore knee and brushing all thoughts of embarrassment aside, rushed forward and swept Charlie up into his arms. This was the cue for the assembled crowd to start clapping. Elvis Ramsbottom cheered wildly.

'I bet you are a parrot over the moon!' exclaimed Mr Schmidt loudly. 'Yes, I am. Thank you!' said Trevor.

Charlie stood on tip toe and kissed him on the cheek. Trevor, at last, felt able to return the compliment and give her a big hug as well.

Elvis Ramsbottom, this time accompanied by the rest of the crowd, cheered again.

Trevor wandered over to Mr Schmidt who was standing on the edge of the crowd with a rather bedraggled Mrs Dussenberg. Trevor took the professional to one side and began talking to him.

The jubilant crowd had surrounded Charlie who was soon hoisted onto the shoulders of some of the less elderly, more stable members of the club. Megan looked on proudly. Willie's arm found Brenda's shoulders and he hugged her to him. Her mascara was streaked down both cheeks and her ridiculous hat was plastered to her sodden hair.

* * *

'Excuse me young lady!' said Mr Schmidt walking up to Charlie, who had by now been lowered back to earth. He shook her firmly by the hand. 'How would you my assistant like to become?'

Charlie's mouth fell open.

'Is that a 'yes'?'

Charlie nodded.

'Good!' said Mr Schmidt firmly. 'Together we will kick some ass, grow a bed of roses and hit the big clock! Yes?'

Charlie nodded again.

* * *

'Do you have to go back to London today?' Trevor asked Megan.

Megan shook her head. 'When I rang my office this morning I told them I was taking a couple of days off,' she said. 'I thought that perhaps you wouldn't mind if I stayed with you. Who knows? Maybe I could get another story out of you! Anyway, we've got some important things to talk about. If I'm coming up to stay with you at weekends you've got to spend Wednesday nights with me in London.'

'It's a deal,' agreed Trevor quickly.

'Congratulations, Mr Dukinfield,' said someone. Trevor turned round. It was Mr Barclay. 'Would you take my card?' he asked, handing Trevor a small white rectangle. 'Perhaps we can do some business together in the future?' He smiled a thin, no-hard-feelings, its-only-business, banker sort of smile.

'Thanks,' said Trevor, slipping the card in his pocket.

'Hurry up, Barclay!' snarled Mr Lloyd from a few yards away. 'I've got to get to Frankfurt.'

Willie, his arm around his wife's waist, turned and yelled to the soaked but happy crowd. 'Come on everyone! Back to the clubhouse. The drinks are on Trevor!'

Appendix

Butterbury Ford Golf Club
Course details
The yardages are for the yellow (ordinary mens') tees.

Hole 1: 457 yard par 4
From the tee a narrow fairway, bordered by thick, uncut rough which is studded with heather and gorse, rises steadily upwards for the first 230 yards before flattening out into a 70 yard long plateau. The final stretch of the fairway then plunges down quite steeply towards a large, undulating green which is protected in front by a narrow but rapidly flowing stream and on the three other sides by three deep bunkers. Players who can drive straight up onto the plateau have a tremendous advantage because they can see the green when they play their second shot. This hole is undoubtedly the most difficult, on the course and many visitors to the Butterbury Ford Golf Club have had a nightmare round after their confidence has been shattered on this hole.

Hole 2: 110 yard, par 3
Players usually sigh with relief with they see the length of this hole marked on their scorecards. But when they see the hole for real the sigh of relief quickly turns into a gasp of horror. The tee is situated about 50 yards below the level of the green and so all the golfer can see is the top few inches of an extra long flag stick. Between the tee and the green there is no fairway at all – just a thick patch of gorse. Twice a year a junior groundsman is sent into the gorse wearing thick, protective clothing. He isn't

allowed out until he has managed to collect a couple of dozen buckets full of balls.

Hole 3: 348 yards, par 4
This left-handed dogleg hole doesn't just turn to the left but actually begins to bend back upon itself. From the tee there is a broad fairway of about 200 yards which ends in a long, deep, grass filled bunker and then turns very sharply to the left, leading towards a wide but shallow green which is protected by a grassy mound at the front and two quite small, shallow bunkers at the sides. To the left of the first 200 yards of the fairway there is a mixed copse of tall, broad-leafed trees, and the distance as the crow flies from tee to green cannot possibly be much more than 200 yards. Occasionally, some foolhardy player tries to lift a ball over the trees to land it directly on the green but as far as anyone knows no player has ever succeeded in doing this, though many balls have been lost in the process of trying.

Hole 4: 422 yards, par 4
The plan of this hole on the scorecard makes it look deceptively simple because it does not show the hillock in the middle of the fairway which completely obscures the view of the green from the tee. Rising about 50 or 60 feet into the air the small hill, which is situated about 80 yards from the tee, and which has the shape of a steamed pudding, can be fairly easily cleared with a decent drive, but its very presence seems to turn good golfers into nervous wrecks. Many members petitioned for the hillock to be removed but Archibald Pettigrew wouldn't hear of it and claimed that the best way to play the hole was to drive off with your eyes closed.

Hole 5: 542 yards, par 5
The longest hole on the course. The tee is situated on a small hill and most players need the extra confidence this gives them in order to clear Poachers' Lake with their drives. The lake, which is circular, has its nearest bank about 20 yards from the tee and

is no more than 120 yards across at its widest. Given the well-known fact that water attracts golf balls like magnets attract iron filings it is perhaps hardly surprising that many golfers find themselves playing a second ball and standing three before they leave the tee. The fairway on the far side of the lake is wide, flat and smooth, but after about 100 yards it starts a slow drift downhill for another 150 yards. It is here that one gets the first glimpse of the green and of the second, smaller lake which guards it. Most players play their next shot short of this smaller lake and then play an eight or nine iron shot onto the green which is fairly large and flat. When it's played like this the hole isn't a particularly difficult par five – it certainly isn't as difficult as it looks. But anyone who attempts to gain a shot here is risking a great deal for to clear both lakes with just two shots requires great skill, strength and courage.

Hole 6: 189 yards, par 3
The second short hole is the last of the holes on which the green cannot be seen from the tee. The first 150 yards of fairway are absolutely straight, as straight and as wide (or as narrow) as a firebreak in a forest which isn't particularly surprising since that is exactly what this once was. The trees on either side of the fairway are a mixture of mature oak and beech and have such thick trunks that hooked and sliced tee shots frequently just bounce back into play. The green isn't visible from the tee because the last 30 yards of the fairway drop down sharply; so steeply in fact that there are steps cut into the hillside for players to walk down. Cut on a natural plateau the green is guarded by a ring of rhododendron bushes. Brave players will aim directly for the green but percentage players know that a shot which is a few yards long is almost certain to result in a lost ball (the hill at the back of the green continues its steep descent and a ball which goes over or through the rhododendron bushes is likely to fly another 70 or 80 yards before stopping). Cautious players prefer to aim slightly short of the green and hope that the ball will roll forwards a few yards and then trickle down onto the putting surface. The green is so large that this becomes a dangerous

practice only in the very driest months of the very driest summers.

Hole 7: 397 yards, par 4
It is a relief to arrive at a hole where the green can be seen from the tee and where there are no natural obstacles to be overcome. There are two small bunkers on the left of the fairway about 200 yards from the pin, and three bunkers guard the green, but apart from that this hole is straightforward if you can ignore the stream which runs along the right of the fairway from tee to green. The stream should not, of course, come into play since it marks the out of bounds line on this hole. However, the attraction of water for golf balls is such that players whose normal tendency is to hook the ball have been to known to start slicing when they play this hole.

Hole 8, 428 yards, par 4
The dogleg on this hole is much less acute than the one on the third hole. There is a raised tee from which players have a clear sight of the first 250 yards of fairway. The fairway then turns gently to the right, climbs up a slight incline and leads onto a green which has two levels. For the last 150 yards the right-hand side of the fairway is guarded by a stone wall, topped with a thick hawthorn and bramble hedge, and this means that players have a choice of either playing their tee shot well to the left, in order to give themselves a clear shot of the green, or else taking a chance and trying to cut a few yards off the length of the hole by hitting their second shot over the wall. If you choose the extreme left of the fairway from the tee the hole is lengthened by about 50 yards. If you choose the right of the fairway your second shot to the green will have to be played blind.

Hole 9, 364 yards, par 4
To the surprise of strangers, who are usually completely disorientated by now, the 9th hole brings players back to the clubhouse. Again a plan of the hole makes things look much simpler than they are. The tee and green are at the same level. There are

no water hazards, no hillocks in the middle of the fairway and very few trees which are likely to interfere with play. But there is a large hill on the left of the hole and this means that much of the fairway, which is closely cut, runs at an angle of about forty-five degrees to the horizontal. The result is that every player has to play his or her approach shot to the green on a downhill lie (or in the case of a left-hander – an uphill lie). The large bunker which guards the front of the green means that poor shots are punished severely and it is virtually impossible to mishit a ball onto the putting surface.

Hole 10, 178 yards, par 3
Although it looks simple the 10th can be one of the most infuriating holes on the course. The green is about 30 yards higher than the tee and since most of this rise occurs in the last 100 yards this means that the fairway which leads up to the green is very steep. The result is that the hole is much more difficult in the summer, when the ground is hard and the grass is cut short, than in the winter when the ground is softer and the grass a little longer. In winter a ball which falls just short of the green will not usually roll back too far. In summer a ball which falls just short of the green can sometimes roll back almost to the tee itself. Players who are aware of this hazard, and who are tempted to over club in order to ensure that they hit the green with their tee shot are likely to discover that the two huge pot bunkers at the rear of the green are so steep faced that for most players they can only be effectively exited by playing out sideways or even backwards.

Hole 11, 299 yards, par 4
This hole is as easy a par four as it sounds. The fairway is straight and flat. The green is level and protected only by three shallow bunkers.

Hole 12, 396 yards, par 4
Players who have already lost balls in the water will view this hole with horror. The fairway, which is narrow, runs to the right

of Poachers' Lake and then turns gently to the left to lead up to the green. Foolhardy players who try to cut the corner and fly a ball over the water directly to the green with their second shot discover that from this angle the approach is a difficult one for there is very little green to work with. If you play safe the hole is fairly straightforward as long as you can resist a hook into the water. The green is three times as long as it is wide and is fairly easy to approach from this angle.

Hole 13, 523 yards, par 5
This is the only hole on the course which dog legs to the right twice! From the tee the fairway turns slightly to the right to avoid a small pond and then, after about another 60 or 70 yards, turns rather more sharply to the right to avoid a clump of thickly growing gorse. These two turns mean that for most players the hole, which looked at from the air would look like a horseshoe, is a genuine par five and no one in the club can remember any player ever managing to reach the green in less than three.

Hole 14, 452 yards, par 4
This hole is as straight as an arrow and almost all downhill. Although the hole looks long, even high handicap players can reach the green in two when the weather is hot and the fairway is dry and hard. Long hitters regularly reach the green with a drive and a pitching wedge. In the winter the hole is much harder and plays much longer and because the fairway is exposed and unprotected from the north easterly winds and even scratch players sometimes have difficulty in reaching the green in two.

Hole 15: 386 yards, par 4
A stream which runs straight across the fairway around 220 yards from the tee makes this hole more difficult than it might at first appear to be. Players who are in any doubt about their ability to carry the water with their drive are advised to play an iron off the tee and play their second shots from the tee side of the stream. The green is surrounded by a ring of tall elm trees and two large horseshoe-shaped bunkers.

Hole 16: 201 yards, par 3
Another tricky one! The stream which runs across the 15th fairway runs right across the front of the green and means that any shot which falls short is severely punished. A circle of bushes around the back of the green make sure that shots which go through the green are also punished severely.

Hole 17: 399 yards, par 4
The view from the elevated tee on this hole is breathtaking. On a clear day it is possible to see for nearly 20 miles in all directions. It is not, however, possible to see the green which is hidden behind a small copse of trees at the end of the fairway. To stand a chance of hitting a long second shot onto the green the player must try to push his drive well out to the right – being careful not to push it through the fringe of chestnut trees which stand between the fairway and Poachers' Lake.

Hole 18: 543 yards, par 5
The course finishes with a long hole that has decided many a match and ruined many a potentially good score. The tee and the green are on the same level but in between the two there is a deep valley. Right at the bottom of the valley, about half way between tee and green, a strong stream flows. Because the green is on the same level as the tee, and is clearly visible, it looks much closer than it really is and the temptation to try and hit a drive right across the valley is often irresistible.

    Invariably, however the player's ball will hang in the air for a few moments before plummeting down into the depths of the valley and then bouncing down the hillside or, more often than not, diving directly into the stream. Sensible handicap players, who know their limitations, deliberately play short of the stream and then hit their balls up the hill with long iron shots. However, one or two players have now shown that it is possible to play the 18th as a par four if you have a great deal of courage. By using a number one iron and playing the ball without a tee it is possible to hit the ball virtually flat so that it flies straight across the valley and the stream and lands half way up the hill on the other side of the valley. The flatter trajectory means that the ball is more likely to stick to the hillside and less likely to roll down the valley. When this shot is played successfully it can take 70 or 80 yards off the second shot and make a four a realistic proposition.

Length of course: 6,634 yards
Par: 71

Also available by Vernon Coleman

The Bilbury Chronicles

A young doctor arrives to begin work in the small village of Bilbury. This picturesque hamlet is home to some memorable characters who have many a tale to tell, and Vernon Coleman weaves together a superb story full of humour and anecdotes. The Bilbury books will transport you back to the days of old-fashioned, traditional village life where you never needed to lock your door, and when a helping hand was only ever a moment away. The first novel in the series.

"I am just putting pen to paper to say how much I enjoyed The Bilbury Chronicles. I can't wait to read the others."
(Mrs K., Cambs)

"...a real delight from cover to cover. As the first in a series it holds out the promise of entertaining things to come"
(Daily Examiner)

"The Bilbury novels are just what I've been looking for. They are a pleasure to read over and over again"
(Mrs C., Lancs)

Price £12.95 (hardback)

Published by Chilton Designs Publishers
Order from Publishing House, Trinity Place, Barnstaple, Devon EX32 9HJ, England

Also available by Vernon Coleman

Bilbury Grange

The second novel in the Bilbury series sees the now married doctor moving into his new home - a vast and rambling country house in desperate need of renovation. With repair bills soaring and money scarce, the doctor and his new wife look for additional ways to make ends meet. Another super novel in this series - perfect for hours of escapism!

"I found the book to be brilliant. I felt as though I was part of the community. Please keep me informed of any more in this excellent series."
(Mr C, Cleethorpes)

"A wonderful book for relaxing and unwinding. Makes you want to up roots and move to the rural heartland."
(Lincolnshire Echo)

"For sheer relaxing pleasure here's another witty tale from the doctor whose prolific writings are so well known."
(Bookshelf)

Price £12.95 (hardback)

Published by Chilton Designs Publishers
Order from Publishing House, Trinity Place, Barnstaple, Devon EX32 9HJ, England

Also Available by Vernon Coleman

The Bilbury Revels

Disaster strikes in this third Bilbury novel when a vicious storm descends on the village. Much damage is done as a result of the storm and the locals band together to undertake the necessary repair work. Money, as ever, is tight and so the idea of the Revels is born – a week of fun and festivities to raise the funds needed to repair the local schoolteacher's cottage.

Price £12.95 (hardback)

Bilbury Pie

A delightful collection of short stories based in and around this fictional Devon village. Every community has its characters and Bilbury is no exception! Thumper Robinson is the local 'jack the lad' and Pete is the taxi driver, shop owner, funeral director and postman rolled into one. Patchy Fogg dispenses advice on antiques to anyone who will listen and Dr Brownlow is the eccentric and rather elderly, retired local doctor.

Price £12.95 (hardback)

Published by Chilton Designs Publishers
Order from Publishing House, Trinity Place, Barnstaple, Devon, EX32 9HJ, England

Also available by Vernon Coleman

Bilbury Country

The colourful characters who inhabit this fictional Exmoor village have yet another battle on their hands when a newspaper article turns a trickle of tourists into a veritable flood! The villagers have a dilemma on their hands – do they give thanks for the much-needed financial boost from the hoard of visitors; or do they try to stem the tide of tourists in an attempt to regain the peace and tranquillity they love so much.

Price £12.95 (hardback)

Mrs Caldicot's Cabbage War

A truly inspiring novel about a woman who embarks on the adventure of a lifetime following the unexpected death of her husband. Pushed from pillar to post by an uncaring family who are determined to rule her life, she fights back with amazing results. Full of the gentle humour and wonderful storytelling for which Vernon Coleman is so well-loved.

Price £12.95 (hardback)

Published by Chilton Designs Publishers
Order from Publishing House, Trinity Place, Barnstaple,
Devon, EX32 9HJ, England

Also available by Vernon Coleman

Alice's Diary

Well over 20,000 delighted readers from around the world have bought this wonderful book which tells of a year in the life of a mixed tabby cat called Alice. She records the year's events and disasters with great humour and insight and at long last give's us a glimpse of what it is really like to be a cat! Delightfully illustrated throughout, this book is an absolute must for animal and cat lovers everywhere.

Price £9.95 (hardback)

Alice's Adventures

After the publication of her hugely successful first book, Alice was inundated with fan mail urging her to put pen to paper once more. The result is this, her second volume of memoirs in which she shares with us yet another exciting and eventful year in her life. Alice's Adventures is full of the wry witty observations on life which so delighted the readers of her first book, and the wonderful illustrations capture the most poignant moments of her year.

Price £9.95 (hardback)

Published by Chilton Designs Publishers
Order from Publishing House, Trinity Place, Barnstaple, Devon, EX32 9HJ, England

Also available by Vernon Coleman

The Village Cricket Tour

This superb novel tells the story of a team of amateur cricketers who spend two weeks of their summer holidays on tour in the West Country. It proves to be a most eventful fortnight full of mishaps and adventures as the cricketers play their way around the picturesque coastline of Devon and Cornwall.

Price £12.95 (hardback)

For a catalogue of Vernon Coleman's books please write to:

Publishing House
Trinity Place
Barnstaple
Devon EX32 9HJ
England

Telephone   01271 328892
Fax   01271 328768

Outside the UK:
Telephone   +44 1271 328892
Fax   +44 1271 328768

Or visit our website:

www.vernoncoleman.com